Praise for the novels of

HANK PHILLIPPI RYAN

"*Face Time* is a superior sexy mystery infused with an insider's knowledge of the wild TV news industry and, at its heart, a rich, well-developed protagonist we can cheer for."
—Sarah Strohmeyer, bestselling author

"*Face Time* is a gripping fast-paced thriller with an important story line and an engaging and unusual heroine."
—Sara Paretsky, *New York Times* bestselling author

"Family secrets, murder, legal shenanigans and evening news power plays— all dished up with Hank Phillippi Ryan's pitch-perfect wry humor and behind-the-scenes accuracy. These characters will stay with you.
Face Time is a winner!"
—Christina Skye, *New York Times* bestselling author

TOP PICK! "Told in the first person, this book has humor, snappy language, danger and a wonderful mystery that will keep you guessing. *Prime Time*... by Hank Phillippi Ryan, has the perfect combination of mystery and romance...
4.5 Stars—highest rating!"
—*Romantic Times BOOKreviews*

"*Prime Time* is current, clever and chock-full of cliff-hangers.
Readers are in for a treat."
—Mary Jane Clark, *New York Times* bestselling author

Also by

HANK PHILLIPPI RYAN

Prime Time

Look for

Hank Phillippi Ryan's

next riveting Charlotte McNally mystery

AIR TIME

Available September 2009

from MIRA Books

HANK PHILLIPPI RYAN

A Charlotte McNally Mystery

FACE
TIME

MIRA®

Recycling programs
for this product may
not exist in your area.

ISBN-13: 978-0-7783-2718-9

FACE TIME

Printed in U.S.A.

ACKNOWLEDGMENTS

Unending gratitude for
Francesca Coltrera, with her keen eye and relentless blue pencil,
who let me believe all the good ideas were mine

Kristin Nelson, the most remarkable agent anyone could wish for

Ann Leslie Tuttle, my brilliant, wise and gracious editor; Charles Griemsman,
patient and droll, king of deadlines.

To the remarkable team at Harlequin and MIRA, Tara Gavin,
Margaret O'Neill Marbury and Valerie Gray.
The inspirational Donna Hayes. Your unerring judgment and
unfailing support make this an extraordinary experience.

The artistry and savvy of Madeira James, Bonnie Katz, Judy Spagnola
and Catherine Jeremko

The inspiration of Harley Jane Kozak, Mary Jane Clark, Elaine Viets,
Amy MacKinnon, Jim Huang, David Morrell, Marianne Mancusi and
Jessica Andersen

The posse at Sisters in Crime and Mystery Writers of America:
Cathy Cairns, Ruth McCarty and Paula Munier

My blog sisters at Jungle Red Writers: Jan Brogan, Hallie Ephron,
Roberta Isleib, Rosemary Harris and Rhys Bowen

My dear friends Amy Isaac, Mary Schwager and Kate Shaplen Kahn;
and my sister Nancy Landman

Mom—Mrs. McNally is not you, except for the wonderful parts.
Dad—who loves every moment of this.

And of course Jonathan, who never complained about all the pizza.

Chapter One

It's statistically impossible that my mother is always right. So why doesn't she seem to know it?

Besides, it's demonstrably true that I'm not always wrong. I have twenty-one Emmys for investigative reporting—won number twenty-one after I was stalked by murderous thugs, threatened by insider-trading CEOs and held at gunpoint by a money-hungry sociopath who I proved was mastermind of a nationwide insider-trading scandal. Every one of them is in prison now. So I must have been right about a lot of things.

But at this moment, struggling for balance on a cushily upholstered chair at Mom's bedside in New England's most exclusive cosmetic surgery center, somehow I no longer feel like the toast of Boston television. I feel more like toast. Once again, I'm a gawky, awkward, near-sighted adolescent, squirming under the assessing eye of Lorraine Carpenter McNally. Two months from now, provided her face heals in time for the wedding, she'll be Lorraine Carpenter McNally Margolis.

"Charlotte," Mother says. "Stop frowning. You're making lines."

Millions of viewers know me as Charlie McNally. I'm not Charlie to my mother, though. As she's repeatedly told me, my news director, my producer Franklin Parrish, my ex-husband Sweet Baby James, admirers who hail me on the street, and certainly Josh Gelston when she meets him: "Nicknames are for stuffed animals and men who have to play sports." After that pronouncement, she always adds: "If I'd wanted a child named Charlie, I would have had a boy and named him that."

Mom and I do better by long distance. Most of our conversations begin with me telling her about something I've done. Then she tells me what I should have done. Then I ask why nothing I do is ever good enough. Then she insists she's not "criticizing," she's "observing." As long as she stays in her skyscraping lake-view condo in Chicago, we do a good job pretending we're a close-knit pair.

But here she is in my hometown, swaddled in a frothy peach hospital gown, surrounded by crystal vases of fragrant June peonies, reclining against down pillows. She insists that I shouldn't come visit her every day, saying she's certain I have better things to do. Patients "of a certain age" who have "extensive surgery" stay here through recovery, minimum fourteen days. So this is going to be an interesting couple of weeks. And by interesting I mean impossible.

At least Mom doesn't look as bad as I expected for a few hours after surgery. No bruises yet, no puffy eyes. She's got bags of what look like frozen peas Ace bandaged to each side of her face to keep down the swelling, and I can still see the little needle marks where her precious Dr. Garth injected Restylane to erase the lines in her forehead.

"All the pretty girls are doing it," she says. She would have given me her trademark raised eyebrow for emphasis, I'm sure, if she could move her eyebrows.

"And if you don't make an appointment with the plastic surgeon at your age…" Her voice trails off, apparently rendered speechless by my continuing refusal to face reality. She settles into her plump nest of pillows, adjusts her peas and pushes harder. "Charlotte, you know I'm right, and…"

Keeping my face appropriately attentive, I begin a mental list of all the things I should be doing at nine-thirty on a Monday night instead of babysitting with my mother. Thinking about a blockbuster story for the July ratings. Calling Franklin to see if he's come up with another Emmy winner. Making sure I have a bathing suit that won't freak out my darling Josh, who has only known me since last November and has not yet encountered my 46-year-old self in anything but sleek reporter suits or jeans and chunky sweaters or strategically lacy lingerie. Under dim lights.

"And local TV is so—*local*…." Lorraine is reprising one of her favorite themes. Why is it, she wonders, that I've never wanted to move to New York and hit the networks? Or at least move home to Chicago, where she could set me up with a handpicked tycoon husband who would convince me to abandon my television career and become a tycoon wife? For the past twenty years I've told her I'm fulfilled by my career and am comfortable being single again. Mother makes it clear I'm wrong about this.

I look dutifully contemplative, nod a couple of times and continue my mental should-be-doing list. Feed Botox, who's probably already ripped the mail to shreds and tipped over her litter box to prove who's boss. E-mail best friend Maysie, who's at Fenway Park covering the Red Sox, and see what I'm supposed to bring to her annual Fourth of July cookout. Call Nora and make sure my younger sister will take her turn at mom-sitting when

Mother finally goes home. Dig up a book about adolescent girls and see how experts suggest I deal with Josh's daughter Penny.

Penny. Right.

I've been to war zones, chased politicians through parking lots, wired myself with hidden cameras, even battled through the annual bridal gown extravaganza in Filene's Basement, but spending my summer vacation days with a surly eight-year-old and her blazingly attractive father? This may be my toughest assignment ever. Not counting the bathing suit.

"Look in the mirror," Mother urges. She starts to point, but then, after a quick scan, apparently realizes the flatteringly lit pink walls of her posh little room—which looks more like plush grand hotel than sterile hospital—don't have any mirrors.

She forges ahead, undaunted by reality. "Well, find a mirror, and look in it," she says. "Charlotte, this isn't a criticism, it's an observation. I'm your mother. If I don't tell you, who will? Your neck is, well, worrisome, and you'll instantly see how your cheeks are drooping."

Happily for our relationship, there's a soft knock on the door. As it opens, Mother's expression softens from imperious to flirtatious. Talk about worrisome. Still, I've got to give her credit for believing she's alluring in that frozen pea and Ace bandage getup. Wisps of her newly reblonded hair escape in a way she'd never allow if there were mirrors, but she's still got the McNally brown eyes and Gramma Nell's good posture. If it's true we become our mothers, I guess I'm not going to be so bad at sixty-eight. Plus, the nursing staff at the New England Center for Cosmetic Surgery is certainly used to women in the awkward stages of transformation.

"Miz McNally?" A romance novel cover-model wannabe in a white oxford button-down and even whiter pants consults the chart clamped to the foot of Mom's bed. His smile is snowier still. "I'm Nurse Justin. How are we feeling?" He clicks some switches on a bedside contraption, checking the heart and respiration monitors the center requires for every patient. Mom coos at him as he muscles a rolling bed table across her lap, pretending she doesn't want to take her latest round of pills because the painkillers make her "silly."

Nurse Justin is just one of the pill-dispensing glamour boys I've seen in the center's modishly fashionable nursing whites. Some are older and gray-templed, some younger with panache-y little ponytails, but they all look like they've just come from shooting the latest Ralph Lauren catalog, and only do this nursing thing in their spare time. I don't know how the center gets away with this obviously discriminatory hiring practice. Plus, who'd want a hunky guy seeing you as a *before?* Mother, apparently, is all for it.

I tune back in to her chitchat. It's about me.

"On Channel 3," I hear Mother explaining. "Charlotte, dear," she says. "I hope you're going to be on the news tonight. We'd love to watch you."

Not a chance, of course. It's now almost ten o'clock, and the news goes on the air at eleven. But Mother has never understood how television works.

"Nope," I say, smiling as if this isn't a ridiculous question. And, I grudgingly realize, she's just being a proud mom, which is actually very sweet. "I do long-term investigative stories," I explain to the nurse, just an amiable daughter joining the conversation. "I'm only on the air when we've uncovered something big. So, nothing tonight." I shrug, smiling. "Sorry."

Nurse Justin's face suddenly changes to a scowl, which is baffling until I see he's pointing at my tote bag. Which is ringing. "No cell phones allowed in guest's rooms," he says, still scowling. "Strict rules. We're all about patient privacy. And quiet. Cell phones are allowed only in the outer lobby."

I cringe. "Forgot to turn it off when I left the station," I say, which is true. I whap it to Off without even checking the number, figuring Justin will forgive me my first transgression, and whoever is calling will call back. His face begins to soften—and then my purse starts beeping.

I dive for my beeper, knowing full well I forgot to turn that off, too. I push the kill button, but the illuminated green letters that pop up are inescapable. CALL DESK, it demands. RIGHT NOW. And if that weren't attention-getting enough, a second screen flashes up at me. NEED U LIVE FOR ELEVEN PM NEWS.

Mom was right again.

Chapter Two

"**W**ho? What? When? Why me?" I leap from the cab, phone clamped to my ear. Roger Zelinsky, managing editor of the eleven-o'clock news, is giving me the lowdown in bullet points: attorney general Oscar Ortega. Announcing for governor. Lead story. Every other reporter out on assignment.

"You're going on the air live," Roger says. "Soon as Oz makes his move."

Oscar Ortega is often called "the Great and Powerful Oz," and word is he likes the nickname. The state's first Hispanic attorney general, he's a take-no-prisoners politician with a big-bucks machine behind him. If he's running for governor, he'll be tough to beat.

The parking lot outside Ortega's redbrick Beacon Hill office is full of scurrying TV types, scrambling to cover this breaking news. Technicians from the four network affiliates, the CW, CNN, a couple of local cable stations and the Emerson College journalism class have staked out spots for their imminent live broadcasts. Masts from a lineup of microwave vans poke into the star-scattered sky like huge yellow forks against the late June night. Technicians inside the vans, sliding doors left open to let in the breeze, briskly read out coordinates to colleagues back in their stations' control rooms, tweaking audio levels and confirming video feeds are clean.

"They're all set for you," Roger assures me. "We've already got a live signal. Find the truck. Thanks for being a team player, McNally. Just let me know when you're ready."

I trot through the maze of vehicles with the phone still tight to my ear. I know I have to hurry, but I can't be sweaty or out of breath on the air. *There it is.* With a fist, I bang on the window of Channel 3's ungainly blue-and-gold mobile studio, then wave at the crew inside the truck to announce my arrival.

"Found the van," I say to Roger. "Talk to you later."

It's got to be less than five minutes until airtime.

Photographers from the other stations are snaking out the extension poles of their powerful spotlights. The parking lot illuminates almost into daylight, as megawattage hits the fidgeting reporters anticipating their face time and their chance to bring home the lead story. Some on-the-air types mutter to themselves, practicing the scripts they've scrawled onto their notepads. Others preen in pocket mirrors, adding lip gloss or a final spritz of hairspray.

A row of cameras perch atop metal tripods like electronic flamingos, set up and ready to roll. One tripod is empty. Ours.

Not good. Not good. Not good.

I snap open my cell phone to send a frantic Mayday. Just then, I see my photographer Walt Petrucelli, sweaty and disheveled in a baggy Channel 3 T-shirt and voluminous khaki shorts, muttering to himself as he lugs his camera from the trunk of a news car. Acting as if there's all the time in the world. The ring of keys yanking down one belt loop jingles as Walt clicks the Sony into ready position and gives one tripod leg an irritated kick into place. "Why me?" He questions the universe as he peers through his viewfinder, adjusting focus. "Buncha bullshit."

Walt looks up, does a double take as if he's seeing me for the first time. "Bringin' out the big shots, huh?" he says. "How'd you get the short straw, McNally?"

Ignoring him, I position myself in front of the camera. Using the lens as a mirror, I take a second to check my reflection. My high-maintenance blond bangs are reasonably straight, my trademark red lipstick reasonably applied, and the black suit I put on for work today— about a million hours ago—reasonably unwrinkled. As good as it's going to get.

Every mosquito and midge in New England dives and swoops across the klieg lights in front of me, probably deciding which ones will go on the attack during my live shot. Happy-go-lucky motorists out on Cambridge Street, also attracted by the lights, honk their horns as they drive by.

I twist an earpiece into place, clicking its cord into the control room connection box I've clipped onto the waistband of my skirt.

"Can they see me back at the station?" I ask Walt, tuning everything else out. I pat my lapel. Nothing. "Where's my microphone?"

Right now, a camera inside at the news conference had better be feeding video to the station. If this all works the way it should, the producer will put Ortega's announcement, live, on the news. I'll know what Oz says because I'll hear it on air through my earpiece.

Right now I'm hearing only silence.

"Yeah, yeah, hold your horses." Walt, molasses, finally clips a tiny black microphone to my jacket. "Control room's got you now."

A deafening shriek screams into my ear though the audio receiver, followed by a blast of static. Then, finally, a voice. Which I can almost understand. Then total silence. "Lost audio," I tell Walt, attempting to stay calm. "What's the control room trying to tell me?"

"Four minutes," Walt says.

I contemplate ripping out my earpiece, yanking off my microphone, and going home. I have no news release. I have no idea what's going on in the news conference, and I'm about to appear live in front of a million people. And undoubtedly, Mother is one of them. They'll all watch this live shot crash and burn.

Suddenly I see a familiar figure power through the revolving door of the A.G.'s office building. He runs across the parking lot toward me, skids to a halt and bends over to catch his breath, hands on his knees. Then Franklin Parrish saves my life.

"It's underway now," my producer pants. "Oz announcing for governor." He looks up at me, one hand still on a knee, confirming. "The anchor's gonna toss to Oz's statement live, then come to you for the wrap-up."

"Three minutes," Walt intones.

In my earpiece, now thankfully static-free, I hear the audio of our newscast. I hear Amanda Lomax, her trademark throaty anchor-voice telling viewers of the surprise candidacy of Oscar Ortega, instant front-runner for governor. And then I hear Oz himself, basso profundo, begin to intone his platform. I imagine he's turned his crowd-pleasing charisma up to full blast. He's clearly not much for exercise, but with his dark wavy hair and killer smile, it's also clear he thinks he's irresistibly charming, and he may be right. Most women seem to vote yes, no matter what he asks for.

Walt holds up two fingers. "Two minutes."

Franklin blots his face with a pristinely ironed handkerchief, pushing his tortoiseshell glasses onto the top of his head, then pulls a piece of paper from his jeans pocket. "Okay, Charlotte. Here's the news release for y'all," he says, smoothing out the wrinkles.

This signals Franklin's just as tense as I am. He always calls me Charlotte, which, instead of carrying Mother's undercurrent of criticism, comes out sounding adorably like "Shaw-lit." But "y'all"? His otherwise usually subdued Southern accent only reappears when he's under pressure. Still, I've worked with him long enough to know he thrives on pressure.

"Just read it," Franklin instructs. "It's got the whole drill, law and order, convictions out the wazoo, death to infidels, all that. Y'all—you know the lowdown on this guy, right?"

I do, in fact. Oscar Ortega: recruitment poster for the prosecution—cool, hot, and politically connected. Known for his outrageous neckties and outrageous legal talent. Scholarship to Boston College. Scholarship to Yale Law. Could cross-examine blood out of a turnip. And some predict, he'll step out of the attorney general's office, percolate for a term or two on Beacon Hill, then head for the Oval Office at 1600 Pennsylvania Avenue.

"Thanks, Franko," I say, taking the release. Less than a minute to go. I'll read it through quickly, then use it to sum up when Oz is finished. Done it a million times. Like riding a bike. "No problem."

Wrong.

I can't see the words. I mean, I can see that there *are* words, but they're a complete blur. I glance over at Franklin, ready to ask if there's a problem with the copy he's offered. I can easily see the crease in his predictably impeccable jeans, the tiny polo pony on his pink knit shirt, even how the ten-o'clock stubble on his face darkens his coffee skin to espresso.

Clearly, what's wrong is me. Without my brand new reading glasses, this is going to be impossible. And even if I could get to my glasses, tucked in my red leather tote bag and back in the van, I couldn't go on the air wearing them.

"Thirty seconds," I hear in my ear.

I can't read this news release, but I have to. Tucking the paper under one arm, I use a finger to pull back my left eyelid and pop out my contact lens. With a brief wince of regret and one flip of a finger, I discard the contact onto the parking lot pavement, and try again to read Oz's formal announcement.

"Four. Three." I hear the countdown in my ear. "Two. Go."

"And that was now gubernatorial hopeful Oscar Ortega," I say into the camera. "As you've just heard, the self-described 'law and order' candidate is promising voters he'll continue his, quote, 'career of crime stopping.' And, as he says in the statement just this minute issued to reporters—" I glance down at the now perfectly visible news release "—I promise to make Massachusetts stronger, safer, and a place where law-abiding families can feel confident their governor is protecting them. A place with a balanced budget. A place with no new taxes. A place where parents can feel safe in their homes, where children can feel safe on the streets and in their schools— and where criminals will never feel safe again."

"Wrap," the control room instructs in my ear. "Toss to Amanda back in the newsroom."

"The primary election is just two months from today,"

I continue. "And as of now, it's open season in Massachusetts politics. Live at Ortega headquarters, I'm Charlie McNally, News 3 at eleven. Back to you, Amanda."

I stand still, smiling confidently into the camera, waiting for my cue. "And you're clear," the control room declares.

I'm grinning as I yank out my earpiece. I hope Mom and Nurse Justin were watching. "I've still got it," I tell Franklin, patting myself on the back. "And I'll buy the beer."

As I retrieve my tote bag from the van, I can hear my cell phone ringing inside its zippered pouch. I flip the phone open, ready for my "Atta-girl!" from the newsroom. "This is McNally." I say, preparing to be modest. I wave thank-you to the crew as Franklin and I leave the parking lot, and then turn all my attention back to the phone.

It's not Roger.

"Well, Mother, I'm sure Mr. Ortega would be very unhappy to hear that." I sigh, then shoot myself in the head with one finger as she continues, summarily changing the subject. "No, I just had my bangs cut. I can see perfectly. Could we—talk about all this tomorrow?"

Charles Street looks like a little slice of London, a brick-and-cobblestone street transplanted across the Atlantic and tucked onto Beacon Hill. Densely packed with elaborate brownstones, it's crammed with tiny storefronts offering antiques and shoes, and peppered with preppy-chic boutiques. Franklin suggested we hit The Sevens, a Beacon Hill institution and our sometime hangout. But now this night seems to be taking another unexpected twist. Franklin has a secret.

"What 'big news'?" I demand. "Tell me now." I see Franklin's face, off-again, on-again, as we walk through the patches of narrow sidewalk illuminated by the wrought iron streetlights. He's got a smile I don't like.

"Not until we get a glass of wine, Charlotte." He points towards The Sevens, smiling that smile again. "Trust me on this."

I hate surprises. Franklin better not be quitting. He and I are a made-for-television team, a well-oiled duo with nicely meshing journalism, curiosity, respect and ambition. I clamp my mouth closed and feel my eyes narrow. I could try to find a new producer, of course. But I most certainly do not want to.

The TV at The Sevens is tuned to Channel 3, as always. Jerry gives Franklin and me a welcoming wave as we pull our stools up to his comfortably pockmarked metal-topped bar. There's never a place to park around here, so the other weeknight drinkers sharing a final beer or brandy are probably all locals, too.

"Saw you on the tube," the bartender says, gesturing with a dish towel toward the oversize flat-screen monitor attached to the wall. "Oz, huh? Wicked tough guy. He's a cinch in November, you think?"

"Who knows," Franklin replies. "Boston politics. Like New England weather, right? Anything could happen."

"Gotcha," Jerry says. "Charlie?"

I've already shredded a cocktail napkin into confetti and made a triangle out of one of those little red stirrer things I found on the counter. Franklin says he has big news and now he's making small talk with the bartender. I have to kill him.

"A glass of cabernet," I decide. "And a Diet Coke. And a water." Franklin is going to quit. My own mother thinks I'm over-the-hill. How did this day go so bad so quickly?

I hook my heels over the rungs of my bar stool, and turn to face Franklin. He's got a new job. At the network, probably. He and his adorable partner Stephen are leaving town to join the other up-and-coming thirty-somethings in the Big Apple. I know it. Now I'll have to talk him out of it.

"Listen, Franko," I begin. "Is it about money? What did New York offer you? What if we can—"

"Charlotte," he says, holding up a hand. "Stop. I can tell you're involved in one of those conversations you have with yourself. I have no idea what you and you are talking about. Whatever it is, I promise we can all discuss it later." He looks at Jerry. "Glass of champagne, please. And one for my pessimistic pal here."

I knew it.

"Don't call me Charlotte if you've got bad news," I instruct. "And I'm not celebrating anything until I decide there's something to celebrate. If you and Stephen are moving out of town," I say though a sip of my red wine, "that ain't something I'm celebrating."

Franklin pushes a flute of champagne toward me and holds his up to make a toast.

I sigh, already defeated. If he and Stephen are happy, I guess I should be happy, too. I put down my wineglass and lift the slender one Franklin's forcing on me. "What?" I ask, expecting the worst.

"Story of a lifetime," Franklin says, looking pleased with himself. "You know how you've been bugging the Constitutional Justice Project to let us in on one of their wrongful conviction cases? Do it up big, inside info, evidence, interviews?"

"Of course," I reply. A tentative smidge of hope emerges. Maybe this will be a good surprise after all. "And so…"

"Well, Brenda Starr, apparently your phone calls convinced 'em. Remember Deadly Dorie? Notorious husband-murdering Swampscott mom? Up the river for life?"

"Yeah, sure." I nod. "Three, four years ago? Bashed her husband with an iron or something, then pushed him down the stairs. But she confessed, right?"

"Wrong," Franklin says. "Well, she did confess, but tonight we got a call from the CJP. We're getting the inside dope. She's innocent. They've got new evidence proving she didn't do it. And it's all ours. Exclusive. They want you, my Emmy-winning friend, to do the story that gets her out of prison."

Two glasses of champagne later, I high-five the air as I trudge up the last flight of stairs to my apartment, the third floor of a restored old Mount Vernon Square brownstone on the flat of Beacon Hill. My live shot was a success, we have our ratings story, and we're going to get an innocent person out of prison. *Not bad for one day.*

I can hear Botox meowing as I unlock the door. She curls her tail through my legs as I enter, purring for attention. I reach down to pet her sleek calico fur and see, as I predicted, she's made a little shredded paper nest out of the mail again. That's to punish me for coming home so late.

"We've got a hot one, Toxie," I tell her. I dump my purse and tote bag onto the dining room table, pushing aside a pile of unread copies of *Vogue* and *The New Yorker,* and hang my black suit jacket on the back of a chair. I wonder, for the millionth time, why I spent so much money on antique dining room furniture I only employ as a magazine depository and an extra closet. I glance around my place, just reassuring myself everything's where it should be. Which of course it is. The navy leather couch, plump taupe-and-white upholstered chairs, elegant Oriental rugs. Splurgy curtains hang over a curving bay window that, if you look in just the right direction, reveals a snippet of the Charles River. I do love it, but I'm hardly ever in it.

"We've got a hot one, Dad." I salute the framed photos on my wall-covering family gallery as I head down the hall. Dad always loved a good story and I wish he were here to hash this one over.

The message light on my bedroom phone is blinking red. I push the playback button, then flip my black leather sling-backs into the closet, and twist my arms around to unzip my slim black silk skirt. I stop mid-zip as I hear the message. I've known Josh for, what, eight months? But still, just hearing the warmth in his voice feels like an embrace. "Hi sweets," I say to the phone. My skirt drops, forgotten, to the floor.

"Caught you on the news," the message continues. "How'd that happen? I thought you were with your mother. Anyway, you looked hot. But then…" His voice gets softer. "You know I always think you look hot." I can picture his hazel eyes giving that full-of-meaning twinkle, his unruly pepper-and-salt hair falling out of place. The moment I first saw him I thought "Gregory Peck as Atticus Finch," and I still think so. A sexy Atticus. Atticus with abs. Atticus with…

"Shall I make this an obscene call?" he continues. Now he's using what I secretly call his "Charlie voice," making me deeply wish we were together tonight. "Ask if you're wearing that little black lace number? Okay, no. But listen, it would be nice if we could talk about it in person, wouldn't it? So, sweets, dinner Thursday, right? We'll hit Legal Seafoods or something, since Penny's now informed me she's a 'fishatarian.'"

There's a pause, and I hear him sigh. "She's off in her room now, still wide-awake, says she has to 'talk' with

Dickens. Her stuffed dog, not the author." Another sigh. "Anyway, I, uh, miss you. Talk to you tomorrow."

The message clicks off, but his voice still hangs in the air. My darling Josh. Though I've never called him that out loud. I sigh, consider clicking my wilted skirt onto a hanger, then toss it into the dry clean pile.

Be careful what you wish for, my mother used to warn. As a little girl I'd always wondered why wishing was so dangerous. Now, I admit, I'm wishing for a future with Josh. Which means a future with his little girl. Which means, I'd suddenly be an English professor's wife and somebody's mom. *Be careful what you wish for.* Maybe Mother was right again.

I throw on my favorite old Rolling Stones T-shirt, and pad off to brush my teeth, Botox trailing behind me. Well, one thing for sure. If I'm ever somebody's mom, I'm sure as hell not going to tell my daughter she needs a face-lift.

Chapter Three

"I have no idea what you're worried about," I say, giving the elevator button another jab for punctuation. The lobby of the office building is chilly and marbleized, and people with briefcases and scowls bustle past us, intent on their own destinations. Our destination is thirty-one floors up. "Of course she'll do the interview, Franko. If Dorinda Keeler Sweeney wants to be a free woman again, why wouldn't she?" I give the button another poke. "Come on," I implore it.

There's a lot to learn in the next few hours. And tonight there's dinner with my darling Josh. And Penny, the newly minted fishatarian.

"The elevator is not going to arrive more quickly no matter how many times you push that button, Charlotte," Franklin instructs, setting his cordovan leather briefcase on the floor. "And as for Dorie, I hope you're right. If we get her to talk on camera, the story is blockbuster. Without her interview…well, let's just say our brand new consultant from the Coast is not going to be too happy."

I pause, mid-push. "You told her? You already told Susannah we're researching this story?" We still have a lot of digging to do, and I never like to promise anything until

I'm sure it's a cinch. That way you don't disappoint people with bad news, you only make them happy with good news.

Franklin gives his briefcase a little kick, looking crestfallen. He runs a finger around the neck of his starched oxford shirt.

"Well, she cornered me in the control room last night. Asked me if we had a July sweeps story yet. It was fun to be able to say yes."

"I'm sure it's fine," I reassure him. Probably fine. Maybe fine. I just don't want to be the one to inform Susannah Smith-Bagley—hired-gun ratings guru and so-called news doctor just assigned to "young up" Channel 3's image and snag more viewers—that our big story fell through.

"Well, sorry, Charlie." Franklin sounds uncharacteristically nervous. He never calls me Charlie. "Oh, sorry, I know y'all hate the tuna ad line. But…"

The elevator doors swish open, and gentleman Franklin gestures me to go first. I lean against the brass railing inside, calculating the potential damage. It's not the best outcome that he revealed our possible scoop too early. Still, what's done is done.

I shift my bulky tote bag from one shoulder to the other in a doomed-to-failure attempt to prevent my charcoal-gray linen suit from wrinkling. Nobody's perfect, I decide, and Franklin's about as close as it comes. "No biggie," I tell him again. I hope I'm right.

Franklin pushes "31" and we ride up a floor or two in silence.

"It's kind of daunting, isn't it?" I ask, changing the subject. "That we could have the power to help an innocent person get out of prison? But what if she trusts us to get her exonerated and then we can't? Which would be worse? To fail? Or not even try?"

The lights on the elevator numbers slowly count upward, making a soft ping every time we pass the next floor.

Franklin nods, considering, then he makes quote marks in the air. "'Effecting positive change' to 'keep the system honest.' That's what they tell you in J-school. It's a lot different when you're actually doing it. When a real person's future is at stake."

The pings stop and the elevator door slides open. This time, I gesture Franklin to get out first.

"We've handled tough stories before. We can handle this one," I say. "If it's bigger, that just means it's better. We'll get the interview and then knock Susannah's socks off."

The elevator door closes, leaving us in a conservatively carpeted entry hall. I know this space is donated, a gift from a celebrated law firm hoping to reap do-gooder points by putting a pro bono face on its pro-business practice. The words "Constitutional Justice Project" are spelled out in bold brass letters affixed to the dark-paneled wall over the reception desk. Matching mahogany side tables, flanked by tweedy upholstered wing chairs, are carefully stacked with *The New Republic* and *Harper's*. Each has a No Smoking sign in a silver picture frame.

The room's focus is unmistakable. On one high-ceilinged wall, illuminated like gospel under a row of pin spots, there's an oversize framed copy of the Bill of Rights.

I look at Franklin with a smile. "Freedom of the press," I say, pointing to the poster. "That's you and me, kid. Let's go get that evidence."

"Would you like to see it again?" Oliver Rankin asks. "Our staff here watched the tape several times, and we feel the evidence is clear and incontrovertible. Agreed?"

Without waiting for our answers, he pushes the rewind button on the video cassette player, then turns to face Franklin and me. We're seated in leather club chairs arranged in front of a television set that glows in the darkened conference room. The executive director of the Constitutional Justice Project is shorter than I'd expected, but other than that he's the fashionisto everyone described: carefully suited in subtle pinstripes and elegantly groomed. He'd choose Denzel to play himself in the movie version, I bet. Or Wesley Snipes.

"Indisputable," he says. He points at me. "Once your viewers see that footage, Dorinda Sweeney's life will change forever. The judge will have no option but dismissal." He leans back on the ledge of the carved wooden cabinet, a lofty antique sideboard that turned out to be stacked inside with an elaborate array of state-of-the-art audio and video equipment.

"And then we'll prove, once again, the power of the truth," Rankin continues. His tone amplifies toward oratory, as if he's delivering the closing argument in a jury trial. "That the cynical, ends-justify-the-means methods employed by unscrupulous cops and prosecutors to manipulate the justice system cannot, will not, be tolerated."

Franklin and I exchange glances. I know Rankin's a zealot, tenacious and passionate. According to research Franklin showed me, Rankin's favorite cousin, years ago, had been convicted of a crime he didn't commit. Rankin battled his way relentlessly through the courts, working to prove his cousin was a victim of mistaken identity and get him released from prison. A shaky alibi emerged, then a DNA test and a new trial. Soon after, Rankin prevailed.

Now, supported by his incessant fund-raising from lawyers, movie stars and political activists, Rankin's CJP has masterminded the exonerations of more than a dozen innocent people. He's obviously convinced Dorinda Sweeney is his next victory.

His self-confidence is reassuring. But we can't put a story on the air unless we're sure it's solid. Commandment One of journalism: First, don't get it wrong. So now, on one hand, I'm wary. Tapes are easy to fake. On the other hand, that video could be journalism dynamite. I'm making a valiant effort to marshal my objectivity.

"Yes," I begin carefully, fidgeting a little in my chair, "that tape appears to be—"

"Watch again." Rankin interrupts. He pushes the play button again. "As they say in law school, slam dunk."

The tape flickers back into life and we all stare at the screen again. First color bars, then a block-numbered countdown, and a screen of black. Then, we see an empty room, smallish, lined with glass-fronted cabinets and rows of shelves and drawers. The camera is apparently mounted high in a corner, so when the door opens, we see only the top of a woman's head as she enters the room. The tape is supposed to be in color, but it's off, as if someone's improperly adjusted the settings, or the tape may have been reused so often it's deteriorating. As a result, the woman's skin appears vaguely green. She's wearing workaday slacks, flat shoes and some sort of smock—blue? green?—covering her clothes. At the bottom of the screen, time-coded numbers flash by, ticking hours, minutes and seconds. A date stamp is burned into the upper right corner of the screen: 05-19-04. *Three years ago,* I calculate. *May.*

The woman's dark hair, which the skewed video settings mutate to look distractingly purple, is pulled back in a ponytail. She appears unhurried, briskly familiar with the room, and has a set of keys clipped to an official-looking ID badge around her neck. At one point, she looks up toward the camera. At that moment, Oliver Rankin pushes Stop. The action freezes.

Rankin loosens his intricately patterned silk tie and allows himself a brief smile. "Every time I see it, it gets better and better. Dorinda Keeler Sweeney, at work, the night of the murder. Look at the date, then the time code," he says, pointing to the screen. "Sixteen minutes after three in the morning and there she is, indisputably, on her overnight shift at the Beachview Nursing Home, half an hour away from her house. According to the coroner's death certificate, at that time her husband Raymond Jack Sweeney was certainly dead at the bottom of their basement stairs. Drunk as a lord on tequila, head bashed in by an iron, bleeding to death in a pile of laundry. Pictures don't lie." He gestures at the screen. "This is alibi with a capital *A*."

He looks at us for confirmation. "Gotta love it."

They say when a story is too good to be true, a good reporter looks for the holes.

"Mr. Rankin," I begin.

"Oliver," he corrects me. He flips on the overhead lights, snapping the room fluorescent bright. Closing the television into the cabinet, he gestures for Franklin and me to take a seat at the long oval conference table.

"Oliver," I say, tacitly agreeing that we're on the same team. That worries me a bit, since a reporter can't take sides. But aren't we always on the side of the truth?

"This tape is beyond compelling," I continue, gesturing to Franklin for confirmation. "But I must ask you— when Ms. Sweeney confessed, why wasn't this tape used to impeach her statement?"

"I can answer that." A voice from the doorway. Quiet. Firm. We look up to see a lanky pale whisper of a man, gray hair a bit too long, cheekbones a bit too high, suit a bit too off-the-rack. *Threadbare,* I think, but that may just be in comparison to the dapper Rankin. He's smoke to Rankin's fire, but the intensity in their voices matches perfectly.

"Will Easterly," Rankin says. "Meet Charlie McNally, and her producer Franklin Parrish." Rankin smiles. "Will was Dorinda Sweeney's court-appointed lawyer."

"Court appointed? So you were with the Suffolk County Public Defenders Office?" Franklin asks. "Did you know…"

While the guys are bonding, my brain is churning out a list of questions. So many, so fast, I'm certain to forget them. I pull out a chair at the long conference table and start writing them in my reporter's notebook. *Motive? Money? Alibi? Battered? Other suspects? Evidence? Why tape not used? Why confess?*

The polished rosewood conference table in front of Rankin is strewn with newspaper clippings, Will's notes and the few files he kept. Picking up one page after another, Rankin's revealing the history of the murder and the local scandal: small-town girl, just graduated from high school, pushed by her single-parent mother into marrying the mother's ambitious boss, a local mover and shaker, a man she didn't love.

I wish he'd just hand over the darn clip file so I could read it myself, but the flamboyant Rankin seems eager to put himself center stage.

"The Prom Queen and the Pol," Rankin declaims. He holds up a two-page photo spread with one picture of Dorie, in a tiara and an unfortunately puffy prom dress.

There's another of B-movie big-shot type Ray Sweeney gaveling a Swampscott town council meeting. There's also a photo of a beribboned little girl, holding her father's hand and clutching some sort of stuffed animal, marching in the town's holiday parade. The caption, Rankin points out, says it all. "Ray Sweeney and his daughter Gaylen Marie back in happier times."

"Dorie's not with them," I observe, reaching across for the clipping.

"My point exactly," Rankin says. He slides the clip away, back into the folder.

Rankin's newsreel continues, a jury-worthy performance of trumpeting headlines, news clips, memories and legal commentary. When Dorinda Keeler Sweeney actually confessed to killing her husband of twenty-some years with their college-student daughter asleep upstairs, it seemed there was hardly room in the paper for anything else. One gossipy neighbor—the apparently libel-ignoring *Swampscott Chronicle* reported—was actually quoted as saying "Him and Dorie had nothing in common. Just the daughter. And everyone knows how Ray was with women."

Will Easterly holds up a yellowing news clipping, its oversize block letter headlines blazing Deadly Dorie Admits: I Did It. "Deadly Dorie," Will says bitterly, shaking his head. "Those headline writers should rot in hell."

I wince, knowing Channel 3's coverage of the story back then was probably just as sensational. "Again, though," I say, turning a page in my notebook and trying to change the focus. "She confessed. Did you ask her why?"

Will tosses the clipping onto the table. "Here's the rest of the story," he says. He pauses, as if composing himself, then runs both hands though his graying hair. "Back when I was assigned Dorie's case—"

I have to interrupt. "I'm sorry, Will, but I wanted to ask you about that." *Money.* One of the questions on my list. "Wasn't Ray Sweeney financially well-off? Why would Dorie need an appointed lawyer?"

"She didn't want a lawyer at all," Oliver Rankin answers. "The Commonwealth of Massachusetts assigned Will to her case. Someone says they don't need legal advice, that's their call. But the courts aren't comfortable if there's no lawyer standing by to make sure the defendant's rights are protected. And if they plead guilty, having a lawyer ensures they did it knowingly and voluntarily. Without coercion from the police, or pressure from someone else. And that was Will's job."

"Which I blew. Big-time." Will says, standing and putting his palms on the table. He looks right at me, his face weary, the picture of defeat. "And that's why you're here, Charlie." He stops, pursing his lips, then starts again. "I had a problem back then. A big one. I hadn't started going to meetings, hadn't admitted I was an alcoholic. When I got Dorinda's case, I didn't even ask how her confession was obtained. When I asked her why she confessed, she said, 'Because I'm guilty.'"

He sits back down, picks up the green glass bottle in front of him and swishes the water back and forth, staring at it.

"I just bought her story. I didn't ask the right questions. I didn't check the evidence, I didn't lift the phone to investigate. Now I know I need to take responsibility for my actions, and I'm responsible for what happened to Dorinda. I have to make it right," he says, his voice taut. "I just hope it's not too late."

I guess his explanation makes sense. And why look a gift story in the mouth? But that's exactly what I have to do. "But why—?" I begin.

Rankin interrupts me. "And that's where the videotape comes in." He slides the cassette across the table toward Franklin, who stops it one-handed. "Before Dorie confessed, police told the proprietors of Beachview Nursing Home, where Dorie worked, to preserve their surveillance tape for the night of the murder. It's a small place. Dorie's the only employee on the graveyard shift in her section. Often it was just her and the sleeping patients. But after Dorie confessed, the tape was no longer needed. The police never asked for it."

"I remembered it might still exist," Easterly picks up the story, his voice earnest. "I knew that might be my ticket to justice for Dorinda. A solid alibi." He locks his eyes onto mine. "Somewhere in my alcohol-soaked brain, back then, I knew she might be innocent. She was…"

He pauses and looks away, perhaps into the past. "She was not a murderer. Now, I need to try to prove it. Of course, if she hadn't been on the tape, that would have at least put my guilty conscience at ease. But there she is. Not guilty. Step Nine—'Make direct amends wherever possible.'"

Franklin, chin in hands, stares at him, transfixed. I realize I'm holding my breath. It's as if Will has made a confession of his own.

Rankin, however, is brusque, all business. "And that's it, right from the source," he says. He continues to tick off his points, one finger at a time. "Will asked the nursing home to search for the video. They found it, still in some file cabinet where they'd locked it three years ago. He convinced them to let him have the tape, and there she was. Will's worked with us on other cases, so yesterday he brought it straight to me."

I'm captivated by Will's quiet passion, his obvious

deep belief. But still, I've got questions. "Will?" I begin, quietly. "Then why did she confess?"

Will throws up his hands, looking frustrated. "I don't know. Maybe she wanted him dead. Maybe she knows something. Maybe someone is blackmailing her. I don't know," he says. "She still insists she's guilty. But now, this tape proves she wasn't there. She didn't do it."

I can't know what the rest of them are thinking, but I'm picturing Dorie locked inside the redbrick fortress of MCI-Framingham, the oldest women's prison in the country. Innocent, terrified, and trapped behind bars for three long years. It's the story I've dreamed about since J-school. I can save her.

"Will she agree to an interview?" I ask. My list is growing. *Find witnesses. Get police report. Where is daughter? Why confess?* "Dorie has to go on camera. And we'll need a copy of that tape. We need to have it authenticated. And—may we take these clippings? We'll need to look at them."

"It'll take two weeks, maybe more, to get this story pulled together," Franklin adds. "But the interview with Dorie is key."

"Once she hears we have the tape, I'm sure she'll want to talk to you," Will says. "And we can find out why she confessed. My guess, the police pushed her into it."

I nod, ticking off another question on my list. "You think they threatened her? Said she'd certainly be convicted, got her to make a deal for a lesser sentence?"

"Happens all the time," Rankin asserts. "All the damn time." He slides back his chair from the head of the table and begins to pace, pointing at each of us, as if he's in charge of Franklin and me, too.

"Will, you call Dorinda. Charlie, of course take those

clippings. And your copy of the tape. Let us know what you find out. Franklin, leave your number with my secretary in case he needs to get in touch with you directly. I'll get my staff to do some digging, but you two are the front lines of Team Dorinda."

I smile noncommittally. Team Dorinda? Situations like this are always sticky. Tricky. Franklin and I don't work for the CJP, we work for the truth. We'll follow the story whether it leads where Rankin and Easterly believe it will—or whether it doesn't. If it turns out Dorinda is guilty, we might even go with that story instead.

It's a fragile equilibrium.

I gather up the newspaper clippings, sliding them into their manila file folder and tucking them carefully into my tote bag. I can't wait to read them all thoroughly, focusing to see if I can put the story together in a different way. In a way that means Dorie's innocent.

Rankin and Will Easterly are moving toward the conference room door. "Oscar Ortega will be ripping some poor sucker for this one," I hear Rankin mutter, patting Will on the back as he guides him through the room. "Governor's chair? I don't think so."

I look up, surprised. "I'm sorry, Oliver," I say. "Did you say Oscar Ortega? Would be…unhappy? Could I ask why?"

"Of course," Rankin replies, changing his tone, affable again. "I thought you knew. You'll see it when you read the articles. Oz was lead prosecutor in the Sweeney case. The A.G.'s office had jurisdiction because Sweeney was a public official. Oz wrapped up the case with that confession, now he touts it as one of his big successes. He says his law and order team is so powerful, miscreants simply surrender." He pauses, then gives a sardonic smile. "If Dorinda's innocent? There goes the law-and-order campaign."

The four of us arrive at the elevator and I push the button. Then, because Franklin's not watching me, I push it again. We hear the click and swish as the mechanism clicks into life. Ha. I wish Franklin had been looking.

"I'll call Dorie right now," Will says. "I'm sure she'll talk with you." He holds out a hand, shaking mine, then Franklin's. "If you can get to the truth, you're going to save her life."

"I—we—" I begin. "Please don't get her hopes up," I urge him. "It would be tragedy on tragedy if she begins to rely on us, and then it doesn't happen."

The elevator arrives, and Franklin and I step in. "Thank you so much," I say. "We'll let you know what we come up with."

The polished stainless steel doors begin to close, but then Rankin steps forward, clamping one confident hand into the opening. He forces the doors apart even as the elevator mechanism struggles to slide them together.

"You two are going up against the Great and Powerful Oz. You know that, correct?" he asks, pretending the elevator isn't fighting back. "Not afraid of him, are you?"

Before either of us can respond to his challenge, he lets go of the door and it slides shut.

"I knew there was something," I whisper to Franklin. We're alone in the elevator, but it feels right to keep my voice low. "Maybe that's what this is really about. Ortega."

Before Franklin can reply, we stop at the twenty-fifth floor. A harried-looking woman tapping a BlackBerry gets on. She pushes 21. We wait, impatient for privacy.

Four floors down, the doors close us into seclusion again. "I mean, Will's obviously obsessed with Dorie," I continue. "What if Rankin's obsessed with Oz? And if Rankin and Easterly hate Ortega, maybe they think—"

I stop as the doors open again. Two young women step on, deep into comparing the nail polish colors showing through the openings of their peep-toed pumps.

I decide to risk it.

"If they think you-know-who being innocent can derail the campaign of 'that guy,'" I continue, talking in code, "maybe they're leaking the story to make him a loser. And manipulating us into helping."

Franklin nods. "But we can't leave her up the river. We can't tell her, like, 'It's June. We'll come back in November, after the election, when it's less complicated.'"

"But if we go back upstairs, and say, hey, we're concerned…" I glance at the girls. Oblivious. "They'll just give the tape to someone else. And we'll be—you know." *Screwed*, is what I don't say out loud. If Rankin and Will give the story to another reporter.

I think about those clippings—and that tape—tucked into my bag. The potentially innocent woman trapped behind bars, expecting us to help her. The persuasively confident Rankin assuming we're on his team. The great and powerful Oz expecting to win the governor's race. My news director and his glossy hired gun Susannah, expecting a blockbuster story in less than a month.

The nail polish girls get off. As the door closes behind them, I suddenly realize what makes this complicated mix not only more volatile, but even potentially dangerous.

"Listen, Franko, there's one more thing," I say. "Getting Dorinda Sweeney out of prison? Of course, it could be off the charts. But here's what else."

"How they got that confession," Franklin begins. "That's—"

"Right," I say, interrupting. "But listen. Ortega's staff and the Swampscott cops investigated the killing right? And if Dorie didn't kill her husband, someone else did. Someone else was in Dorie's home that night. And that same someone else bashed Ray Sweeney on the head with an iron, and pushed him down the stairs. Question is—who? And why didn't anyone know that?"

Chapter Four

What do you wear to interview a convicted murderer?

I'm almost late. I know I should be getting dressed for this morning's mandatory "hear Susannah's strategy to win the ratings" meeting at the station. I know I can always figure out what to wear to interview Dorie when the time comes. But thinking about Dorie is so tempting. She's just six years younger than I am and I'm overwhelmed at how different our lives are.

I open my closet door, flip on the light, and plop down in the curvy white wicker chair in the corner. You don't need three bedrooms if there's only one of you, so I converted the one across the hall into my office and this one into a closet. My contract includes a clothing allowance. If you don't spend the money, you lose it. That means twenty years of purchases—minus, of course, the few years' worth of unfortunate shoulder pads and irreparably short skirts that faced a quick demise—that need to hang somewhere.

I park my mug of coffee on a shoe box next to the chair and retie the belt of my terry-cloth bathrobe.

Dorie. I imagine the interview to come, the innocent and unfairly imprisoned woman sitting across from me at a battered table, bleak daylight attempting its way through the prison's barred windows. She'll be nervous, maybe, at first. Or defensive. Tears will well up, as she reveals—what, I wonder? Anyway, soon after our story airs, she'll walk out of Framingham State and into the sunshine, probably in one of those prison-issue jumpsuits. Our cameras on the scene catch the dramatic moments, as—I come out of my daydream and frown, picturing it. I hope she's not wearing stripes. That could make the camera jumpy. We'll need one camera on the door, to shoot the critical video of her as the doors open. And one camera on me.

I pick up my mug just in time to prevent Botox from knocking it over. My neurotic calico jumps onto my lap, demanding attention, as I scan the closet's "on the air" section. Black suit. Then, black suit. Black suit. Black suit. Okay, then. Another life decision successfully made. And easier than I thought.

I'm mulling over shoe selection when I hear my desk phone ringing. Sliding in my stocking feet across the hardwood hall, I slip my way toward my office. Botox scampers after me, then hops up to her spot on the windowsill.

"This is McNally," I say, grabbing the receiver and landing safely in my swivel chair. I can never remember how to answer the phone at home. "I mean, hello."

"Hey Charlotte, it's me. I'm at the station. We've got a…"

Franklin pauses, so of course I interrupt. "Hey Franko, what's up? Do we have a photog for today? After we hear from our no-doubt fabulous new consultant, we should head right out to Swampscott. Get exteriors of the Sweeney house. And the high school. And the bar where Ray was last seen. Maybe we can get some neighbors to talk. And we can see if—"

"Charlotte." Franklin says. "Stop. Listen to me. We've got a situation."

I hear something in his voice I really don't like. "Yeah?" I say. I lean forward in my chair, elbows on the desk, and realize I'm clenching the phone. "You're scaring me here, Franklin. What situation?"

I can hear Franklin take a deep breath. For a moment there's only silence on the line.

I wait. As long as he's not saying anything, I'm not hearing anything bad. The silence doesn't last long.

"She's not going to do the interview," Franklin says. "She's not talking. Period. End of story. I just got off the phone with Will Easterly. Apparently Dorie got back to him early this morning. And she told him to tell us two words. Drop. Dead."

Kevin O'Bannon claps his hands once, twice, and calls out to the newsroom full of Channel 3 staffers. "Gang? Hello?" the news director pleads. He takes off his trademark navy-blue double-breasted suit jacket as he speaks, hanging it over the back of a nearby computer monitor, loosens his paisley tie, turns back his cuffs. I watch him in amusement. He's so management school. This is supposed to telegraph he's one of us. He so isn't.

"Can we settle down, please?" Channel 3's news director taps on the microphone clipped to a stand in front of him, but all we hear is a tinny thunk. It's dead. The tawny blonde seated beside him, ropy pearls and multi-hued bouclé announcing her allegiance to the Chanel mother ship, crosses one toned leg over the other, and pretends not to notice. Susannah Smith-Bagley. The newest darling of news-consultant world. Waiting for her chance to bestow her cutting-edge wisdom and change our lives.

Franklin, Maysie and I are among those leaning on the mezzanine railing that overlooks the crowded newsroom below, watching Kevin continue his struggle to get his troops to stop chatting with one another and pay attention to him. So far, the news director is failing, and the three of us railbirds aren't helping.

"So how much you think that suit set somebody back?" Maysie whispers, pointing to the newcomer at Kevin's side. "Not to mention the boob job?"

"Queen Susannah wears what she wishes," I answer softly. "We, her subjects, must do as she bids. You hear anything about what she's gonna say? Besides, of course, that we should all come up with more on-the-air cleavage." I look down, doomed. "Somehow."

"You're the brains of the operation, Charlotte," Franklin puts in. "No one is looking at your…" He pauses. "Anyway, I hear from my sources in San Fran, Susannah's all about the brand. Give a bad story a good title and it sells. Who cares about the content? Give a story a good title, and ka-ching. Ratings gold."

"Speaking of suits," I say, turning to look at Maysie. "What's up with you? I can't remember a time I've seen you in anything but black jeans. Suddenly now, you have legs. And lip gloss."

"Well, I just found out," Maysie begins. "I tried to call and tell you this morning but your line was busy."

An ear-splitting squeal fills the room, as an embarrassed-looking tech guy adjusts Kevin's microphone. Everyone snickers. A few cynics applaud.

"You'd think a TV station could get the mic to work," Franklin comments.

"Tell me what?" I turn to face the ponytailed sports reporter beside me. Maysie and I have been pals since we bonded years ago while divvying up the junk food left in the station's cafeteria during a sudden blizzard. I'm like her older sister. I can read her better than anyone, except (maybe) her husband Matthew. I can tell she's holding back.

Kevin claps his hands again. Now there's no way to ignore him. As he begins his introduction of Susannah, I give Maysie a wide-eyed entreaty. *What?* I silently mouth the word, trying to look as beseeching as possible.

Maysie points me to Kevin and Susannah, then her watch. *Later,* she pantomimes.

The only sound now is the jingle of Susannah's multiple charm bracelets clanking against the mic stand as she confidently adjusts it higher, instantly proving she's taller than Kevin. She gives him a seemingly apologetic shrug, which serves only to underscore her prominence, and claims center stage.

"Hello, all," she says. "Get out your calendars, folks."

Flipping open a logo-covered folder, she holds it up in front of her. I guess it's a calendar, I can't see details that far away. Every eye in the newsroom follows her, as she pivots, surveying us. She waits until we're all silent. "July? Is the new November. The ratings holy grail. We're gonna milk those demos till the other stations can't see straight. You're age twenty-five to fifty-four? A woman? We want you watching Channel 3. And we'll do anything to get you here."

The murmuring buzz picks up again as a roomful of newsies begin individual calculations. *How will that affect me? Am I in? Or out?*

"Dollarwise, Envirobeat. We've discussed your roles," Susannah continues, pointing to the franchise reporters and producers of those segments. "Now. Charlie Investigates." Susannah scans the room, apparently looking for me and Franklin.

I give a tentative wave. "Up here," I call out.

Every face in the room turns up to look at me and Franklin. I can feel my face tighten as I stoically keep smiling, pretending I know what's coming next. Susannah consults her folder again, then looks back up at us, too.

"I'm simply thrilled to announce that Charlie and Frank have come up with another…" she pauses "…very important story. We're keeping the details under wraps, because those investigative types are such secret squirrels! But we want you to know we're going all out to promote their superdynamite July scoop. We're counting on it for big, big numbers." She taps her folder. "You're the first to know. We're branding it Charlie's Crusade."

Susannah nods, self-satisfied, as if she's just invented alliteration and now expects someone to applaud.

I give Franklin a tiny kick in one ankle. "Nice one, *Frank*," I hiss. "We're screwed. She doesn't know about Dorie's 'drop dead' decision, I imagine."

Franklin, frowning, opens his mouth to answer. I wave him off, as below us, Susannah continues to outline her grand scheme.

"Now, one more agenda item before it's time for the noon news," she says. "With the Red Sox grabbing such a huge fan base this season, I'm happy to announce a decision made just last night. We're starting a new weekend show. We're branding it—Red Sox Nation. And it will feature our newest anchor, Maysie Green, the Sports Machine."

I turn to Maysie, shocked, my jaw slack. Franklin has

lost it and is laughing uncontrollably. His reaction is all the more difficult because he's trying, unsuccessfully, to hide it from the room below. "Ma-chine?" I hear him say.

Susannah must be wrapping up the meeting, but I have no idea what she's saying. Maysie's good news trumps everything, even the impending doom of losing our story.

"So you've got your own show," I whisper, grinning. "Hot stuff. A little TV face time for the queen of radio." I give Mays a hug. "Congratulations," I say. "Ignore Franklin. You deserve it. Now I understand the suit and lips, video girl."

"And it'll keep me home this season, too," Maysie says. Her brown eyes shine, and there's a satisfaction—or something—in her expression I haven't seen before. "No more two-week road trips with the boys of summer. Matthew is so psyched."

"The Sports Ma-chine," Franklin repeats. He adds a dancing little hip-hop move now that the meeting is over. "Ma-CHINE." He looks at Maysie, his dark brown eyes twinkling teasingly behind his glasses. "Did you come up with that? Or did old Susannah?"

"Like I said, ignore him," I tell Maysie, laughing. "But listen, it's so funny. I thought you were pregnant. That's what I thought you wanted to tell me. You know me, Miss Suspicious, anything to make the day weirder. Just what you and Matthew need, a sibling for Max and Molly." I hurry to reassure her. "Not that there'd be anything wrong with that."

"Yeah, well." Maysie replies. I detect the beginnings of a blush, and that satisfied expression returns. "Good thing. Because—yeah. That *is* what I was trying to call you about. Baby Green number three is on the way. Don't make plans for New Year's Eve, okay?"

* * *

The car window beside me powers down by itself, letting in a blast of salt air and a faint stench of something as we drive up the North Shore Parkway. We're half an hour out of Boston, destination—at last—Swampscott.

"Smell that?" Franklin asks. He has one hand on the steering wheel of his Passat and the other on the window controls. "Welcome to the north shore of Massachusetts. The good news—you get to live by the ocean. The bad news—every summer, some disgusting algae stinks up the beach."

I sniff, then buzz my window back up, nodding. "Never fails," I agree. The Parkway is taking us straight to our destination as the expanse of Atlantic Ocean, white-capped and sparkling, stretches endlessly beside us. Above a weather-beaten boardwalk, gray and white seagulls swoop between skateboarders, diving at remnants of leftover clam rolls. "But it's so beautiful here. You probably get used to it."

Franklin makes a dismissive face. "I suppose it could happen," he says. "Turn right after the ball field?"

"Yup," I say, confirming. We'd put in multiple and increasingly urgent but unanswered calls to Will Easterly and Oliver Rankin, then realized we couldn't just stay at the station and worry. We decided it couldn't hurt to check out Dorinda's hometown, even though we have no camera with us. The assignment desk Nazi informed us he couldn't spare a photographer except for breaking news, so today we're on our own. Cross fingers we don't miss out on some once-in-a-lifetime interview because Channel 3 refuses to provide the resources we need.

"This takes us to Swampscott. The Sweeney house is off Humphrey Street," I continue. I tip my new red-striped reading glasses into place from the top of my head and check our map. "Alden Street, then turn onto Little's Point Road. It's number three twenty-seven, but the clerk at town hall said it was for sale again, so I'm thinking we can just look for the sign."

We drive through the seaside neighborhood, patches of ocean grass and hydrangea keeping houses politely private, and pull up in front of an unpretentious two-story white-shingled cape with dormer windows, weathered shutters, gray front door. A bright yellow For Sale sign flaps silently in front, the yard's only color. Someone's mowed the lawn, but the garden is suffering, azaleas parched, splay-petaled tulips defeated by the June sun. The bad vibes surrounding the place are just my imagination, I know, but I hesitate to get out of the car. I wish Will or Rankin would call.

"So now what?" Franklin asks. "You want to check with some neighbors? See if anyone knows anything? Remembers anything?"

I check my watch, back-timing, frustrated that we have to hurry. Franklin insisted we have lunch, and I wasn't going to argue with that. But it's now two o'clock. I've got to meet Josh and Penny at six, a kid-friendly dinner-time. Before that I've got to change clothes. And before that I've got to stop by the Center for Cosmetic Surgery and check on Mom. This workday feels over before it's even started. "I wish Will or Rankin would call," I complain, staring at the house. "And I figure we still have three hours or so. Well, two, since we have to drive back to Boston. We could—" I stop mid-sentence.

The Sweeneys' front door is opening.

Chapter Five

Poppy Morency, oversize black-rimmed sunglasses holding back her snowy-white pageboy, pulls a jangling ring of keys from a navy-strapped canvas boat bag. Where there's usually an embroidered monogram or a sailboat name, Poppy's bag says Morency Real Estate.

"House has been on the market for two years?" She tilts her head, calculating. "Three? We sold it once, after the—well, of course you know." She focuses on the keys, choosing. "Anyway, the buyers never moved in, and asked us to sell again. So it's still furnished, pretty much the same as it was when—well, of course, you know that, too."

"Thank you so much," I say. Franklin and I did some fast talking after we found out who she was, and convinced her to take us inside. Maybe our luck is changing. But it stinks that we don't have a camera. "We won't be long," I assure her.

Poppy finds the key she's looking for, inserts it into the front door lock. "You do have a point," she says, turning the key. "If you were in the market for a house, I'd let you in to look around. So, as you say, there's no harm. And I've always admired your work, Charlie." She stops and looks back at me. "And I do remember Dorinda

Sweeney, of course. Little snip of a thing. Ray. It was all very sad. You know…"

She pushes the door open, and gestures Franklin and me inside without finishing her sentence. "We have a service that keeps it tidy, in case we have to show it," she explains, all real estate business now. "Personal items, someone took most of them away. They had a thorough cleaning done of certain, um, areas, of course, after the, um, incident."

"We know," Franklin says, crossing the threshold.

I follow him, stepping into Dorinda's life. Poppy leads us through a tiled entryway, empty coat hooks establishing more emptiness to come, and into the living room. Square, white-walled, silent. Dorinda's house is—*was*—standard issue, unimaginative, matching. Seems like the Sweeneys' money wasn't spent on style or comfort. Straight-armed, dully plaid couch that matches stolid side chairs. Walnut coffee table that matches unhappy end tables. Ashtrays. It's stripped of all personality, no photographs, no art, no mirrors. A curtain rod, empty, stretches across the wide rear windows, a strip of ocean visible just at the top. A home—now just a house. Waiting to see what will happen next.

Poppy looks at her watch, an oversize clock face tied to her wrist with a preppy green ribbon bow, and begins flipping through what looks like an appointment book. I get the message. *Hurry.*

"May we take a quick look upstairs?" I ask. Then I casually ask the clincher as if it's no big deal. "And the basement?"

Poppy perches on the couch and pulls out a cell phone. "I have a couple of calls to make," she says. She's already focused on dialing. "Look around, and then—

Hello, this is Priscilla Morency, can you hold a moment?" She interrupts herself, looking at me apologetically, and waves us along. *Go ahead,* she mouths the words. She holds up her hand, fingers spread, pantomiming. *Five minutes.*

"Want to split up?" I turn to Franklin, keeping my voice low. "You take the kitchen, I'll go upstairs, then we can meet in a few minutes." I point down the hall. "Figure out where the basement door is, okay? Then we'll go down there together." I glance at Poppy, who now has the phone tucked between her cheek and shoulder, and is consulting her notebook. "She'll forget about the five-minute thing," I predict. "But we should hurry."

Franklin nods, checking his watch, and turns down the hall. I trot up the stairway, trailing my fingers on the wall over a patchwork of faded, then bright paint. Square outlines on the wall remember where pictures used to be. Family portraits? Souvenirs from Ray's political campaigns? Little Gaylen's first finger painting? I think of that newspaper snapshot of Gaylen and her father. Except Gaylen would be older now, of course.

I'm upstairs. A narrow hall. The afternoon sun struggles to make it through the four-paned window at the hall's end, but a partly closed shade shapes the light into fluttering shadows on the closed doors, two on each side of me. There was a murder in this house. *Did someone scream? Panic? There was a struggle, certainly. Violence. Passion. A body, battered and bleeding, crumpled and lifeless at the bottom of the basement stairs. The murderer, and the victim, might have walked this hallway.*

The intensity of the vision surprises me a little. I pause, hand on the banister, keeping my connection to the real world and the live people downstairs. As soon as Poppy finishes her calls, my time is up. There's no cleaning solution potent enough to eradicate bad karma.

I banish the ghosts and choose a door.

Bathroom. Hand still on the doorknob, I take a quick scan and decide to come back if I can. I close the door and choose another, opening it quickly now, aware of my time limits. The master bedroom, this one must be. There's a double closet, its doors faced with sliding mirrors. Hesitant at first, I slide open one closet door, setting off a soft clatter as a row of wire hangers rustles with my gesture. I look quickly. Nothing. I reach up to the closet's upper shelf, patting my hand along the top in case the cleaners missed something. I check the floor. Nothing.

Now that I've given myself permission, I head for the armoire. One door open, two. A few limply empty plastic cleaning bags on hangers, an empty shoe box on the floor. Even on tiptoe, I can't see what's on the top shelf, so I pat across it with my hand again. Nothing. Damn.

On fast-forward now, I quickly open every bureau drawer, hearing the scrape of the metal rollers as each slides open. Still nothing. I close the final drawer, reminding myself there are still two rooms to explore and not much time to do it.

The drawer won't close. I try again, but there's something jamming it. Have I broken the bureau? That'll be fun to explain. I open the drawer again and close it more slowly, almost hearing the clock ticking. It still won't close.

I reach underneath, searching blindly for some mechanism that'll release the wooden drawer from its bracket. Finding what feels like the switch, I click it open, and the empty drawer slides completely out. Holding the drawer in one hand, I stretch my other arm into the opening, reaching for whatever obstruction might have been in the way. My fingers feel a crinkle. Like a piece of paper.

"Charlie?" I hear Poppy's voice from the bottom of the stairs. I hope from the bottom. It's going to be very unpleasant to try to defend why I'm standing in a convicted murderer's bedroom with a drawer in one hand and my other arm deep in her dresser. And I've still got to see the basement.

I grab the paper and carefully ease it out. Don't want to tear it. Fumbling with haste, I tilt and wiggle the drawer to get it back into place. "*Do* it," I mutter at the drawer.

"Be down in a moment," I call out, still continuing to jiggle the drawer handle, trying to sound casual. Poppy's still all the way downstairs, it sounds like, and I don't want her joining me up here just yet.

With a metallic click, the drawer finally rolls all the way closed. I look at the document in my hand, and then I hear my name again. The voice is getting closer. I grab my tote bag and dig out my cell phone. This had better work.

"I promise you, there wasn't anything to see down there," Franklin reassures me as we pull out of the Sweeneys' cul-de-sac. "You were taking so long upstairs, I just went down to the basement myself, figuring you'd arrive sooner or later. Too bad it was too much later," he adds. "You should have checked your watch."

I know he's teasing, but it drives me crazy that Poppy threw us out before—well, she hadn't exactly thrown us out, but even though she'd politely tucked my business card into her files, she had made it clear our time inside was up. Luckily Franklin was resourceful enough to investigate the basement himself. So far, he hasn't stopped talking about what he saw downstairs long enough for me to show him what I found upstairs. Just as well, since I'd rather wait until we can get somewhere private. And I do want to hear about that basement, even if he thinks it wasn't revealing.

"It was all…" Franklin wrinkles his nose, remembering. "Bleachy. The concrete floors, all spotless." He glances at me. "You know, spot-less. No stains, if that's what you're imagining."

I had been, actually. He knows me too well. "What's at the top of the stairs? Are the steps steep? Were there railings? Are the floors all concrete?"

I'm wondering about Oscar Ortega and his investigators accepting the story that a woman of Dorinda's size, a "little snip of a thing" as Poppy had called her, got control of her hulk of a husband and managed to push him down the stairs. Not to mention how she bashed him with an iron. "According to the news articles," I continue my thoughts out loud, "they'd gone home after having an argument in that bar. The Reefs? Dorie hit him with the iron while he was passed out on the couch, then dragged him to the basement steps and pushed him down."

I pause, imagining the scene, and Dorinda, and how heavy her dead husband would be, and why the daughter didn't wake up, and how much blood and evidence there would be on the path from the couch to the basement steps. "You'd think Oz's crime-scene people could easily tell," I begin, "whether someone actually—"

"She confessed," Franklin reminds me, interrupting. "Oz and the Swampscott police probably didn't even bring in a trace evidence team. Wouldn't have needed to. Case closed, you know?" Franklin clicks on the car's turn signal. "Dunkin's okay?"

"We've got to talk to her. Got to." I say, probably for

the millionth time, as we head into the parking lot of the coffee shop. There's a line at the drive-through, so Franklin pulls up to the front door. "Wait," I say, turning toward him. I make a quick check around the parking lot, although with Poppy long gone, who's going to be watching us? I zip open my purse.

Franklin looks at me inquiringly. "Did you forget to go to the bank machine again?" he asks. "I'll spring for the lattes."

"Nope," I reply. I pull out my cell phone, and click into My Photos. "I just want to show you something. Look what I found in the Sweeneys' bureau," I say, holding up the phone so Franklin can see it too. "It's a picture of Dorie from high school. See? It had slipped behind a drawer, you know? Underneath. I took a snap of it with my phone. She's wearing a Swampscott High hoodie sweatshirt, so it must have been taken years ago. You can tell how young she is. And she's giving the peace sign. Very eighties teeny bopper."

"You took it? From a drawer?" Franklin is focusing on the process, not the picture. I'd hoped he'd ignore that part. "You opened their drawers?"

"Yeah, yeah, so I opened the drawers," I say, trying to dismiss him. "I couldn't help it. But I didn't *take* it. I put the picture back, so if anyone knew it was there, which they don't because everything was cleaned out, it'll be there when they check. Which they won't. And now," I say, pushing the cell phone closer to him, "we have a new picture of Dorie."

Franklin squints at the admittedly fuzzy photo. "Which," he says, "we won't be able to use, not only because it's basically out of focus, but also because how will you—and I do mean *you*—explain where you got it?"

"I know we can't use it on the air. But once I found it, I couldn't just leave it, you know? And I couldn't swipe it, although I admit the thought crossed my mind. Anyway, we have it. For whatever it's worth. And to prove I didn't totally fail as Nancy Drew." I flip the phone closed and zip it back into its pouch. "Now let's go get those lattes, Franko. I need a little caffeine courage before I face my mother."

Opening the door of the coffee shop, I walk into a fragrant den of cinnamon and vanilla and sugary just-baked doughnuts. A *little* caffeine courage? I need an extra large. Because after my hospital visit, I remember, there's my tête-à-tête-à-tête with Josh and Penny.

I smile at the pink-jacketed teen behind the counter. "High-test," I say. She looks at me, blank and confused. I try again. "Low-fat no-foam no-sugar triple latte, two Splendas, double cup."

This, she comprehends. Good thing I'm in the communications business.

How am I supposed to get an eight-year-old girl to fall in love with me? Penny's wearing what I recognize as Josh's old Beach Boys T-shirt with a pink leotard underneath, black leggings and pink ballet shoes. Her frosty pink nail polish is chipping from her bitten fingernails, and her pin-straight brown hair is held back with a sparkly black headband. She deigned to acknowledge my presence when I arrived at the restaurant, but since then, I've obviously been about as enthralling to her as the salt shaker. So much for the communications business.

What's making this more complicated, I still have to explain to her dad—the heart-flutteringly handsome man across from me—that yet another news story is coming between us.

Right now, though, it's Penny who's coming between us. She's sitting next to Josh in our maroon suede booth, her spindly preteen body tucked into him as closely as possible. I'm on the other side of the red-checked tablecloth.

Two, plus one. I'm so clearly the addition, the newcomer, the intruder. This is going to be a difficult dinner.

And Penny isn't making it any easier. As I pretend to examine my seared tuna, Josh's daughter begins to make bread pellets from the mini-baguette on the plate in front of her. So far her conversation with me has consisted of: "Fine." "Yuck, who could eat raw fish?" And "Mom always lets me have pasta with butter." And that comment was mostly to Josh.

Using her thumb and one finger the same way my sister and I used to play marbles, she flips a bread pellet sideways across the table, and it lands in Josh's water glass.

I burst out laughing, then cover my mouth with my napkin to hide my reaction. I know I'm not supposed to laugh—it will encourage her. But on the other hand, it's harmless, and pretty funny. If you're eight. Which, of course, she is.

"Think you're a comedian, huh?" Josh tries to rumple her hair, but she flattens herself into the corner of the booth, laughing, and pulls her knees up to her chest, tucking those little shoes under Josh's thigh. She obviously adores him. "Gotcha, Daddy," she says "Two points."

I might as well not even be in the room.

"On the floor," Josh says, affectionately pushing her feet off the suede. I'm watching the bread pellet fall apart in Josh's glass. Disintegrating. Just like our relationship, if I can't find the secret words to break through Penny's no-trespassing barrier.

"So Mom says to tell you both hello," I begin, attempting to make us a table for three. "I was just at the hospital, and the doctors say she's recovering nicely." Then I stop. Talk about the elephant in the room. My first venture into conversation, and I've brought up the M word.

Penny pulls a lock of hair across her mouth and looks at me from under her lashes, her smile vanishing. "*My* mother is a doctor," she says. "She's on a cruise." She briefly turns back to pellet-making, then looks at me again, challenging. "To Montserrat. It's French."

Okay, I'm going for it. She's eight. I'm a grown-up. Lots of kids even like me. I can do this. "Yes, I know," I say, putting down my chopsticks. "I actually covered the story in Montserrat, after the volca—"

Two waiters in sleek black T-shirts arrive, their steaming platters cutting off what might have been my best chance to finish an actual sentence. Penny's plate is white, her scallops are white, her pasta is white, and she looks skeptically at the green flakes sprinkled on the sides of the dish.

"I hate—" she begins.

Josh twists the end of his napkin into a point and with one swift gesture swipes the parsley out of existence. "There, fussy bird," he says, touching her nose with one finger. "All white again." He shrugs, looking at me apologetically. "Not worth the struggle, you know? White food. Victoria says it's a phase."

I hate—when he says her name. I know it's silly, they've been divorced for two years now. But if Victoria told him it's a phase that means they must talk. And of course they have to talk—they share Penny. And Penny will always be both of theirs, no matter that Victoria married Elliott what's-his-name. No matter if Josh and I—

I sneak a foot under the table, slide a toe under one leg of Josh's jeans. "How's your—salmon?" I ask.

Josh flickers a look at Penny, who's focused on twisting her spaghetti, and then winks at me. "The cottage in Truro has a private outside shower," he says, leaning across the table. His voice is PG matter-of-fact, but his look conveys an unmistakably X-rated double meaning. "Did I tell you that? Warm summer nights, in the moonlight, you can wash the sand out of your hair. Or wherever."

And there's the rub. Here's where I'm supposed to look dreamy and seductive, perhaps mention my new and frighteningly small bathing suit, perhaps allude to coconut-scented suntan lotion. And it would all be from the heart. I'm longing to try out that shower, and see just how X-rated one summer vacation can be. Just one hitch in the potential passion. Dorinda Keeler Sweeney is stuck in prison. And I can get her out. Does that trump spending time on Cape Cod with the man of my dreams, shower or not? Wouldn't any other decision be selfish?

"Um," I reply. "That sounds perfect." I move a bit of gingered sea bass around my plate, stalling. It's usually my favorite, but now I'm too tense to enjoy it. I bring a bite of fish to my mouth, then put it back down. "But you know," I begin. Dorinda's potential innocence pesters me like an insistent child, never far from my side. "You know I told you about Dorinda Sweeney?"

Penny is out of it. She's strapped by the seat belt into the back seat of Josh's Volvo, mesmerized by some Play-Station gizmo, the real world muted into muffled background by her iPod earbuds. Oblivious to the intense conversation in the front seat. We're all parked outside of my apartment, the car windows open, letting in the summer as the last of the daylight fades. Tourists with cameras around their necks stroll along the twisting narrow sidewalks, pointing and gesturing, locating the architectural quirks and oddities of the oldest part of Boston. A blue-uniformed police officer in BPD shorts bicycles slowly past, giving me a quick appraising glance, and salutes as I return a reassuring wave—I'm fine. I hope that's true. I've got to go inside soon. Josh and Penny are going home.

"It's fine, sweets," Josh reassures me. He runs a finger down my cheek, tracing my jaw, then tilting my chin. "Got to get you another Emmy, right? And get Dorinda Sweeney out of prison. Penny and I will be fine in Truro. And you can be our special treat. Come see us whenever you can. It would be…" He pauses, cocking his head back at Penny. "Well, if someone had unjustly taken me away from her, I'd be unstoppable. Whatever. Do your stuff, Brenda Starr. Truro can wait."

I glance into the back seat, see the child Josh loves so much. They have such a connection, a bond, a certainty. Right now, she looks sweet, clicking intently on her computer game. And loving. And eight. And what little girl wouldn't worry about the other woman, essentially a stranger, threatening to take her dad away? How can two be three?

Reaching over, I take Josh's hand. "I need you to understand, I'm not choosing my job over you two. It's just—Dorinda. That videotape is a perfect alibi. She should not be spending one more day behind bars."

Without another backward glance, Josh pulls me toward him, his eyes locked into mine. "We'll be here for you," he says, giving me a delicate kiss on the forehead. "Me, and even little Penny. I'm proud of you."

The complicating combination of a stickshift and an eight-year-old means I can't melt into his arms. Or slide my hand under his shirt. Or slide his hand under mine. But I trust him. Victoria is completely out of the picture, thousands of miles away, cruising happily with her husband. Penny will come around. And Josh would tell me, I reassure myself, if he was upset. Maybe, maybe it could work.

Chapter Six

"Before." I'm peering into the oversize makeup mirror, illuminated by the unforgiving perimeter of frosted bulbs surrounding it. Maysie, ponytailed as always and hands on hips, is looking at me in the mirror, too. Since she's the only woman working for Channel 3's all-sports radio station, she's claimed this fourth-floor ladies' room as her private salon, the place where we convene for high-level gossip and general life discussions. Today, it's face time.

"And after." I use two fingers on each side of my face to yank up what Mom insists are my worrisomely sagging jowls. "Is it that much better? I mean, don't I look like a lizard with blond hair and red lipstick?" My voice sounds a little lispy, since pulling on my skin spreads my mouth out of its normal range. I let my face drop back from fantasy-35 into reality-46.

"Well?" I demand, still contemplating the mirror. "Do I need a face-lift?"

Instead of answering, Maysie leans forward toward the mirror, too, trying the two-finger jowl-lift demo on her own actually-35 face. Today she's back in her trademark black jeans. And I still can't tell she's pregnant. I smile at the memory. They hadn't been trying. Apparently, the impending new kid was just as much a surprise to her and Matthew as it was to me.

"I think I look better, you know? Fixed?" Maysie's voice now has the fake face lift lisp. "I'd do it in a heartbeat, too. After little whoever is born. Maybe get a tummy tuck, while I'm at it. Bye-bye baby fat. And I've got to be on TV soon, after all. My days of hiding behind radio have come to an end." She focuses on her reflection, first tugging at the corners of her eyes, then pulling up her eyebrows. "Can't hurt."

"Margaret Isobel Derosiers Green," I turn to her, my own face forgotten. "You wouldn't. Would you?"

"You wear contacts, right? Had braces? And might I ask, in my role as your best friend forever, whether you know the true color of your hair? As my preteen queen Molly so often puts it when she's angling for pierced ears, 'what's the diff, dude?'"

Maysie's now checking for loose skin under her neck. I check my own. Suddenly I'm envisioning a rhinocerous. Maybe Mom was right.

I tear my eyes away from the mirror and boost myself onto the counter, leaning my back against the wall, knees drawn up, feet on the counter. My mind flashes to Penny in just this position in our booth at dinner. "So like I said," I say, changing the subject. "Penny acted as if I were invisible. She's devoted to Josh, and he dotes on her. I felt like such an outsider. I mean, I *am* an outsider."

I stare at the toes of my little black suede flats, unseeing. Franklin and I are heading back to Swampscott in a minute. We decided to make it a casual day. The power reporter look can work in the corporate world, but high heels and Armani are sometimes too daunting when you're trying to extract info from cautious—and potentially suspicious—neighbors. But first I needed to talk to Maysie. And not just about my face.

"So you didn't *study* to be a mom, did you? Seems like Molly arrived and you somehow knew what to do next. Sleep, diapers, crying. You just—"

"There was no sleep," Maysie says with a smile. "For about two years. Then Max arrived. And there was even less sleep."

"You know what I mean," I say, waving away her digression. "Do I have a heart-to-heart with Penny? Am I her friend? Do I tell her what she can and can't do? Do I always have to agree with Josh? What's my attitude about Victoria? What if Penny, I don't know, hates me?" I twist my gold-linked bracelet, a three-month anniversary present from Josh, around my wrist. "I hate surprises," I say. "I'm better at things I can control."

"You want a real answer?" Maysie asks. She sits across from me in her black director's chair, leaning toward me, her face earnest. "I didn't plan on little number three here. Talk about surprises. But I love her. Him. Already. Love is not about control, that's one of the joys of it."

She stops, and it seems as though she's considering her own words. "You'll never know unless you have your own child."

My eyes turn teary, emotion unexpectedly washing over me. Of course I'll never have my own child. Those days are gone.

Maysie jumps up, throws her arms around me. "Ah, my hormones, I'm so sorry," she says. She steps back and holds her arms out, apologizing. "I sound like one of those Chicken Soup books, I know, and I didn't mean…"

"Oh, honey, you know I've crossed that bridge," I say,

reassuring her. "Years ago." At least I hope I've crossed
it. I swing my legs down from the counter and brush the
wrinkles out of my black slacks. "But that's Victoria's
connection to Penny, you know? And Penny's to Victoria.
And I don't want to change that. Couldn't. I just hoped I
could be Penny's best friend, confidante, role model, or
something. And maybe stepmom. But if last night proves
anything, it ain't gonna happen."

From inside my tote bag, my cell phone begins a
muffled rendition of "You Can't Always Get What You
Want." Franklin's and my theme song. He must be ready
to leave for Swampscott.

"I've gotta disagree with Mick Jagger this time,"
Maysie says giving me a quick hug. "Sometimes you can
get what you want. Just let yourself love her. And she'll
eventually love you back."

You can tell it's summer at Swampscott High School
even with your eyes closed. No footsteps from packs of
students giggling down the halls. No bells insistently
clang for classes. No muffled unintelligible public address
voices proclaim the day's schedule over the teenage din.

Not only is the reception desk at SHS deserted, the
halls are empty. Some lockers flap open. Hand-lettered
"Good luck to the Big Blue graduates" and "Go Seagulls
4-Evah" posters are beginning to untape themselves from
the institutional beige walls.

On the counter in front of us, the *Swampscott Chronicle*'s headlines blare what's fast becoming the biggest
story in Massachusetts. *Oz Tops Pols Polls*. Franklin picks
up the paper, reading the story out loud as we wait for
someone to answer the hotel-desk bell on the counter we
pinged, hoping for attention.

"This law-and-order thing seems to be resonating," Franklin says, picking up the newspaper and flapping it open. "Listen to this. 'Oscar Ortega, now an unprecedented seventeen points ahead in the polls, says his history of convictions is unmatched across the country.' And, he told a crowd of cheering supporters, quote, 'an Ortega administration means parents can be—'"

"Let me guess. Safe in their homes and safe in the streets," I finish the sentence. "You'd think he'd get a new stump speech. Although this one seems to be doing the trick with voters."

I peer across the counter and around the corner, checking for open doors in the line of offices that's tucked on the other side. I ping the bell again. Its tinny jingle resounds hollowly through the room. No answer. "He's not going to be happy when he hears we're looking into Dorinda. What Oliver Rankin said at the elevator is an understatement. Bad publicity is death on the campaign trail, so Oz will certainly try to stop us. Though there's nothing he can do, I suppose."

Franklin puts the paper back. "Time, as they say, will tell." He takes a few steps into the long hallway. "You know, there's got to be someone here. Someplace. I mean, we just walked into the building. It was open."

"How about this," I say. "Franklin, you take the car, and hit the Swampscott paper. See if they have archives, a reporter who covered the case, old photos they didn't use. I'll check around here. Maybe someone's in the library. Or the gym. Even if no one's there, I bet there'll be yearbooks. Names, pictures, all kinds of stuff. If someone asks what I'm doing here, I'll…" I pause. "I'll think of something."

"Good luck with that," Franklin says. "You're probably guilty of trespassing, if someone decides to be a hard-liner about it."

I look at my watch, ignoring him. "Call my cell in two hours," I say. "We'll compare notes over clam rolls at the Red Rock."

I still have nightmares that I didn't study for some exam, or I'm not ready for a test, or I can't find my class-room. Those dreams have nothing to do with high school, I'm told, and everything to do with my struggle for per-fection. Still, I'm probably in for some heavy sleep drama tonight. The smell of leftover pencil sharpenings and notebook paper and industrial-strength floor wax inside the Swampscott High School library time-travels me back to Anthony Wayne High in suburban Chicago, home of the Fighting Red Devils and my four misfit years of high grades and low self-esteem. High school—get through it, then forget it. For me at least.

The glass and metal door opens without a sound and clicks back closed behind me. The fluorescent lights buzz and hum as I scan the long, narrow room. This place is deserted, too. A dark wood librarian's desk, looming and massive, protects one end. In its sights, long pine tables with stocky chairs are lined up with geometric precision. A forest of pale wooden shelves stands in well-ordered lines, each displaying a brass and paper bracket, block lettered to show the range of Dewey Decimal numbers it contains. I'm on the prowl for yearbooks. And since there's no one here to stop me, I'm going to find them. I head for the stacks and search until I see a line of tall, narrow, identical dark blue books. The gilt-lettered year is on the spine of each.

I grab the wooden ladder, and slide it closer, doing the

math in my head. Dorinda Sweeney. Class of 19—she's
forty-three years old, so that would mean—82. I climb up,
spot the book and pull it from the shelf. The *Seagull*.
Almost ceiling-high on the ladder, I prop my open book
against the row of closed ones. No index. *Rats*. But I can
start with the senior class, that's always alphabetical.

If I find something, though, that's a dilemma. I stop,
mid-search, and lean against the shelf. There's no one
here, so there's no way to check out a book. I'd have to
steal it, and although tempting, that's not the best plan.
Then, a brainstorm. I'll just use my cell phone camera
again. I'm a genius.

I flip through pages of lip-glossed girls with overpermed
hair and unfortunate leg warmers. Power chicks with
Dynasty shoulder pads. Boys with surfboards, cars, guitars.
At the beach, in the bleachers, in the back of a white convertible. I hurry to the *K*'s. And there's Dorinda Keeler.

"Might I inquire," says a prim and birdy voice from
three feet beneath me, "who you are and what you
possibly think you are doing?" It sounds like "enquiah"
who you "ah," but there's no need to translate her intent.
She's in charge, I'm the interloper. I hope she's not
packing pepper spray or something.

Still holding the *Seagull* in one hand, I twist myself
around on the ladder. Now I'm looking down at a polka-
dot headband, a gray bob and brown sensible-looking
shoes. Someone who, with one shake of this already
unsteady ladder, might be able to dump me onto the
scuffed linoleum. Headband tilts her face up to look at
me, inquisitorial.

"Would you like to get down and leave quietly?" she
asks. "Or shall I call security?"

Tucking the book under one arm, I begin my descent,

talking the whole time in the most reassuring tone I can muster. I'm grateful I wore those flats. "I'm Charlie McNally, Channel 3 News?" I take a step more, trying to look right at her and not my feet, so she can see how unthreatening I am. "The building was open, and the library, too. I looked everywhere for someone, I'm so sorry, and when there was no answer, I just—" I wind up with one arm hooked over a ladder rung and one foot on the ground, face of a grown-up but feeling like a teenager nabbed in some after-hours mischief.

I pause, entreating the journalism gods to play ball. "Do you remember Dorinda Keeler?"

A pack of laughing teenagers, reef sandals and baggy cutoffs, sweeps into the Red Rock clam shack, their boisterous laughter filling the circular glass-walled restaurant. It smells of fried everything—clams, potatoes, onion rings—plus ketchup and tartar sauce. Out the window, the Atlantic Ocean touches Swampscott Beach on one shore and the white cliffs of Dover on the other. June sun glints on the water, its glare darkening figures walking on the sand into flickering silhouettes. Franklin and I have commandeered a table for six so we can spread out his loot— old newspaper articles and photographs. He even managed to snag Dorinda and Ray's photo from the wedding section. Her childlike white-gowned figure, veiled and tiny, is tucked under her tuxedoed husband's shoulder. He's holding a glass of champagne. She has only a bouquet of white rosebuds. He's beaming. Her face is obscured by the frothy veil.

"Here's one for the psych books," Franklin says, covering the newlyweds with another page from his black leather folder. He turns the photo toward me, pointing.

"This was spray painted on the sidewalk in front of All Saints Church."

"Where Dorie was—"

"Married, right," Franklin continues. "And it was on her wedding day. Some newspaper photog got a shot of it before the city power-washed it away. See? It says 'Dorie and CC 4-Evah'. Spelled like that, 'evah.' The archives guy, a real walking history book, remembers that Dorinda dumped her devoted boyfriend CC Hardesty for Ray. He figured this paint job was CC's last cry of un-requited love, like Dustin Hoffman in *The Graduate* yelling "Elaine," pounding the glass. But Dorie 'chose the Sweeney money and power,' so says Mr. Archives. And apparently that was the end of Dorie and CC."

A miniskirted waitress, polo shirt with collar flipped, annoyingly long tanned legs and bouncing hair, arrives at our table. She's carrying two waxed-paper-lined red plastic baskets, and hesitates as she dubiously eyes the documents strewn across the plastic tabletop. Franklin sweeps his copies together, tamping the edges to make them straight before he inserts them into his folder. "I like the boy-friend," Franklin says, snapping the folder shut. "He's—"

"You like the boyfriend?" I raise my eyebrows and pretend to be shocked. "What would your adorable Stephen say—"

"Clam rolls?" The waitress interrupts, eyeing Franklin first. "Extra tartar, extra lettuce, extra onion rings? Coke?"

Franklin nods. She hands me the light mayo, no fries and Diet Coke. Damn Franklin and his cooperative metabolism.

He nibbles a few onion rings, meticulously peeling the batter-dipped strips away from one another and dipping each in a puddle of ketchup. "So," he says. "You scored at the library?"

My clam roll is oozing mayonnaise. So much for "light." I try to tuck escaping clam shards back into the buttered, toasted hot dog bun while relating my encounter with Marybeth Gallagher, Swampscott High's enduring librarian and uncompromising guardian of her well-ordered domain.

"She was not happy to see me," I say, holding the clam roll in one hand and my napkin in the other. I'm alternating taking bites and dabbing bready morsels from my lipstick. "Told me in no uncertain terms I was trespassing and it was only because she had seen me on TV that she didn't call security. I explained we were trying to help Dorinda Keeler. Sweeney. I could tell she was curious, you know? But even then, no way she was going to let me stick around. She actually took me by the elbow, propelled me to the door, and then she—kind of begrudgingly—let on that she did remember Dorinda. And her 'beau' as she called him, the star of the senior play, Colby Carl Hardesty."

I sit up straighter and flutter my eyelashes, mimicking the librarian's dramatic intonation and Down East accent. "'CC, just like Romeo, was every girl's dream and every mother's nightmare.'" I smile, myself again. "Muthah's nightmayeh, I love it. Then she tossed me from the place faster than you could say no comment."

"She loaned you the yearbook, though?" Franklin asks. His clam roll, extra tartar sauce and all, is not dripping. Somehow his clams are staying nicely inside their boundaries. Even Franklin's food is neat. "Bring it out, girl."

I wipe my hands on my pile of paper napkins and draw the *Seagull* from my tote bag. By now I know exactly what picture to show him. "'Up Where We Belong'" was the prom theme, can you believe it?"

Holding the yearbook with both hands, I turn it so Franklin can see, then point to each picture. "That's Dorinda. That's the CC person, her 'beau.' Look at that updo. And the tiara? I like her better with the sweatshirt look. The one in my phone snapshot."

Frowning briefly, I stare at the hauntingly dated photograph, feeling the wrinkle between my eyebrows nestle itself in a little more permanently. My toe starts to tap. I slowly push my plate of congealing clam roll remains out of the way.

"You know," I say, "she has that prommy dress, and the tiara and those banana curls. And no one looks like themselves at the prom, but—"

"Yeah, I've seen your prom picture, in the Farrah-wannabe getup," Franklin says. "You looked like you had two heads. That clump of fake curls." He smiles. "How much did that thing weigh? And your dress—was that a color found in nature? "

"It was 1978," I say, my voice muffled because I'm digging into my purse. I need my cell phone. "It was cool." There's a beep as my phone powers up. More beeps as I click to my photos. I scroll down to the one I snapped of Dorinda. I was right.

"Check it out," I say, holding my phone up next to the yearbook shot. "This picture of Dorinda I took? From the photo in the drawer? It's not Dorinda."

Chapter Seven

Franklin and I look back and forth between the two pictures, my fuzzy out-of-focus phone snapshot and the elaborately unrealistic prom photo. They look similar, but they're clearly two different teenagers. Either one could have grown up to be the person in the nursing home surveillance tape. Or neither.

"Maybe Dorinda had plastic surgery? For some reason? And that's why she looks different on the tape? It drives me crazy that all we have are pictures—the yearbook, my phone, that video. What can you tell from a picture? We have got to talk to Dorinda in person."

"Could be a friend of hers." Franklin takes the yearbook and begins flipping the pages. "We could compare your phone photo with all the faces in the yearbook. See if we get a match." He reaches for my phone. "Let's see it."

I stare at the cell phone's tiny screen, then I flip it closed, shaking my head to get my thoughts in order. "Wait. Why do we have to know who's in the picture? Let's not lose sight of our goal here. I just found it in the drawer—it doesn't have to be some big clue. We need to advance the story. Find out what happened to Ray Sweeney. Why Dorinda was convicted."

Franklin hands me back the yearbook, then scoops up the last bit of ketchup with a shred of onion ring. Only he would eat onion rings with a fork. "She confessed," he says, examining his final bite. "That's why."

"Remember what Rankin and Will said?" I ask, ignoring the confession remark. "Dorinda's mother forced her to marry Ray Sweeney. Maybe she knows something? Is she still alive? She'd be—how old now?"

Franklin shrugs. "Well, if Dorinda is forty, her mother is probably at least, I don't know, sixty. Or older."

I put my elbows on the table, put my forehead in both hands, and look up at Franklin through my laced fingers. "My mother," I say, remembering. "This is bleak. I can't believe I forgot. I still have to go see her today."

I check my watch, feeling smothered by the unrelenting deadline pressures of Mom, Josh, Penny, Dorinda. Will and Rankin, who want Dorinda out of prison. Oz, who wants to keep her in. And Susannah, who wants a ratings boost. And that's not even counting myself.

"Let's get this show on the road," I say. "Since we're in Swampscott, let's track down some of the people in the yearbook photo with Dorie and CC. See what they can tell us."

Franklin looks skeptical, one eyebrow raised. "How do we know they're still around? Needle in a small-town haystack, I say. I suggest we go back to the station, check computer databases, run some names." He waves a hand around the crowded restaurant. "We can't just go up to people and say, hey yo, do you know anyone in these photos? Wish I'd brought my laptop."

"Good old-fashioned reporting," I say, shaking an admonishing finger. "Never fails. Hand over that *Seagull*. We don't need no stinkin' computers."

* * *

Myra Matzenbrenner is wearing pink-and-green flip-flops with flamingoes on the grosgrain ribbons criss-crossing her tanned feet. Her toenails match the flamingos, and her fingernails match her toes. She flip-flops across her kitchen linoleum carrying three plastic flowered glasses of iced coffee, one in each hand and the third balanced in her fingers between them. The names of the prom princesses listed in the yearbook had been Donna Mill, Sheila Fortune, Bitsy Bergman, Sharon Freeland, and Linda Sue Matzenbrenner.

With a name like Matzenbrenner, who needs a computer? How many Matzenbrenners can there be in town? And if there's more than one, I told Franklin, they're certainly related. One quick flip through the local phone book brought us to prom princess Linda Sue's home. Turns out, Prom Princess Linda is long gone. She has a husband and children and a house of her own outside Detroit, we've learned, but her mother's memories have remained.

Myra Matzenbrenner slides pink napkins toward Franklin and me and sets down our coffees. Continuing her nonstop newsreel of Swampscott High history, she pulls up a white rattan stool and sits down to join us at the kitchen counter. Her living room is set with three card tables, each topped with a poof of carnations, a dish of chocolate-covered almonds, a stack of notepads and tiny pencils. It's bridge club day at the Matzenbrenners', but Myra has agreed to talk before the "gals" arrive.

"And I don't mind telling you." She rips open two pink packages of sweetener and pours them into her coffee, stirring carefully. "My Linda Sue was not happy when Dorie and that CC were crowned prom king and queen. My Linda Sue had practiced wearing a tiara, you know? Had her hair done just right, so the queen's crown wouldn't slip." She taps her spoon against the rim of her glass, puts it on a napkin. "That CC, though, he was a slick one. Charmed the pants off everyone—teachers, Principal Webb, coaches. He was used to getting anything he wanted. He wanted to be quarterback, he got it. He wanted the lead in the school play—*Romeo and Juliet*—and he got it. And when he wanted Dorie, he got her, too. She was the cutest little thing, I've got to admit. What we always called a good girl. Never smoked, never drank. And her poor mother, of course."

She looks between us, confirming. "Well, I can tell you this. Dorinda was pretty enough, smart enough, but she'd never have been prom queen without CC. That's what *I* say." She makes a tsking noise. "It would have been Linda Sue."

"You said 'her poor mother,'" I begin.

"So why'd she marry—" Franklin says at the same time.

Both our half questions hang in the air. Myra Matzenbrenner absently pats her pepper-and-salt curls, finding the fuchsia-framed glasses on the top of her head. She pulls them off with a look of surprise, as if she'd been looking for them and had forgotten where she put them. Flapping the glasses closed, she points them at Franklin, then me.

"Well, it's the same answer," she says. "When Dorie's father died, that left Colleen on her own with Dorie. They didn't have much."

Colleen. I make a mental note. I've left my reporter's notebook in my bag, keeping it casual. I'm hoping whatever I don't remember, Franklin will. But my increasingly unreliable short-term memory (did I pick up the dry cleaning?) is still pretty solid when it comes to research and reporting.

"Colleen worked at Bay State Insurance. It's still there on King Street? And Ray Sweeney, of course, ran the place. Took over from his father." Myra narrows her eyes disapprovingly. "Ray was a piece of work. Piece of work. All bluster and no brains. Just waiting to take over from his dad. Sniffed around Dorie when her mother brought her to the office."

She stops, then frowns. "Dorie must have been fifteen when he started paying attention to her. Fifteen. Ray was what, twenty-five? You catch my drift? But he had money, no doubt about that. The Sweeneys had money." She points to me with one pink acrylic fingernail, making sure I understand. "Money."

"So Dorie's mother—how do I put this—arranged? Pushed? Convinced? Allowed her daughter to marry Ray Sweeney?" I ask.

"Whatever word you choose," she replies. "The prom. Then graduation. And before you could say, 'oh promise me,' Dorie was Mrs. Ray Sweeney. And before you could say 'Uncle Sam wants you,' CC had signed up for the Navy."

I glance at Franklin, remembering his words in the Red Rock. *I like the boyfriend.* Maybe Franklin had something. Or maybe Colleen Keeler, in a fit of remorse over pushing her daughter into marrying a sleazy local pol, had bashed her predatory son-in-law with an iron and pushed him down the stairs. I like it.

And for a moment, I almost believe it. But a grandmother in her sixties is not the likeliest murderer, no matter how unhappy her daughter might be. Of all the suspects, I sadly realize, the most predictable murderer is Dorinda herself.

Myra looks away. I see she's checking the green numerals of the clock on the stainless steel microwave. Our time is up.

"Mrs. Matzenbrenner, you know them both. Knew," I say. "Do you think Dorie Sweeney killed her husband?"

Myra Matzenbrenner slides off the padded chintz cushion of the stool, one foot hitting the floor, then the other, not looking at me or Franklin. She picks up her coffee, then wipes the counter with her napkin, back and forth, back and forth.

"Why do you think Dorie worked the overnight shift, all these years?" she asks, still focused on her shredding pink napkin. "To stay as far from Ray Sweeney as she could. That's what I think. He had money, she wouldn't have to work. She was getting out of that house. A man like that, catting after teenagers. Colleen should have realized Dorie wasn't Ray's first and wouldn't be his last. She died years ago, in some nursing home. Dorie never forgave her. She told me once she swore she'd never allow her own daughter to end up like she did. Trapped. Ignored. Like I tell Linda Sue, money can't buy you a loving family."

Crumpling up the last of the napkin, Myra looks at Franklin and me. "Did Dorinda kill Ray Sweeney? Who knows. If I were Dorie? I certainly would have."

This is not what I was hoping to hear. We're on the trail for evidence to exonerate Dorie. Myra isn't even skeptical of her guilt. We're getting nowhere. My brain races through possibilities while Myra shows us out. I hand her my card. What did I forget to ask her?

"CC Hardesty," I say, turning back to Myra as we reach the front door. "Where can we find him?"

Myra has one hand on the doorknob. She pushes it open, letting in the still bright afternoon. "Arlington National Cemetery, I would think," she says.

* * *

"And so much for the boyfriend theory," I say, as we dump our newly collected files on our desks. At least, I'm dumping. Franklin is using a sharp-pointed black marker to make labels to put on a set of manila folders.

I stare at my phone, willing the red message light to go on. I wish Will Easterly would call to tell me the story-saving news that Dorinda has agreed to talk to me, that she'll go on camera and spill the real saga of Ray Sweeney's death. If she even knows it. "Should we, maybe, call Will? See whether he's gotten anywhere? And aren't Rankin's people supposed to be coming up with evidence, too? Or do they just think the tape is enough to get Dorie exonerated?"

Franklin adjusts something in his file array. "Maybe we should—"

"Yes, absolutely," I interrupt. "We need to hit that nursing home, the one where Dorinda worked. See how the surveillance tape system operates. See why no one checked it out."

"Go to the bar," Franklin continues as if I hadn't interrupted him. "Is what I was attempting to say." He turns away from his files to look at me. "We need to track down the customers and the bartender, don't you think?"

"Good idea," I agree. "Try to get some sense of that night, perhaps someone overheard what Ray was saying. Better yet, find someone who can positively identify who Ray was with, and not just from seeing a photograph. If Dorinda was at the bar, arguing with Ray, it's likely she wasn't at work. Which makes that surveillance tape incredibly suspect. And the murder—"

Poison. I'd know it anywhere. My nose wrinkles, testing, as a plume of fashion's equivalent of toxic waste announces a visitor to our office. I know it's oh-so au courant, and most people adore it, but to me, the perfume smells like bug spray. I sneeze once in involuntary olfactory protest, then again, as the clack of stilettos comes to a stop in our doorway.

"This is no time to get a cold, Charlie." Susannah waves a French-manicured finger at me. "Be sick in August, if you must, or at least not until after we get your story on the air. Now look." She flips open her lizard-bound clipboard. Two interlocking capital letter *C*'s look like an advertisement for something Chanel. "Here's my little surprise for you and Frank."

"Franklin," he mutters. "Not that it matters."

Susannah doesn't seem to hear him. She continues her show-and-tell, her signature gold bracelets clinking as she points to the page. "This is our brand new graphic for Charlie's Crusade." She shows it to me, then Franklin, her face fairly luminous with her outstanding achievement in marketing. "You see? We've run this by design, and Kevin, and of course the general manager. It's green-lighted to the top. Do you love it? I mean, do you *love* it?"

"I—" I begin.

"And that's not all," Susannah continues. She turns to the next page on her clipboard and holds it up. "Here's the end page. It'll be the final frame of all our video promotions. 'Truth. Justice. The Charlie McNally Way.'" She shakes her head, apparently unable to comprehend the extent of her prowess and the potential for her own success. "The demos are going to eat it up."

"I—" I begin again, then pause to see if she's going to allow me to talk this time. She's looking at me, expectantly, so I continue. "Susannah, you know I'm thrilled with the promo campaign." This is actually true, because if you're getting promos, you're not getting fired. "But I'm just the slightest bit concerned that we're a little ahead of ourselves."

And actually, I think ripping off the Superman slogan is embarrassing. I keep that to myself.

Susannah's face is hardening unpleasantly. She snaps her folder closed, and her nails tap, briefly, on its lizard skin cover. "Ahead? Of ourselves?"

"It's just that Dorinda Sweeney hasn't agreed to do an on-camera interview. Yet." I'm trying to temper my annoyance with my understanding of office politics. But protocol aside, the news department should be telling the promotion department what to do, not the other way around. "And as I've discussed with Kevin, if we promise the viewers a story and then it doesn't make the air, well, won't that be difficult to explain?"

Susannah looks downright combative. Gold buttons at her wrists flashing in the fluorescent light, she pushes up the sleeves of her black-and-white houndstooth bouclé cardigan, seemingly in preparation for her return salvo. Before she can open fire, Franklin's phone rings.

He looks at me questioningly. I wave him to answer. The interruption will give us all a chance to regroup. Especially me.

"Parrish, Action News."

Susannah turns her attention to Franklin. So do I.

He tucks the phone into his shoulder, picks up a pencil and opens his spiral notebook.

Still listening to whoever is talking, he holds it up to show me the word he's just written: WILL.

I look at Susannah, whose semi-snarky expression telegraphs *I told you so.* Fine with me. If she's right that would solve a lot of problems.

Franklin continues the frustratingly impossible-to-gauge one-sided conversation. I can't see his face. His only reactions are murmured and emotionless "mmm-hums" and "okays." He writes again, then holds the notebook up a second time.

It's two letters.

NO.

Chapter Eight

Ethan Margolis has sent Mom even more peonies. I can see she's had the newer ones placed on her nightstand. The older ones, still in full pink-and-white glory in their frosted-glass vase, have been relegated to the dresser. A suburbanista in tight jeans hosts some interior decoration show Mom has on, volume off, brandishing paint swatches and gesticulating mutely at a lineup of couches. The chrome-and-glass heart-respiration monitor beeps softly as Mom gives me a play-by-play of her day.

Tiny welts of blue-black bruises now underscore her brown eyes. Even the frozen peas haven't successfully held down the unavoidable puffy eyelids, overplumped cheeks and angrily red still-healing lips.

"Does it…hurt?" I have to ask, taking my assigned seat by her bedside. "It looks like it might."

Mom shakes her head, wincing after her first motion. She carefully pats the pink blanket covering her, indicating where her thigh would be. "A little," she admits. "The lipo. And the tummy thing. Those, I must admit, are making me a bit more uncomfortable than I might have expected. But you know, they're making me take these pills, four every four hours, and so it's not so bad."

Then she holds up her left hand, waggling her

fingers and points to the multi-carat rock sparkling dazzlingly on her ring finger. "Here's my secret," she says. "Every time I feel like complaining, I simply think—it's all for Ethan and me. It's all for the wedding, and our honeymoon. Then I ask myself, is it worth it? And, of course, it is."

She pats the blankets again. "Hello, size eight," she says, almost to herself. "I can't wait till they let me have a mirror. And when all the bruises are gone, Ethan will get his first look at his bride-to-be." She looks up at me. "Your appointment with Dr. Garth is soon, right? This week?"

I'm happy to see her happy, of course. And Ethan is a perfectly nice guy. It would be silly for her to be alone the rest of her life. I wrap my arms across my chest, stopped, for a moment, by the realization that unless I can untangle the Josh and Penny situation, it's more likely that *I'll* be alone the rest of my life than she will.

"When do I get to meet your Josh?" Mom asks. "And his little daughter?

She's reading my mind, of course. I'm not even surprised. Maybe she could explain to me how I'm supposed to turn sullen into sunny, and bread balls into domestic tranquility.

"Have you ever seen him drunk?"

Now I'm surprised.

"Drunk?" I ask. I can't even imagine where she's going with this. "Him? You mean—Josh?"

Mother nods. Even puffy, I can see she's wearing her "pronouncement" expression. Like Rumpole. She who must be obeyed.

"Before you marry anyone," she says, reciting gospel, "you must see him drunk, sick and with his mother. If not mother, then offspring."

I can't help it. I'm fascinated. Where does she come up with this stuff?

"Drunk?" I repeat. "Sick. And—offspring? Offspring?" I'm about to laugh, but I know Mom will not be amused.

"Drunk, so you can see whether he becomes affectionate. Or angry. It's undoubtedly going to be one or the other," she says. "Drunk reveals your true personality, without any filter. Sick—same thing. Is he needy? A complainer? And how they treat their mothers and children is how they're going to treat you. They can't hide or pretend, that's their true colors." Mom reaches over, and almost pets the petals of one fluffy white peony. Peonies are her wedding flowers. I know she's thinking of Ethan. And maybe, Dad. "Trust me on this, Charlotte."

Reluctantly, I admit—to myself, of course—she may have something here.

"Well, Moms, is this your own philosophy? Or something from your pal Oprah?"

"It's from your Gramma Nell," Mother says, flickering a glance heavenward. "I promised her I would pass it along to you when I thought you needed to know it. And from the look on your face when you speak of your Josh, I decided it's time for you to know it."

I wonder if Dorinda Sweeney had ever seen Ray drunk, or sick, or with his mother, before she married him. I wonder if her mother, Colleen Keeler, cared as much about her daughter's future as my mother seems to about mine. By all accounts, she forced Dorie to marry him. For money and security. What if Colleen hadn't felt pressure to make sure her daughter made the "right" decisions? What if Dorie had said no? And no question, Dorinda saw Ray with their own daughter. Maybe she didn't like what she saw, somehow. What if that's when

Dorie finally fought back? Took action to protect her only child? But from what?

"You know the story we're working on about the woman who supposedly murdered her husband?" I say. "Protecting her daughter—if he was inappropriate, or something—that would be a motive, mightn't it? From a mother's perspective, I'm wondering, how far would one go to keep a daughter safe?"

Mom reaches out her hand, placing it gently on my arm. The lines of the heart monitor attached to her wrist and finger stretch along with her movement. "Charlotte, sweetheart, I'm surprised you're even asking. A mother—"

Bing bong. A bell rings and the door to Mom's suite swings open. "Hello, Mrs. McNally. And—hello, Charlie." A white-coated attendant pushes a wheeled tray into the room. On it is a single white rose in a vase, several china plates with steam spiraling though the holes in their silver covers, and a white cloth napkin wrapped with a twist of pink and white ribbons.

"Dinner for one, I'm afraid," the attendant says, his face concerned. "Did we order for two?" He pulls a pad from a shirt pocket, checking.

I stand, gesturing *no problem.* "I was just going," I say, leaning down to give Mom a careful kiss on the one silvery-blond patch showing through the bandages stretched around her head. I gather my tote bag and purse, then turn back to Mom as the obviously moonlighting movie star begins to remove the plates' covers.

"Drunk, Josh passes the test," I say with a smile. "We all had a lot of champagne last Emmy night. But don't tell him I told you. Sick? Not yet. And with Penny?" I pause, remembering. "She idolizes him, that's for sure.

And he's wonderful with her. Adores her. He'd do anything for her."

I stop, realizing what I've just said. What if Dorinda's guilty?

"Guilty. Or not guilty. It just makes the whole thing more interesting," I say, trying to believe it. Franklin and I are in my Jeep, on the way to Swampscott again. We're headed for The Reefs, the bar where Ray Sweeney had his final tequila. If we have time, we'll hit the nursing home to check out their taping system. My turn to drive.

"So Dorinda turned down our request for an interview. We can ask again." I go on. "I refuse to give up on this story."

The morning sun disappears as we enter the narrow gloom of the Callahan Tunnel, fritzing our all-news radio station into static. I snap it off. The tunnel is not my favorite. I finally remember to remove my sunglasses, which allows me an even clearer view of the cracking and soot-streaked Cold War era tiles lining the tunnel walls. I keep picturing the billions of gallons of Boston Harbor sloshing menacingly above us. I would have preferred taking the bridge, where at least you can see the water. What makes this trip even more unpleasant, I'm beginning to envision Franklin and me as victims in a pretty diabolical political plot.

"Just a thought," I say. I'm trying to make sure I know where the emergency exit doors are located without letting Franklin know I'm doing it. "What if—what if this is all some sort of a trick? By say, Oscar Ortega and his cohorts? To make the Constitutional Justice Project look bad and his campaign look good? See what I'm getting at? You know they loathe Oliver Rankin and all the CJP stands for."

I'm also monitoring the life-threatening zigzag of a pack of teenagers, all wearing Red Sox caps, who seem to think their convertible deserves both lanes of the tunnel. As a result, I can't see Franklin's face, but his voice sounds skeptical.

"You mean, trying to lure Rankin and Will Easterly to champion Dorinda's case—then lower the boom later? Prove she's guilty and make the CJP look soft on crime? That's quite a conspiracy theory, Charlotte. And how about that surveillance tape?"

Still watching the teen-mobile, I lift my latte from the cupholder in the console, and take a lukewarm sip. The more I think about this, the righter I am.

"That could be part of it. Let's just play out the scenarios, both ways. First, say the tape is fake. Doctored, somehow. Planted. It didn't cross your mind that it was pretty darn—convenient?—that just as Oz announces his candidacy, a blockbuster piece of evidence shows up in Rankin's hands? And remember, those people in the bar identified her from the police photos. If she was in the bar arguing with Ray, she wasn't at the nursing home. Dorinda's actually guilty. The CJP looks like idiots, backing a guilty murderer, and Ortega looks like a winner."

"On the other hand," Franklin says, "if the tape is real, Dorinda is innocent. Oliver Rankin and the CJP come out heroes, and Ortega—"

"Not to mention you and me, Franko," I interrupt, putting my latte back. The teenagers swerve to the other lane. "Here's the potential disaster. If the tape is fake, and we fall for it? Put something wrong on the air? We're going to look like idiots, too." I shake my head gloomily, imagining it. "Oz takes down the liberal do-gooder lawyers and the liberal do-gooder reporters, all in one election-sweeping swoop."

We finally come up out of the tunnel, thankfully back into sunshine and fresh air. I buzz down my window to hand my money to the toll taker. A lanky-haired woman with sagging shoulders looks up, languidly, from a tiny black-and-white television that's flickering Regis and Kelly inside her glass-booth domain. She does a double take, then slides the half window wide open, leaning head, shoulders and both arms outside to accept my three dollars. She holds on to the three bills without taking her eyes off me.

"Aren't you—that McNally? On television?"

"Yes, I—"

"I had Danny DeVito in my lane once," she says with a face-crinkling smile. "And that cooking lady. But you're one hundred per cent my favorite. You always get the bad guys. And you still look one hundred per cent terrific." She pulls a piece of paper from a drawer and hands it through the window. A Bic pen follows. "Sign this for me? Put, from Charlie McNally to Edythe. With a *y* and an *e*."

I takes me a second to figure out how to spell Edith with a *y* and an *e*. By that time, several cars have pulled up behind us and are honking their impatience at whatever is stalling the flow of traffic. Which is us.

I hand her the paper, properly autographed, and she waves us through.

With a glance in the rearview mirror and a newfound determination, I yank the Jeep across two lanes of highway. Instead of heading north, I turn right into the twisting streets of East Boston, planning my strategy for a U-turn. Not only of our car, but of our morning plans.

"Forget about Swampscott," I say. If I have to go back into the damn tunnel, so be it. That toll taker expects me to get the story, and that's exactly what I'm going to do.

Franklin's grabbed what he calls the "Charlie strap" as the Jeep careens around the cloverleaf exit. "Good Lord, Charlotte," he says. "This is why I don't like you in the driver's seat. Mind telling me what's going on in that brain of yours?"

"The bar can wait. The nursing home can wait," I say. "We need to find out if Dorinda's innocent. We need to find out whether Dorie was really in the bar. And I know one way to do it." The more I think about his, the righter I am. "We need to go to Oscar Ortega's office. Into the lair of the Great and Powerful Oz."

Chapter Nine

"Appointment?"

Apparently the flame-haired sentinel behind the expanse of government-issue wood and metal desk doesn't feel it's necessary to waste a whole sentence—subject, verb, object—on two strangers who have entered her kingdom. Taped to the file cabinet behind her is a curling-edged cartoon of three Shmoos, holding their Shmoo-tummies and laughing. Their thought balloon says "You want it when?" I've always wondered why someone would post their flip and trivializing attitude about their jobs in plain view of their visitors. Not to mention their bosses. Over my desk, there's a quote about persistence.

I use my friendliest, most amicable tone. "We don't have an appointment, no," I say. "But as I said, I'm Charlie McNally? From Channel 3? And we were hoping Mr. Ortega, or one of his staff, might give us a moment."

"We tried to call," Franklin adds, glancing at the lineup of flashing red Hold buttons on the receptionist's phone. "But the line was always busy."

"McNelly. TV. No appointment."

"McNally," I say. I wish we had called. But he's a public official and I'm the public. Someone has to talk to me.

The receptionist raises one finger, as if putting me on hold, and then uses it to punch a few buttons on her phone. She swivels in her chair, halfway turning away, and cups her hand over the tiny receiver microphone in front of her mouth. She listens, then turns back to us.

"Consuela Savio will be out in a moment," she says. She glances at her watch, then turns back to her computer. "Take a seat."

Franklin and I head for a yellowing plastic couch. Its original color was probably somewhere between leftover mashed potato and aging mustard.

"I'm starving," I whisper to Franklin. The upholstery creaks unhappily as the two of us sit down. The cracking plastic instantly pinches the backs of my thighs. I shift position, trying to tuck my black skirt more securely between me and the attacking couch. "We should have gotten lunch."

"Read a magazine, distract yourself," Franklin says, turning over the selection on the low wooden table in front of us. "Here's one you probably missed. '*Law Enforcement Product News.*'"

"Give me that," I say, taking it from him. "That's not a real magazine." It is. I flip through the pile nearer to me, seeing if I can go one better. "Wait here's one for you. '*Consolidated Municipal Infrastructure.*' Read it. Know it."

I'm starting to get impatient with reading obscure publications when I sense someone standing over us. I quickly put down *Police Chief* and stand up. Franklin does, too. I'm not short, but my view is of a column of pearl buttons on a silver charmeuse blouse. The tiny buttons are clearly strained to the limits of their overburdened threads struggling to keep them from popping into the conversation.

"Well, Charlie McNally, of course I recognize you. And this is?"

If this is Consuela Savio, she probably spells her name in all caps. She has big hair, big shoulders, big lipstick. And somehow it all works. I can picture her in the beauty pageant, tiara'ed and teary, while the losing contestants whisper—*"Her?"* There's a lot to be said for unabashed sex appeal and I'm betting Consuela says it all the time. I'm sure that could be a plus for a public relations mouth-piece. But her come-hither technique is not going to work on me. And, though she may not know it yet, certainly not on Franklin.

"My producer, Franklin Parrish," I say, making sure I'm looking up at her face. "We're just doing some research on a story and were thinking that…"

Consuela, all smiles, focuses on Franklin. This'll be amusing.

"Frankleen," she says, ignoring me. "Have we met?"

"As Charlie was saying," Franklin says, ignoring her question and coming around from behind the coffee table. "We're researching a story. And hoping to talk to Mr. Ortega. It's about—Dorinda Keeler Sweeney. Can you tell him we're here?"

Consuela's face darkens. She glances disapprovingly at the receptionist, whose faltering skills have clearly let in two troublemaking gate-crashers.

"The attorney general is in a meeting," she says, making sure, with studied inflection, that we know this is not true.

"That's fine," I say agreeably, opening my tote bag and pulling out a manila file. I glance at Franklin, attempting to telegraph my tactics. Reporter gambit: the bluff. I clear my throat, make my voice a little louder. "We'll just talk to you, then, about the possibly questionable procedures in the Sweeney arrest. Then you can pass the word on to the A.G." I look around the lobby, inspecting the five or six other waitees, all of whom by this time are not even pretending not to be listening. "Shall we discuss it here in the lobby?"

Consuela flickers a glance at the folder. She has no idea it holds copies of potential maid-of-honor dresses Mom sent me. I know she's wondering what we've got. And if it's bad, she doesn't want everyone else in the room to hear a reporter spill the beans during the heat of a political campaign.

Suddenly she's no longer a contender for Miss Congeniality.

"All right, Ms. McNally," Consuela says. She smiles to the waitees, silently signaling there's no *60 Minutes* confrontation coming up. "You can both follow me."

We're in.

We walk down a dingy hall, Franklin giving me a surreptitious thumbs-up. Consuela creaks open the door to a conference room and waves us inside. Judging from the hazy windows and discolored slant-slatted blinds, it must have been home to years' worth of smoke-filled meetings and confabs. Gray and grayer upholstered chairs, sagging and mostly threadbare, are twisted randomly away from their places as if a rogue burst of wind gusted through and departed. A few paper clips are scattered on the conference table, a scarred wooden monster that swallows up most of the room.

Consuela closes the door with a little more force than necessary, the silk blouse stretching perilously across her broad back. She whirls to face us. "What's this all about?" she says. Her lilting touch of Hispanic accent has disappeared along with her PR niceties. "You two know better than to show up like this. This is the attorney general's office. You want something, you call in advance."

She holds up a thumb and forefinger, almost touching. "I'm this far from calling your news director, asking *him* what the hell is going on."

Though Consuela doesn't invite us to take a seat, I do anyway. I put my tote bag between me and the increasingly agitated flack, hoping it will feel like a potential mysterious arsenal of documents. When Franklin also sits down, leaning back in the swivel chair, Consuela has no choice but to join us.

"The photos used in the Dorinda Sweeney case," I say. I keep my voice uncontentious and pleasant. "The ones police showed to the witnesses in the bar. We'd like to see them."

"Not a chance," Consuela sputters with the absurdity of my request. "They're sealed. The court sealed all the evidence after your Miss Sweeney confessed to murder in the second degree."

I feel Franklin swivel in his chair, then see him stop himself by putting his palms on the table. He looks at his hands, then at Consuela. His voice is almost apologetic. Franklin the gentleman. "I'm afraid that's incorrect," he says. "I've checked with the court clerk. The docket file is not sealed. We were told the evidence is being held by your office."

Consuela considers this, but only briefly. "Those photos are private," she says, moving on to her second attempted excuse. "Property of the attorney general's office."

It's hard to hide my smile, so I unzip a side pouch of my tote bag to refocus her attention. This is good news in the making. If she's putting up roadblocks to the photographs, there must be some reason she doesn't want us to see them. Which means I want to see them even more.

"Ms. Savio." I say, looking back up at her, "Property of the A.G.'s office? That's simply not true. As a matter of fact…" I pause, rummaging though my tote bag. I find what I'm looking for, and hold it out to her. "As a matter of fact, while we were waiting for you, I found this copy of *Police Chief* magazine on the coffee table in the waiting room."

I hold it out to her, hoping she won't accuse me of petty larceny. She doesn't make a move to take it, so I place it on the conference table. Not guilty.

"There's a whole feature article about police lineups. I leafed through it while we were waiting. It includes a lot of background about photo array evidence. You know?"

I look at her encouragingly, as if I really want her to answer. She doesn't say a word, but gives me a bitter little gesture to continue.

I flip open the magazine and point to a page. "After conviction, photos are public records. You have to keep them. And you have to let us see them." I shrug, to let her know it wasn't my idea, it's law enforcement reality. Which, of course, we both already know.

"You have to," I repeat.

"In some cases, that may be correct, Char-lie," Consuela says. I can hear the sneer as she drags out my first name. "But in this one, you're wrong. She confessed. It's a breach of attorney-client confidentiality." She looks at me challengingly, wondering if I'll fall for excuse number three.

I won't. "Consuela, look. We can go back and forth over this all day. Or not. But whichever. Your office will have to hand over the photos."

"You said in the lobby—you indicated you had some documents." Consuela is not going down without a fight, and has fallen back on the "change the subject" method. "You said this was about the Sweeney arrest."

"It *is* about the Sweeney arrest," Franklin says.

The room goes quiet.

I watch Consuela's chest rise and fall as she calculates her next move, her buttons even more in jeopardy. Without exchanging a glance, Franklin and I know we've won this battle. We also know we don't need to say another word. All we have to do is wait.

"I'll get tech," she says. And with a flounce of curls, she sweeps out of the room.

"Tech?" I ask, watching the conference room door click closed.

"Perhaps the lineup photos are JPEG files on computer disk," Franklin theorizes. "She's got to get the techies to burn us a copy. But Charlotte, talk to me about those pictures. I thought we were here about the tape."

"Well, here's what I was thinking," I say. "And that *Police Chief* magazine made me all the more suspicious." I hop onto the conference table and stare down at the institutionally neutral carpeting, examining the shadowy patterns cast through the window blinds.

"Remember, Rankin and Will said the witnesses in the bar identified Dorinda from her picture." I pause and look back at Franklin. "Let me ask you. What's your understanding of how they got that ID?"

"I'm not sure what you mean by *how*," Franklin says. "The police showed witnesses a picture of, well, I suppose, it would be pictures, plural, of Dorinda, and a few other people. To see if anyone picked her out. The usual. A lineup."

"Correct," I say, nodding. "But has anyone told us they used a lineup? Anyone ever said that word? Maybe we just assumed it, because that's what the cops are supposed to do. But what if they just showed one shot, a photo of Dorie? Because they suspected her, figured it was her, so might as well confirm it?"

There's a sharp rap on the door, then whoever's knocking opens it without waiting for our response. I scoot myself down from the table, briefly wondering how long whoever is out there had been out there.

A taut trip wire of energy strides in. Shoulders courtesy of Gold's Gym. Suit courtesy Signore Armani. Attitude courtesy Clint Eastwood. His hand, still white-knuckle tight on the doorknob, claims all this as his territory, and us as his prisoners. A thin black cord around his neck shows off a daunting array of what must be security clearance badges. I read one bold-lettered name tag as our visitor snaps out his introduction.

"I'm Tek Mattheissen," he says. "You two have a lot of nerve."

A blast of early-summer sun hits us as we take turns revolving out the front door of the air-conditioned building. Chief of Staff Tek Mattheissen's long strides force me to trot a few steps to keep up with him in a two-block march to the statehouse. Oscar Ortega's number-two man had an appointment "in the corner office," as he put it, making sure we'd infer it was with Governor Landsman. He only had time for a "walk and talk," he'd said, between the A.G.'s office and Beacon Hill. Franklin headed back to the station. I agreed to the on-the-move discussion.

Unfortunately for my strappy city sandals the two-block walk is entirely uphill. This is forcing Mattheissen to do most of his "walk and talk" going forward and glancing backward at me straggling and puffing along.

"So as I explained," I say, finishing my recap of the encounter with Consuela, "we'd just like to see the photo you used for the witness identification of Dorinda Sweeney." I wish I had a better view of his face. I wonder if he picked up on *photo*. I wonder how he'll try to weasel out of showing me what's in their files.

"Are you familiar with the case at all?" I ask. "Because we'd also like the names of the witnesses involved." I'm deeply regretting this interview method. I'm sweaty, I can feel my T-shirt clinging to my back, and I'm certain the shoe-chewing Boston cobblestones have claimed another pair of victims. I sneak a glance at my heels as we, thankfully, reach the corner of Park and Beacon Street, where the outline of a red figure on the pedestrian signal instructs us to stop. An ungainly turquoise-painted open-air tour bus marked *Beacon Hilda* chugs by us with its load of visitors, heads all turned toward the statehouse across the street. I can hear the driver's voice booming about "oldest statehouse in the country" and "gold-leaf dome."

"Know something about it?" Mattheissen turns to me as I finally get to stop walking. He puts his narrow leather briefcase down on the sidewalk and peels off his Euro-chic sunglasses. His eyes are slate, the color of smoke and flint, and his gaze is intense. He's all edges, no curves. That makes it all the more shocking when he smiles. Not only because it's the first time he's done it, but because it transforms him. In a good way. *Mattheissen, Tek Mattheissen.* I can easily picture him delivering the lines, sleek and Bond-like, as the leading man. *License to…*

"I was lead investigator on that case, thought you knew

that," he says. "Assumed that's why you came to see me. They tell you at the Swampscott PD that I was with the Ortega campaign now? " That smile again. Lower wattage.

I see the red Stop figure has turned to a green Go. Mattheissen makes no move to walk.

"Know that case inside and out," he continues. "Deadly Dorie. Confessed. Now I hear, Rankin's people are poking around. Sent you, did they?"

Here's where the interview ends, I predict. But, surprising me, Mattheissen stays put, so I persist. I need to make sure he's aware Franklin and I are on our own. And the best way for a reporter to talk to a cop is to be honest. For as long as you can.

"Not at all, Mr. Mattheissen. The CJP did contact us, of course. People who want stories investigated do that all the time." I turn on my most winning expression. "People constantly hit you up, too, when you were on force?"

He raises an eyebrow, acquiescing, so I continue. "It's all about the truth. Wherever the story goes, we go. I just want to see the photo that was used. We have a right to see it. And if Dorinda Sweeney's innocent, well, I'm sure you'd want to know that, too. Right?"

"Look, Charlie. I can call you Charlie? You want pictures. I get that." He looks out over Boston Common, the historic expanse of well-kept trees and lush grass that opened in 1783. It's been green—and covered with tourists—ever since. The light changes back to red as we stand on the busy corner, horns honking, trucks rattling, air conditioners in the top floors of the brownstones beside us humming and plopping drops of condensation on the concrete sidewalk. Mattheissen checks the crosswalk light. Still red.

"Names of the witnesses?" he says, turning his attention

back to me. "Photo array? All in the files. Archives. Could take some time." He puts his sunglasses back on, discussion over. "Might want to make a public records request."

Damn. Time is exactly what I don't have. And if I make a formal records request, all kinds of bureaucratic quicksand could delay our story until *next* July.

Briefly touching Mattheissen's arm, I give my last-ditch pitch. Power-broker wannabes love to show their power. I play damsel in distress.

"Look, Mr. Mattheissen. Can you help me with this? You're really the only one who can cut through the red tape." Even I'm gagging, but Mattheissen's demeanor seems to soften. Come on, Tek, make my day.

"Nothing to hide," he says. He seems to be weighing his options. "Public documents. Closed-case evidence like that's in the archives though, deep storage, in the new building. No way to get them today."

And tomorrow, I remember with annoyance, is Saturday. Monday will be the Fourth of July, when every state office in the country will be closed. Tuesday is my inescapable appointment with Dr. Garth. I'm certainly not going to mention that. Plus, Mom would pop her stitches if I canceled the appointment she was so pleased to arrange because I had some other silly commitment. Like my job.

The light goes green. This time, Mattheissen picks up his briefcase.

"Charlie?" he says.

"Wednesday," I say quickly. I'll use the unavoidable delay to make it appear I'm being flexible and cooperative. "So you'll have time to contact your people at the archives. So how about Wednesday? I could meet you there."

"Ten a.m.," Mattheissen says, stepping into the white-striped crosswalk. "At the state archives in Dorchester. Front desk." He takes two more steps, then stops in the middle of Beacon Street. Rows of cars idle on either side of him, ready to hit the gas as soon as the light changes. He turns to me, ignoring the traffic. His eyes are hidden behind those glasses, but his smile is amped to the highest power and aimed straight at me. "Maybe we can have coffee afterward."

Chapter Ten

"He said what?" Maysie's scooping a second spoonful of pickle relish onto her foot-long and completely barbecue-blackened hot dog, melting the mustard that's already slathered on it into yellow rivulets that pool onto her sagging paper plate.

"Ketchup?" I offer. I mean it as a joke, but Maysie accepts the red plastic container and squirts a line of red on top of what now looks like a condiment sandwich. I glance over at Josh. Blindfolded, he's stumbling around the Green's expanse of south shore backyard in a raucous twilight game. Penny's latched on to Maysie's twelve-year-old Molly with the tenacity of a pop-star stalker. The two of them, plus Franklin and Stephen, Maysie's husband Matthew, and their five-year-old, Max, are taunting and dodging. Their shouts of "Marco" and "Polo" escalate in hilarity, floating across the muggy summer evening.

Max drops to the grass, rolling away when Josh gets too close, leaving one untied thick-soled shoe behind. Dave the Dog, their hyper but protective black Lab, leaps from his spot on the deck to retrieve the shoe, then single-mindedly dashes after Max to return it. Dave the Dog bumps the blindfolded Josh, who spins away, startled and confused by the unexpected commotion.

We're surrounded by laughter and chaos, but even in the midst of the Fourth of July festivities, Maysie and I have a slice of privacy.

"I know," I say. I pull a bottle of diet iced tea from the bright green ice-filled cooler next to the round wooden picnic table. Big wet drops from the bottom plop onto my white pants. Even this late in the evening, the spots will evaporate without a trace in the heat. At least the pants have escaped Maysie's mustard. "He's incredibly handsome, about my age, a little older? And that double-oh-seven look, more Euro than you'd predict for a local cop. Anyway, he didn't even wait for an answer, just walked off into the sunset."

"Sun doesn't set until, like, nine, " Maysie says. "I thought it was—"

"I was being funny," I say. "Like in a movie. You know." I twist off the cap to my iced tea and take a sip. It's more like metallic chemicals and imitation lemon than tea. "So you think—I mean—no question I have to go meet him at the archives. That could produce some key evidence for our story." I flicker a glance at the still-blindfolded Josh. "You don't think he'll expect me to go out with him, do you?"

"Why don't you?" Maysie asks. "Is he married? Did you check his finger?"

I look at her, blinking, trying to process whether she's kidding. And I had, in fact, checked. But more out of habit than specific curiosity.

"Mays, you're killing me here," I say. "I thought you loved Josh. Thought he was perfect. You said you were shopping for maid-of-honor dresses, right? Even though I warned you not to count weddings before they're hatched. So what's up with the ring-checking question?"

"*Did* you check?" Maysie persists, looking at me inquiringly from under the bill of her Red Sox cap. She drags a picnic bench away from the table and straddles it, elbows on knees, her face unreadable. She's wearing what looks like one of Matthew's madras shirts over a denim miniskirt.

"And who knows what'll happen with Josh. You've been all worried about Penny's reaction to you, and whether Victoria is still in the picture, and whether you've got what it takes to be a mom. Maybe this "Tek" would be a good love backup. He's not just an ex-cop, he might be on the fast track to the governor's office, then the White House." She shrugs. "You know. The big time. Your mother would love him."

I twist the top of my iced tea back onto the bottle and place it on the red-and-white checkered tablecloth. The condensation from the bottom makes an instant ring on the paper. I stare at the spreading damp spot, wondering what I should say. *No.* I don't wonder.

"I love Josh." I say it before I even realize it. And it doesn't sound strange to say it out loud. "Ring, no ring, no matter if he's the most attractive ex-cop in the world. I'm done with all that. Me and Josh. Done deal. Penny. It'll work."

The gang has now moved to touch football, racing across the backyard, pursuing the plastic ball that's bouncing and rolling with a wobbling mind of its own. I look back at Maysie and see the beginnings of a sly smile.

"Just wanted to hear you say it," she says. She looks pleased with herself. Maysie the backyard psychotherapist.

"You—" I don't fill in the actual word that first came to mind. What she is, is a true friend. Sneaky, but a true friend.

"Marshmallows," she yells. "Fire's ready."

As the footballers brush themselves off and clamor toward dessert, Maysie stands up, then selects a long wooden-handled fork from a pile beside the cast-iron barbecue. She points it at me, then at Penny and Josh, who are walking hand in hand, swinging arms, laughing. "What'd your mom say? Drunk, sick and with their kids? Look at the two of them, kiddo. I'll wait till after New Year's," she says, patting her stomach. "But then—I'm buying a dress."

"Hi, Daddy." Penny bounces back into view. Her two pigtails are now festooned with red, white and blue bows, apparently the result of her visit to newfound role model Molly's preteen domain. The full-of-herself twinkle vanishes as soon as she acknowledges me. She downshifts into perfunctory, polite. "Hi, um."

My name's been "Um" ever since the dinner at Legal's.

Not waiting for a reply, Penny plops onto the navy-and-black plaid wool blanket we've spread out onto the lawn in a line with all the others, positioned in just the right spot to view the Duxbury town common fireworks over the trees. After a brief assessment, she parks herself strategically, back to me and facing Josh. Stretching out her bare legs and leaning back on her hands, she scans the night sky. "When's the fireworks thing start?"

I gaze at the quickly darkening sky, too, wondering if I should reintroduce myself somehow. She obviously knows my name and I can't help but believe this is some kind of eight-year-old power play. If she doesn't say my name, I don't exist.

"Sweetheart?" Josh says.

"Yes?" I answer.

"What?" Penny answers at the same time.

"Sweetheart Penny, this time," says Josh, smiling and touching her nose. "But I'm talking to Sweetheart Charlie as well. And that's what I wanted to say. You can call her Charlie, you know, if you like."

I scoot around, tucking my legs under me, getting ready to join the conversation. Maybe I'll suggest we can all come up with something else she can call me. Charlotte? Aunt Charlie?

Penny purses her lips as if she's considering how to respond to her father, but then, instead, she starts making faces at him. Widening her eyes, making pretend fins with her hands, cheeks sucked in, now-bowed mouth opening and closing. "Fish face," she says, her words distorted though her moving lips. She points to Josh. "You do one."

There's a sound like a sizzle and a pop, and the night clicks into darkness as someone snaps off the spotlights that had illuminated the backyard. A shower of glittering orange plumes of light explodes overhead, illuminating the line of tilted-up faces watching from suburbia below. A Sousa march, courtesy of the Boston Pops radio broadcast, blares through speakers Matthew set up on the deck. I can hear the clash of brass and drums repeating down the street, each family with its own version of the celebration. Fireworks beginning. Conversations over.

Penny splays herself out, flat on her back, arms beneath her head and one flip-flopped foot propped on her knee. She's made herself a boundary between us.

"Come on, baby girl." Josh scoops up his dozing daughter, cradling her drowsy little body in his arms. One ribbon droops from a lank pigtail. There's still a line of white marshmallow sticking to her half-open lips. The combination of football, sugar and staying up past her bedtime has zonked Penny into oblivion. We trudge across the lawn toward Josh's car. And mine. The two of them are heading back to the vacation cabin on the Cape. The one of me is heading to Boston.

"I wish you were coming with us, sweets," Josh says. He glances at Penny, lolling in his arms. "I was hoping you two could…"

"Me too," I say. "Maybe Penny could even figure out my name." I touch his arm as we walk. "I'll be there this weekend, I promise. And I'll take you up on the outdoor shower offer. Thanks for being so understanding about my story."

"So what's next? The nursing home, you said? To check on the tape?" He stops briefly and looks at me, his eyes narrowing with concern. "You've got to be careful, Nancy Drew. You and Franklin. Are you going to that bar tomorrow?"

In a time-honored gesture probably more age-appropriate to Penny, I cross my fingers and prepare to lie. Luckily, we arrive in the driveway's parking cul-de-sac, where our cars are the only two left. Luckily, now Josh is distracted, and I don't have to answer. Somehow, I'm not comfortable telling him about my complicated rendezvous with Tek. *Meeting,* I correct myself. Not rendezvous.

Josh opens the back door to his silver Volvo and slides Penny into the backseat, pulling a safety belt across her chest. Her eyes flicker open and she gives a groggy smile. Overtired and exhausted by fun, she sighs back to sleep as the belt clicks into place.

Gently Josh closes the car door. Leaning against the window, he takes both my hands. "It's a hard time for Penny," he says. "I have to tell you that there's something more."

Pausing, he looks down at the asphalt driveway. His face darkens as the combination of headlights and streetlights cast slashes of moving shadows, but I can still recognize his expression. He's worried. And I don't know why.

My brain races with possibilities. A hard time for Penny? What could that mean? I hear the final sounds of the neighborhood celebration—laughter, a slamming door, a car's ignition cranking into life—but all I care about is what Josh will say next.

"Victoria and her husband Elliott are not at a resort in Montserrat," Josh continues. His voice is even and unemotional. "They're having some problems. And they needed some time alone."

"Does Penny know?" I ask softly. Poor thing.

"No," he says. "At least, they haven't told her. But kids recognize when something is wrong. I'm wondering if that's why she's so clingy, so needy. When parents aren't happy, that's difficult to disguise, no matter how you struggle to pretend. I always hope Penny wasn't really old enough to remember when Victoria and I—"

He breaks off. "Thing is, Victoria has this—idea—that maybe she and I should have stayed together."

Slowly, I take my hands back, one at a time. I stare up at the night sky. The last of the fireworks have long faded and now it's sprinkled with stars. Choosing one, I dispatch a fervent wish. And then the star moves. I've just wished on an airplane.

"For Penny's sake, though," I begin, stepping into uncharted territory. "Do you think it would be—"

Josh reaches out, touching my check, turning my face back to him. "Charlotte Ann McNally," he says carefully. "Victoria's wrong, of course. It's absurd. Her perception of what's 'right' is whatever she happens to want at the time. But if you and I are, if you and I are going to be together, we can't have secrets. Penny, Victoria, your job. It's all part of who we are, right?"

I search his face for clues, still unable to answer. Josh's eyes soften and he gently takes up my hands again, one, then the other. Then, one at a time, he touches each to his lips, tenderly kissing my fingers.

"Fireworks," he says with a smile. "And with you, not only on the Fourth of July." He draws me closer, cradling me in the curve of his shoulder. We're both leaning against the car, once again looking out at the sweep of stars above us. I feel his breath near my ear, feel his lips on my cheek.

"I love you, Charlie McNally," he whispers.

A set of tiny twinkling lights moves through the sky, and this time the distant roar of the jet engines reminds me what I'm really seeing.

I nestle closer, almost convinced Victoria does not exist. Josh says he loves me. Maybe wishes on airplanes do come true.

Chapter Eleven

I look good. I didn't even have a glass of wine at Maysie's last night, so my eyes aren't the slightest bit puffy. My hair actually looks the same on both sides. I'll be out of here in five minutes, no question. Mother satisfied, me off the hook. And armed with a do-not-pass-go from her precious doctor: I get out of surgery, free.

"So what do you think, Dr. Garth?" I'm swallowed up in a gargantuan barbershop chair with metal footrest, padded headrest and wide flat vinyl arms. There's a massive floor-to-ceiling mirror right in my line of sight. I'm trying not to stare at myself too obviously, so I turn to the white-coated physician sitting at a mahogany side desk nearby. "Am I getting past my sell-by date?"

Dr. Garth looks up from examining the yes or no boxes on the medical history chart I painstakingly filled out. His French cuffs, each monogrammed MDGIII, peek out from under his starched lab coat. "Dr. Malcolm Duncan Garth, III" embroidered in blue, is stitched over the pocket. His carefully knotted and conservatively striped tie is held in place by the silver and black rubber tubing of the stethoscope draped around his neck. I'd bet that stethoscope is engraved with his name and birth order, too.

He puts a finger on the chart to mark his place, then

tilts his metal-rimmed glasses up onto his forehead,
peering at me, his latest specimen. "Sell? Buy?" he asks.
He gives a sharp nod and his glasses fall back into place
on his nose. "I'm afraid you've lost me, Ms. McNally."

He smiles engagingly. In the outside world he'd be described as "skinny" and "the runt of the litter." Inside the
Center for Cosmetic Surgery, he's the elegant and patri-
cian king of the operating room. Power doctor. Protector
of Beacon Hill's best faces.

I try a flirty little gesture, crossing one leg over the
other. My splurgy new red patent pumps signal I'm successful and professional. Reliable, but with a certain flair.
A young flair. "Like at the grocery store? Time's up?"

He gives an uncomprehending smile. He probably
hasn't been in a grocery store in, well, maybe not ever.

I try again. "When you pass the sell-by date, the
product is too old." I smile what I imagine is adorably.
This is really going well. I'll have time to do a quick
check in with Mom after I bid adieu to Dr. G., then
possibly Franklin and I can arrive at the nursing home in
Swampscott earlier than we planned. Franklin thinks I'm
at the dentist.

"Ah," Dr. Garth says, looking at me from under one
eyebrow. "Of course."

I'm drawn to the mirror. I can't help it. The lights in
the examination room are soft. A few are even pink. I
know that's designed to boost and flatter skin tones, like
looking through rose-colored glasses. It works.

I'm sure he's going to tell me *Oh, no, Miss McNally.
You're here much too soon.* He'll gesture me out of this
contraption of a chair and wave me to the door. See you
in five years, he'll say. Maybe ten. You're only forty-six.
Right now, you look terrific.

And sure enough, Dr. Garth puts down his cigar-size pen and gets up from his swivel chair. I lean over to pick up my purse and tote bag from the floor beside me, anticipating our swift goodbye and my even swifter exit.

"What I'd like to do now, Ms. McNally," he says, pulling a spindly three-legged stool in front of a blank white wall, "is have you take a seat here, please, if you will. And please remove your jacket, if you will." He looks at me expectantly. I have no choice. Mom is going to owe me big.

I abandon my purse and my plans and climb down from my medical high chair, uncertain. As I drape my blazer over the back of the chair, Dr. Garth pulls a braided cord, lowering what looks like a navy-blue window shade. Except there's no window.

He repositions the stool in front of the blue background and, again, points me to sit down. "Now, if you will face me for a moment…" Dr. Garth flips open a panel on the mahogany desk. A contraption like Mom's old sewing machine rises up from its hidden storage cabinet underneath. It's a camera. He fusses with some dials and switches, and looks through what must be a viewfinder. "What I'm doing to do—" he's almost talking to himself "—is get a couple of baseline befores."

Befores? Oh. Like before and after. "So you think," I begin, "that—"

Dr. Garth rolls a metal cart in front of me. On it is a curving black apparatus that looks like a plant stand. "And if you'll please put your chin in the positioner," he instructs, "we can get underway."

I drop my chin into the molded rubber gizmo. I suppose this is to keep my head in place for the dreaded befores. At this point, I don't know if I'm more worried about the befores or the afters. Not to mention the "durings."

With three snaps of brass-plated wall switches, he clicks off the soft-focus lighting and clatters open the window blinds. The morning sunshine blasts through. I sneak a sidelong glance in the once-reassuring mirror beside me. The sight startles me so much, I sit up, right out of my chin perch, and stare at the wrinkles and lines of the stranger in the mirror. Me. Instantly aged by lighting reality.

"Ms. McNally?" Dr. Garth gestures pointedly to the chin holder, and I obediently get back into position. I wince as a flashbulb pops, then again and again. Dr. Garth rolls the table around beside me, and positions me for what I assume is a profile.

"And once again," he mutters. "Please hold still." I stick out my chin, see another flash, hear the pop. "And that's all we need."

Dr. Garth rolls the cart away and stands in front of me, hands in his lab coat pockets. He surveys my face, pleasant but appraising. "We'll just give you a little re-freshment," he says. He puts two fingers along my jaw, turning my face back and forth. He tugs up the skin at my jawline, then lets go. Again he lifts, then lets go. I feel like a piece of clay. Really old clay.

"Mini," he says. "To reshape the line of the mandible. Two weeks' recovery." He uses a thumb and forefinger to pinch that rhinoceros-worthy fold of flesh under my chin. "This can also be removed. Mentoplasty," he says. "Two weeks."

I still haven't said a word. I'm not sure what to say. I thought I'd be saying "no," but now I'm beginning to wonder. Maysie's right, I wear contacts. I can't even imagine what my natural hair color would be. And if Dr. Garth's waiting list is any indication, most women think this is no more a big deal than highlights and a blow-dry. With anesthesia.

"What would it look like?" I ask. Maybe Mom is right. Maybe Maysie is right. Maybe it's face time. "After it's all changed? Would I still look like the same me? Or a different me?" I get an even more alarming thought. "And what if I don't do it—what'll I look like then? And in how long?"

Dr. Garth shakes his head, as if he's answered this one before. "Do it now, do it later. You can't stop the aging process any other way," he says. He goes around behind his desk, and begins to steer a sterling silver mouse across a thin foam pad bearing the black and red crest of Harvard Medical School. The motto says Veritas. Just what I need.

"If those befores I just took were entered into the system, I could show you on the computer," he says, watching the monitor. "I've installed a state-of-the-art age progression software that manipulates photographs. It essentially speeds up time." He looks up. "However, if you have a snapshot of yourself, I can scan it in right now," he says. "Any size."

Do I want to see me ten years from now? I do. I don't. I do. I definitely do. I head for my tote bag, knowing the only photo I have is my station ID card. But how will I know if it really works? He could be running some sort of scam to stampede vulnerable baby boomers into clamoring for a surgical savior. Unless you waited a decade or two, you would never know if his software time machine was truly accurate.

Contemplating my misgivings and sniffing a possible story, I snap open my bag and dig to excavate my ID card. Though tethered to a black cord and clipped to my contraband mini-canister of pepper spray, it's still buried itself somewhere in the black hole. I instantly see, however, the blue-and-gold binding of the 1986 *Seagull*.

Now there's an idea. And it may be the first good news of the morning.

I have a picture of Dorinda Keeler Sweeney. From twenty-five years ago. What's even better, I pretty much know what she looks like now. Let's just see if Dr. G's fancy software is so much smoke and mirrors. My face can wait. It's Dorie's I'm interested in now.

I hold out the yearbook, open to the page of Dorie and her prom court. "How about the queen," I say, pointing to the wide-eyed and wrinkle-free teenager. "Can you make her twenty years older?"

I pause, then bait the hook. "Or would that be too difficult?"

Dr. Garth takes the yearbook with both hands and turns it facedown onto a squat black and silver metal box beside his computer, adjusting the photo until he finds the correct place on the top. "This scanner is a V7200, with 6400 dpi optical resolution and 48-bit color," he explains, as if I know what that means. "The scan feeds directly into my AP—age progression—program. It will create a stream of images as the face evolves through time."

He pushes a button, and the scanner begins to whir. "Its wrinkling and aging algorithms are based on photographs of a population cohort of two thousand people," he continues. "Once we download the photo, the AP morph will take just fifty-five seconds to generate the final product."

"Fascinating," I say. Skip the jargon, Doc, let's just see if the thing works. "I'm so eager to see the results."

"I can't look at it now, I'm trying to drive," Franklin says.

Franklin had picked me up at the corner of Cambridge and Blossom streets, near the "dentist," and as we head for Swampscott I've described how Mom's plastic

surgeon demonstrated his age progression software. So
far, Franklin hasn't questioned why I happened to be in
Dr. Garth's office. He may think it's all part of Mom's re-
cuperation, since he knows I just paid her a quick visit.
Fine with me. Franklin knows a lot about my life—hard
to avoid since we share an office—but my personal con-
sultation with Dr. Garth can stay private.

I stare again at the peculiarly haunting images gener-
ated by the AP computer. Dr. Garth had put the whole
page on the scanner, so it's not just Dorie, but her whole
prom court that transformed through computer magic
from eighteen-year-old high-schoolers to thirty-eight-
year-old whatever-they-ares. They still have lithe and
toned teenage bodies, wearing wannabe-sophisticated
gowns and embarrassing tuxes, but now they're unsettlingly stuck with middle-aged heads. Puffing jowls,
receding hairlines, narrowing eyes, the early etchings of
lines and wrinkles.

"It's creepy," I say. "But I have to tell you, this
computer version of Dorie is right on the money. You'd
recognize her from it. You'd think it was a real photograph, you know? I guess it really works."

"Did he do you? Charlotte at sixty-six?" Franklin asks,
making a woo-woo face. "Maybe you just don't want to
go there. Might be too scary."

"Very funny," I say. "Ve-ry funny. But since you're
being so unnecessarily mean to me, I guess it's time to
tell you I had him do a shot of you, too. I was going to
save it as a surprise for Stephen. So he could see what he's
in for." I pretend to rummage in my bag. "Want to see it?"

Ignoring me, Franklin turns his Passat into the parking
lot in front of a yellow brick building, low and stubby and
vintage 1950s. It's as boxy as a file cabinet and just as

interesting. A soldier-straight row of identical shrubs lines the extra-wide concrete path to the entrance. Instead of steps, two wheelchair ramps lead to the double framed glass front door. A stolid white sign announces Beachview in boldly painted black letters, although the nursing home where Dorinda Sweeney worked is nowhere near a beach.

We push a plate-sized silver button and the automatic doors swing apart, allowing us into an overbright lobby. It's insistently cheery, so resolutely upbeat it instantly makes me sad. A massive arrangement of fake yellow gerbera daisies and white carnations sits on a lace-covered round table in the center of the room. Clusters of uphol-stered couches, chairs and love seats, empty, await absent visitors. Some decorator no doubt pitched them as "con-versation areas," but there's not a person to be seen. I sniff, trying to identify the familiar yet unfamiliar fragrance. Disinfectant? Onion soup?

Franklin is already checking out what appears to be the reception desk, though there's no one there to receive him. A phone and a guest book sit unattended on a curving wooden counter. The swivel chair behind it is empty.

He turns to me, questioning, and points to a doorway behind the counter. "Should we knock?" he whispers. "There's no bell or call button."

I dig into my tote bag, and pull out my cell phone, flipping it open and hitting redial. "I told her we'd be here at eleven," I say, tucking the phone between my shoulder and my cheek, and checking my watch. From behind the door, we hear a phone ring and then someone answering.

"Beachview," I hear it first, muffled, from somewhere out of sight, and then clearly in my ear.

"This is Charlie McNally," I say. "I'm in the lobby? We had an appointment with Miss Soltisanto, and—"

The door behind the counter opens. A harried-looking woman in a thin beige cardigan, white blouse and a dowdy flowered cotton skirt bustles into the lobby. She seems to be carrying her entire office with her—legal pad tucked under her arm, pencil behind one ear, and eyeglasses on a chain layered on top of a necklace of jangling keys. Another brass key bounces from a plastic spring around her wrist as she offers me the hand that's not holding her cordless phone. With that motion, the legal pad plops to the ground. "Amelia Soltisanto," she introduces herself as she leans down to pick up the pad. "Administrator of—" She glances at the phone, a flashing green light signaling it's still on. With a brisk gesture she clicks the cell to Off.

"Sorry," she says, "Emergency with the water heater. Luckily, laundry time is over and we—" She holds up one finger, as if she's just thought of something. She ducks behind the reception desk, picks up the phone and punches three buttons. "It's me," she says. "Plumber's on the way. Twenty minutes." She hangs up, uses her pencil to make some sort of notation on her legal pad, then turns her attention back to Franklin and me.

"Sorry," she says again. "It's only Virginia on duty today. And Joe B. of course. And Kiley, in at two. If she decides to show up." She smiles brightly and tucks her pencil back in place, patting her spirals of gray hair as if checking to see if more pencils might be stored among the curls. She's a combination of pack rat and air traffic controller.

I'm exhausted just watching her. I risk a glance at Franklin, who's leaning against the counter and taking in the whole performance. I can tell he's trying not to smile.

I open my mouth to remind her of what we need, but Amelia Soltisanto's phone interrupts, trilling insistently.

She holds up one finger, and this time Franklin actually laughs, which he quickly transforms into a cough.

"Hold please," the administrator says. Putting one hand over the phone's mouthpiece to shield her voice, she gestures with her head toward a door marked Client Services. "I pulled the records you asked for. In there. That's all we still have." She sighs as if trying to make a decision, her eyes darting to the phone, to the door, then back to us. "I have to—I can't—" Back to the phone. "Hold please." She holds up a finger, then points us to the door. "Fifteen minutes."

We're getting nowhere fast. Franklin and I, shoulders touching, are sitting at the client services desk, turning the pages in an oversize logbook, a ledger-lined compilation of time sheets. It contains the hour-by-hour arrivals and departures of every employee at Beachview. A page per employee, a page per day. Thanks to the efficient Amelia, the book including the night of the murder was already pulled from the shelves of similar forest-green volumes archived behind us. I figured there'd have to be some record of who was on duty that night. Turns out there is—and there isn't.

"The good news—doesn't this handwriting all look the same? It does to me." I turn the heavy logbook to Franklin, pointing out several daily entries. I twist it back to me, and flip to the front to reconfirm the date. "And for the entire seven months, back to the beginning of this group of time sheets, Dorinda K. Sweeney signed in at midnight, and out at 7:00 a.m. And looks like no one did it for her." I turn the book back to Franklin, keeping my fingers in place to mark several of Dorinda's pages. "See? Every day. Including the night of the murder."

"The bad news…" I pause. "The bad news, who knows when these pages were filled out? They're not numbered, and—look."

It takes both hands for me to flip the book over so we're looking at the back. A back that reveals two flat metal discs. I know they're what's holding the book together.

I pull open the desk's narrow top drawer, scanning for a letter opener. Slipping the thin blade under one silver disc, then the other, I pop the circles off, which allows me to pull the book's pages apart. "See? It would have been easy for Dorie to create a fake page for that night and insert it in the right place. Instant alibi." I snap the book back together, hoping Franklin can come up with a reason we're not one step forward with the logbook, two steps back with its easy-open binding. "She could have done it before the murder."

For a moment, the only sound is a soft swish as Franklin turns the pages of the employee time sheets. Just as I had done, he folds one page over to the next, comparing signatures.

"Still, 'could have done it' doesn't mean 'did do it,'" he says, looking at the time sheets. "More to the point, if she did, why didn't she make a big deal about it? You'd have to think police checked them. And yet they still arrested her. And she confessed."

"But if detectives had the time sheet and held it back— that's huge." I'm beginning to see a glimmer of hope for our story. And for Dorinda. "Law enforcement misconduct like that, withholding exculpatory evidence. That's enough on its own to get Dorie a new trial. Rankin and Will are going to love…wait a minute."

I lean back in my chair, then grab on to the desk when the chair tips back precariously farther than I expected. I carefully let go, keeping a toe on the floor and trying to keep at least my physical equilibrium. Our search for answers is only unearthing more questions. I'm beginning to realize why they call it a deadline. The reporter's career is on the line, and if she fails, her career is dead.

"Will Easterly," I say. Even though he's the one who's brought us this story, we've never really checked him out. His background. His connections. His motives. "I know he told us he was trying to redeem himself for his negligence in Dorie's defense, but why didn't he think to examine this book? I mean, it's the definition of reasonable doubt."

"Vodka, I'd say," Franklin replies. "Or whatever his alcohol of choice was at the time. As he told us, he was probably so buzzed back then, or hungover, he just didn't think of it."

"And of course," I say, my voice bleak, "let us not forget the two words that continue to haunt us—*she confessed*. And after that confession, no one was looking for evidence of anything."

The door to the Client Services office clicks open, and I look up, expecting to see Amelia giving us a time's-up. But it's not just Amelia.

A battleship in a pin-striped suit, lapels wide and electric-yellow tie even wider, takes up all the space in the doorway. Amelia is attempting to peek over his shoulder, but all I can see are her feet, on tiptoe, and the top of her head.

"This is Mr. Bellarusso," I hear Amelia say, as she darts her head back and forth, up and down, trying to be seen around the apparently immovable object blocking the view. "Head of our security."

Mr. Bellarusso reaches over to crush my hand, then

Franklin's, giving Amelia just enough room to sneak by and enter the office one shoulder at a time. "Mr. Bellarusso wanted to make sure—"

"Joe," he says, interrupting. "Joe B." Joe Bellarusso wears an American flag as a lapel pin. His pink scalp shows through his thinning colorless hair, and when he claps one hand onto the door frame, his sports coat opens to reveal the straps and pouch of a shoulder holster. Empty. "Charlie McNally, right? Do for you?"

I translate this to mean that he's asking what he can do for us, and actually, there are a few things I'd like to know. I point to the logbook and turn it to face him.

"Did the police ever look at these time sheets? After Ray Sweeney's murder? Or maybe recently?" I'm wondering if Oscar Ortega's office, knowing Rankin's on their case, might have gone back over their investigation, retracing their steps to make sure they crossed all the legal T's. Tek Mattheissen had been lead cop for the Swampscott PD. If the Sweeney case blows up, his past and his future would both be on the line.

"A Detective Masterson, name like that, looked at the time books. His partner Clay Gettings looked, too. Back then," Joe B. says. He takes out a tiny spiral-bound notebook from his inside jacket pocket, gives his thumb a lick and uses it to turn over the pencil-covered pages, one at a time. "Insurance company fella. Just the other day. And it's Mattheissen, not Masterson." Joe B. closes the notebook and tucks it back in place.

"You worked here?" I ask. "Time of the murder?" I'm starting to talk like Joe B.

"How about the tapes?" Franklin's talking at the same time.

Bellarusso lumbers to a row of cabinets lining one

wall and slides open one floor-to-ceiling door. Behind it are a row of tiny television screens, most of them turned off. The one in the upper right corner, however, is showing, live, the same view of the meds room we saw in Rankin's office. And the one next to it shows what must be the back door of the building.

Bellarusso gestures to the array of screens. "Course, we're not up to speed on this," he says. "Right now, we still got just the meds room and the back. We keep them for a week, then tape over them."

"It's a cost-saving measure," Amelia puts in. "We simply don't have the money to expand our security system. It's always on the list," she says, "but something else always seems to come first."

"And the tape for the night of the murder…?" Franklin asks, looking at Mr. B.

"I yanked it," he says. "Couple of days after the arrest. Locked it away. Only been on the job a week, just moved up here. Figured they'd need it for the trial." He shrugs. "Then, you know."

"She confessed," I say. I hate those words.

"Yep. First week on the job, this happens." He smiles, a cherub on steroids. "Never a dull moment."

Chapter Twelve

I slide Dorinda's time sheet across the conference table toward Will Easterly, offering it as if we're sharing. But I'm really testing him. I had confided my latest suspicions to Franklin on our way to CJP offices. Unfortunately for my paranoia, Franklin couldn't come up with a convincing reason that I'm wrong.

Franklin's off feeding his e-mail addiction, and then he's going to call the Swampscott PD, seeing if he can track down Mattheissen's partner. My job is to see if we're dealing with a hoax.

I'm worried that Will Easterly is a plant—a fraud—paid off, maybe, by the D.A. to trap us. What if Will forged the time sheet? He'd certainly have enough of Dorie's signatures to copy with all the legal documents she must have signed. What if Will was the "insurance guy" Joe B. mentioned? Went in "just the other day" and tucked in an alibi? Down on his luck, gets signed up by the Great and Powerful Oz to bait the do-gooder Rankin into championing a losing case. And takes Franklin and me down as collateral damage in their battle for political power.

I watch Will's reaction. If this time sheet existed at the time of the murder and he hadn't looked for it, it's a jaw-dropping dereliction of duty. If he had looked back then and it wasn't there, it's a jaw-dropping complication.

"Damn it." Will rolls his chair away from the table, knocking into Oliver Rankin, who had been looking over his shoulder. Rankin steps back, surprised, as Will stalks toward the closed door. I see his fists are clenched, his head lowered. He reaches for the doorknob—is he going to leave? And what will that mean?

Then he turns, facing us. His fists are so taut I can see the blue veins on his pale hands. He swallows, holding his chin high. "Step Ten," he says. "Continue to take personal inventory and when we are wrong, promptly admit it." He shakes his head, looking rueful, one lock of lanky gray hair falling onto his forehead. "Funny how there's a step for every occasion. And this one—well, hell. I thought I was on the right road, you know? Getting the tape? One step forward in my recovery. Now this. One step back."

Rankin drapes an arm across Will's shoulders, an almost affectionate gesture I wouldn't have predicted. "It's all a process, Will. And it's a process you initiated," he says. "And Charlie and Franklin found the time sheet. It's just another proof Dorie is innocent, is it not? Don't be so harsh on yourself. This is not a step back, it's forward."

He turns Will's chair around, gesturing his colleague to sit down. "Let's focus on what this can mean. And how to use it."

"I know. I'm being selfish." He pulls away from Rankin. "It's not about me, it's about Dorie," he says, but he heads for the door again. "I need some water. Or coffee. Can I bring you…?"

Rankin and I shake our heads, no. Will leaves, closing the door behind him. Is he really going to get water? Or to call someone? Rankin's CJP could be in real jeopardy if Will turns out to be a—what? Double agent? I don't have much time to float my suspicions, but for the sake of the CJP and of our reputation, I have to try.

Rankin's picked up the time sheet and is holding it to the light, looking at the back, then the front again. It's now or never. I perch on the conference table and outline my theory, quickly as I can.

I hop down and walk to the still-closed door, still talking, and stand in front of it as I wrap up my impromptu presentation. I'm my own early-warning system. If the doorknob clicks, I'll step away and quickly change the subject.

Rankin started shaking his head, disagreeing, when I was halfway through my first sentence, and he hasn't stopped since. It's like talking to a pin-striped power-tied bobble-head doll, except this one is now talking back.

"I 'preciate your candor, Miz McNally," Rankin says. He's suddenly cordial, as if I'm a juror he's trying to charm. "But you must know we don't enter into these cases without thoroughly vetting every aspect. Our reputation is, of course, at stake every time." He smiles, confident and untroubled. "Don't worry yourself about Will. His story is solid. Of course the time sheet's upset him. It's just another reminder of his shortcomings."

"But what if—"

"You're a good reporter," Rankin interrupts. "I admire your caution. But we're full speed ahead here, no doubt in my mind. We can trust him, Charlie. If we're going to defeat Oz, we've got to derail his law-and-order platform. Without flinching. I'll need to make a copy of this time sheet for our files, so—"

"Defeat Oscar Ortega?" My turn to interrupt. That's

not what I thought the goal was. And Franklin and I can't afford to get nailed in some political crossfire. "I thought this was about Dorinda. Listen, Mr. Rankin, we're not about politics, we're about the truth." I sound a little like a made-for-TV movie about crusading reporters, but then, I am made for TV. "Crusading" reminds me of Susannah, which reminds me of the promos, which reminds me if this story blows up, we're the first casualties.

The doorknob clicks, and I take two quick steps away, glancing at Rankin, hoping he'll understand the subject is closed. At least for now.

Franklin and Will come in, each holding two bottles of water, apparently deep into a discussion of their own.

"But what about the eyewitness identification?" Franklin is saying as he hands me one of the bottles. "According to the paper, witnesses all picked out her picture. Pointed out Dorinda as the person arguing with Ray Sweeney in The Reefs Bar. At half an hour after midnight. According to the time sheet, she was at work. Can't be two places at once."

"Just a minute," Rankin says, joining their conversation. He takes a bottle from Will. "Here's something else we need to confirm. 'Picked out' her picture? From an array of photos?"

I fill them in on my meeting with Tek, set for tomorrow at the archives. "That's what I wonder, too. We should find out exactly how it went down," I say. "If the photos are in the D.A.'s case files. But from what I recall, the witnesses were describing just one picture."

I nod, confirming my own memory. Then I remember one more thing. The article in *Police Chief.* I look at Rankin, then Will. "They're not supposed to do it that way, is that what you're getting at?"

"Correct. Indeed they are not," the CJP director says. "Police are not supposed to do a 'show up,' where they just show one picture—that's suggestive, and often causes witnesses to assume the person must be guilty. As a result, they pick them out. They're supposed to do a serial lineup—show an array of pictures. Placeholders, ringers, people who could not have been at the scene. Certainly not just the one the police think is guilty. If we can prove they showed a bunch of drunk and tired people, late night, in a bar, just one photo, Dorie should get a new trial right there."

"But bottom line, a photo is a photo, right?" Franklin says. "No matter how they show it? Do we know if any of the witnesses actually knew Dorie? Did they say, yes, that's Dorinda Sweeney? Or yes, that's the person I saw?"

"And what if police said her name? Said she was the wife?" I ask. "People might assume—"

"You could fill this room with the studies proving the unreliability of witnesses' memories," Rankin says. "And eyewitness ID is often wrong. It's almost impossible for police not to telegraph the answers they want. People remember what they think they should remember and, even more dangerous, what they're led to remember."

"Close your eyes," I instruct Franklin. I'm remembering something else from the article.

"Do what?" he says. "Can't you just tell me whatever it is while I have my eyes open?

"Indulge me," I say. "Close them. Tight."

Franklin puts his bottle of water on the conference table, then picks it up, centers a napkin underneath and puts it down again. After looking at me skeptically, he slowly closes his eyes. He manages to still look skeptical. "Okay, they're closed," he says. "Now what?"

"Is my jacket black or brown?" I ask. "Keep your eyes closed."

"Um, black." Franklin answers.

"Open 'em," I say, glancing at Will and Rankin. "It's blue."

Franklin, eyes now open and hands on hips, looks perplexed. "That wasn't one of the choices."

"Exactly," I say. "You chose black because I suggested it as one of the choices. Not because you remembered seeing it."

The room is silent for a moment. All this talk of photos and lineups and what a witness might or might not say. What the police might or might not have done. Tek is supposed to show me the case file with the actual photographs tomorrow anyway. It's really only about one thing. Dorinda Sweeney. And there's only one person who can get me to her.

"Will," I say, hoping I'm not taking a fatal step into journalistic quicksand. "I've got to talk to Dorie. Let me ask her about the time sheets." I bite my lip, contemplating an unpleasant option. Without an on-camera interview, our story is dead. Is it worth it, to go in with just a notebook? Newspaper reporters do it every day. Easy for them. I wish Franklin and I could discuss our next move, but there's no time.

"Off camera, even," I say. As I say the words, I know I may be setting myself up for trouble. It's in the top-ten dilemmas of television journalism. "Tell her—I won't even quote her unless she agrees." Off the record, worse and worse.

This could be the last card we have to play. From the concern apparent on Franklin's face, he knows it too. I shrug, acknowledging my unilateral last-ditch effort and hoping I haven't given away the farm. "It's better than nothing, isn't it?"

"I sure hope so," Franklin mutters.

Chapter Thirteen

Ten minutes until I'm supposed to meet Tek. I'm parked in front of the fortress-fronted state archives building, a haphazard sprawling boondoggle that looks like it was designed by committee.

Franklin had no luck working the phones yesterday, so he's at the Swampscott PD checking on Tek's old partner—the one Joe B. mentioned—and seeing if he can get a copy of the 911 call Dorinda made after finding her husband's body at the bottom of the basement stairs. Or where she says she found it. Maybe we'll hear something on that tape, something police missed.

I check to see that my cell phone is on, just in case Will calls to give me the good news about a visit to the Framingham women's prison. Tucking the phone back into my tote bag, I check for pad and paper in case I need to take notes. My pager, in case there's an emergency. Quarters, in case the copier is one of those ridiculous pay-in-advance numbers. And lipstick, in case Tek is as ruthlessly handsome as I remember.

Then I smile. This visit is all business. Pleasure comes later. I'm driving to the Cape tomorrow night to catch up with Josh, and Penny, and grill lobsters on the beach. My smile of anticipation fades as I imagine another audition in front of my preteen nemesis. I lock the door of my Jeep and step into the present. Story now, Penny-worry later.

I'm walking on tiptoe, trying to prevent my black leather sling-backs from getting chewed up in the too-wide spaces between the bricks on the pathway leading to the entrance of the archives building. I decided to wear jeans, in case it's dusty or I have to sit on the floor, but I know I look better in higher heels and figured there's no need to sacrifice style. With a click and a whoosh, the imposing glass doors automatically slide open, then swish closed behind me. A blast of air-conditioned chill replaces the July morning.

A marble-topped counter, waist high, stretches the width of the lobby. An ungainly metal detector, stuck in like an afterthought, blocks the entrance to the rest of the building. Behind the desk, a massive painted mural extends floor to ceiling, someone's garishly outsize and perspective-challenged take on local history. Lobster boats, a galloping Paul Revere, the *Mayflower* and a huge codfish. The committee probably designed that, too.

And there's Tek. Waiting for me. Black T-shirt, black jeans, his array of security badges around his neck, sunglasses on top of his head. He's his own silhouette, stark and sleek in front of the color-saturated walls. He's leaning on the counter, proprietary and serene, oozing ownership.

I give a casual wave, all business, as I walk toward him. I instantly hear my heels echoing through the cavernous lobby, so I go back to my tiptoe technique. The journey to the desk seems to take days. Though I'm keeping my expression upbeat, I'm regretting my shoe choice with every clackety step. Why does this guy make me so self-conscious?

"I've already signed in," he says, gesturing to a computer keyboard on top of the counter. "You need to show ID, and then we'll get started. Shouldn't take long."

The blue-coated security guard looks up from an array of tiny television screens arranged in a flickering patchwork in front of him. Beneath it, a single, smaller, separate screen, plugged into an extension cord snaking under the desk. The Red Sox game. "Bags," the guard says, half an eye still on the game. "Have to lock 'em up. Electronics? Phone, pager, beeper? Metal? Has to stay here."

"Playing the Yankees, right?" I'm trying to be congenial. "Not a big archive day, I guess." I hand him my purse and tote bag, silently lamenting the loss of my connections to the outside world. I'd better not miss a call from Will.

"Yup," the guard answers. He drags his eyes from the screen as he waves me to the metal detector. "Place is pretty deserted."

I walk slowly under the metal structure without a beep, but the guard still brandishes another detector wand down my front, and up my back. From my quick tour through the Mass.gov Web site, I know the building holds three-hundred years of history, documents from the original thirteen colonies, Civil War muster lists, handwritten transcripts of the Salem witch trials. I guess the security is understandable. The guard, straining toward his tiny TV, seems more interested in hitting than history. I watch for Tek to pass inspection, but he flashes his attorney general's ID, and the guard opens a metal gate and lets him pass.

"Here you go, gotta wear these at all times inside," the guard says. He reaches under the counter and pulls out two pale blue packages, handing one to each of us. They look like just-washed shirts from a commercial laundry. I'm confused, but Tek rips open the plastic and shakes out a cotton dust jacket with buttons up the front, and long sleeves.

"Government issue," Tek says, putting his arms through the sleeves. He ignores the buttons. "Probably not up to your usual fashion standards. But it's all about protecting our taxpayers. Can't have people leaving here filthy with the dust from long-untouched document boxes."

I hold up my archive-wear by the shoulders, imagining *I Love Lucy* in that candy factory scene. "Very retro," I say. "Do we get special shoes, too?"

"Gloves," the security guard says. We're each issued smaller white packets. "Wear 'em if you want to, got to if you're headed for the historicals." He checks what looks like a schedule book, open on the counter. "You're not registered for that, though."

Tek tucks his gloves into a pocket, and I follow his lead. "No," Tek says. "We're only going to the attorney general's section."

"Dump 'em all in the linen chutes when you're done," the guard says, opening the door to the rest of the building. "Check out here before you leave. Getcher stuff." He's back at the ball game before the door closes behind us.

Tek and I enter a long straight corridor. White-painted cinder-block walls are interrupted by a series of doors, identical except for stenciled letter and number markings. Tek walks confidently, apparently certain of where he's leading me.

"It's a couple of pods away," he says, as if I know what a pod is. I wonder how he can still look so cool, even wearing what could pass for a 1950's housecoat. "We'll have to dig out the boxes from an inside section, but that shouldn't be too difficult."

I accelerate to a little trot, working to keep up with his long strides. We walk through the archives' institutionally monotonous and monochromatic halls. I see only a few other visitors, all dressed in identical government-issue blue jackets, some wearing the white gloves. "It's kind of like the *Twilight Zone*," I say, partly because it is and partly because it seems we ought to be having a conversation. "Or a hospital." This reminds me I haven't called Mom yet today. Next on my list.

We approach a stainless steel elevator and Tek swipes his ID card through a bracket by the doors. A square button lights up red, then flashes green. "You come here often?" I try again to connect, hoping he'll be amused by what's usually a pickup line.

"Swampscott PD files aren't stored here, but I've been around," Tek says, looking at his watch. "When the A.G. needs records, he usually just sends a messenger." He cocks his head. Suddenly his demeanor changes. I remember the smoldering look he gave me in front of the statehouse. "You're getting the special treatment, though, *Miz* McNally. Your tax dollars at work."

The doors slide open, not to an elevator, but revealing a moving walkway like the ones between terminals at Logan Airport. "Hop on," Tek instructs. "And hold the rail. Most visitors have to walk. But this takes us right to the annex. Like I said, your tax dollars at work."

The walkway carries us past a bank of windows. At least now I don't have to try to keep up. For someone I once thought was trying to win me over, even flirting, Tek's now harder to read. Maybe he's changed his tactics. Maybe he's still devising them.

"Tek's an interesting name," I say, partly because I'm curious and partly because it's the only thing I can think of that's not business but not too personal. "Is it—short for something?"

The walkway is ending. With a quick motion, Tek steps off, and onto solid ground. He holds out a hand, offering to assist me.

"Detective," he says. He keeps my hand infinitesimally longer than necessary as I hop off the moving conveyor. "*Tek* is short for Detective. And I'll tell you my real name—if you tell me yours."

Taking my hand back, I'm briefly flustered by his touch, and somewhat frustrated, because what should be an uncomplicated situation seems to be getting more complicated by the moment. And just to prove I'm right, now I have to go to the bathroom.

Where's Tek? Frowning, I look both ways as the door marked W clicks closed behind me. Peering down the hallways, I realize that's about the only door with an understandable designation. The others all have those letters and numbers. Except, of course, for the one marked M, which is probably where Tek's gone.

I lean against the wall, waiting for him to emerge. The low-ceilinged hallways, lined with low-watt fluorescent tubing, are silent, uninhabited. I briefly wonder about the annex Tek was talking about. How long will it take to pull the documents and photos I need? My frown returns. This is taking too long.

I wonder if he's all right. There's no reason for him not to be all right, of course, and checking my watch, I see it's only been five minutes. Maybe seven, since I came out. But that's too long. If something is wrong, he's sick, or he fell, or, I don't know. And if I was just standing here the whole time…

I turn and knock, tentatively, on the door marked *M*.
"Tek?" I say. I pause, waiting for him to yell he's okay.
But there's no response. Maybe I didn't knock loudly
enough. Taking a deep breath, I knock again, louder, and
again call his name. "Tek? You in there?" With a final
breach of everything we learned in grade school, I push
open the door, looking but not looking. Of course if
anyone else is in there, they would have answered when
I knocked. Probably.

The room is stark and silent. And empty. No sprawled
body on the ground, no feet showing under the stall doors,
no invasion of privacy for a surprised ex-cop.

Okay, fine. Plan B. So what's the deal? I play back our
conversation and remember Tek said we were "almost
there." Maybe he's just gone on to the storage room.
Thinks he told me where it is or figures I can find it.

I continue in the direction we were walking, examining the look-alike doors to see if there's anything I recognize, or any sign of where I am or where I should be
going. But all the doors are identical. Indistinguishable.
And closed. No sign of anyone.

I try a couple of doors, at random, figuring someone
might be inside, or there might be a phone, but one after
the other, they're locked. I'm having some sort of
Through the Looking Glass moment, in a place that
should feel safe and ordinary but instead is tauntingly
surreal. Tek can't just vanish. And what's behind all these
locked doors? I rattle each doorknob in turn, annoyed,
frustrated, and getting angrier by the second. Damn Tek.
He couldn't wait two more minutes for me to come out?
And now I'm—a door opens. And I take one step inside.

The murky and flickering fluorescent lights are on and
the windowless room is filled with steely gray file

cabinets, identical, floor to ceiling. I hesitate, listening. "Tek?" I say. The sound echoes though the room and I can hear it's not quite my normal voice. No answer.

Leaving the door open, I check an elaborate fire exit chart in the hall. "You are here," I read. "Right. I know that. Question is, where is everyone else?"

I head back through the warren of file cabinets, noticing they all seem to be labeled with numbers and dates. I give a halfhearted tug at one file cabinet handle. Locked. As the map in the hall promised, there's another door in the rear. That opens, no problem, and I'm out in another hallway intersection. Left, right and straight ahead. Who the hell knows which way to choose?

Ahead it is.

I'm infuriated. The fronts of my thighs ache from trying not to slide on the linoleum-slick hallways. My heels are noisy. I'm starving. And I'm lost, lost, lost. In one more minute, I'm going to retrace my steps and head back to the guard's desk. And there'll be some explaining to do.

Was that—footsteps?

"Tek?" I call again. I stop, listening. No answer. The only sound is the buzz of the lights and some faint hum of air-conditioning. Shaking my head, I begin my trek back to the lobby—and then, unmistakably this time, footsteps.

My shoulders sag in relief. Tek's probably looking for me, too. We should have made a plan. At least this will be a funny story. If we decide to tell it. "Tek?" I call out. "Not funny! Where'd you go?"

Trying to track the sounds, I walk slowly, one tentative step at a time, toward the footsteps. At the hall intersection, I see a fish-eyed traffic mirror, set almost ceiling high. Reflected from far down the dimly lighted hall, I see the blue jacket I know Tek's wearing.

Shaking my head, ready to share our archives adventure, I feel my whole body relax. The blue-coated figure comes closer. Walking faster, then breaking into a trot. Then I see he's also wearing the white gloves. And a ski mask. The man—I guess it's a man—begins to run. Holding something. A gun? I'm not going to wait and see.

I turn, confused and terrified, and blindly run in the other direction. Down one hall, then another, my bearings, if I ever had any, completely lost. My damn shoes, clopping like castanets, amplify every step and echo thorough the corridors. I pause, catching my breath, and rip them off. Barefoot and terrified, and holding both shoes in my hands, I race around another corner, touching the wall to keep my balance as I careen through the maze of corridors. This has all got to come out somewhere. Someone's got to be here.

I skid around another corner. My blue jacket flapping, my T-shirt coming untucked, my bare feet sticking to the cool linoleum, one shoe in each hand.

And there he is.

Two strong hands grip my wrists. I squeeze my eyes closed and snap my hands down and away, the one move I remember from a self-defense class. "Use what weapons you have," I can hear the teacher saying. And I do have weapons. I clench my shoes, heels down, and with a yell that's half fear and half rage, bash both stiletto heels right into his crotch.

I hear a satisfying howl as—whoever it is—doubles over in what I can only hope is excruciating pain. I manage to yell "get away from me" at him as I take off down the hall.

Minutes go by. I know I can't keep running. I pause, listening intently. Nothing. Maybe I should find another open door—but that's stupid, if I can get in, he can get in. If whoever it is gets in, I'm trapped. I prop myself up against the hallway wall, breathing hard, palms on my knees, one shoe still dangling from each hand.

Was it Tek? I try to remember how tall the person was. I can't. I know he had on jeans. I think he did. Some eye-witness I turned out to be. That blue jacket, and the gloves, certainly. Like everyone else in the building. I know Tek wasn't searched after he showed his badge, so he could have had a gun. And if it isn't Tek, where is he, anyway? And what might have happened to him?

Maybe he's waiting. Waiting until I make a move. But I have to move. I dash down another hall, my eyes swimming with tears. Am I going toward "out"? Or farther in? Am I going in circles? And is whoever it is waiting for me? Or gone? Doesn't know who I am in the first place? Just hanging around the archives in a ski mask. Right.

Where the hell is everyone? The flashing red lights of a smoke alarm give me one idea—a worthless one. I have nothing to set on fire. I run nearer the red light, figuring where there's a fire alarm, there's an exit. Instead, there's a smoke alarm with a red light and a—what?

A security camera. Problem is, if I scream for help, it'll only let whoever it is know where I am. And the damn security cameras have no audio anyway. Hoping the security guard's not completely transfixed by baseball, I pretend to scream. I plant myself in front of the camera lens, jumping up and down. Waving my hands. "Help! Help!" I silently mouth into the camera. Clutching my throat with both hands, I pantomime disaster, which isn't so difficult, since this is a disaster. I look in all directions, making sure no one's coming up behind me. Or in front of me. I have to keep running. The guard should be seeing me. Where are the damn exit signs?

I pick another hallway, trotting now, realizing with an additional flash of concern that running might just bring me closer to whoever is after me. If he—she?—is still after me. Every time I see a security camera, I stop, waving and holding my throat, silently screaming for help. But there's nothing. And no one. The bad news and the good news.

Just another length of hallway, door after door, stretching out. And then I see one more thing. A metal opening in the wall. A silver door about the size of a big-screen TV with a black knob that's labeled Pull.

Linen Chute, it says.

Where the security guard told us to—where is he anyway? Told us to drop our jackets. I stand in front of the shiny metal door, my lips pressed tight together, assessing the odds. I know the building only has one floor. How far can it be to the basement? And there's gotta be a basement exit.

What are the chances there's a big fluffy laundry basket at the bottom? Pretty good. If today's pickup hasn't already been made, the sane part of my brain reminds me. Still, at least I know where this door goes.

I swing it open. Yeah, I know where it goes. Down. Down into the yawning darkness. Like an evil, narrow, suffocating tunnel. I flash back to my fan the toll taker, who was so supportive and enthusiastic and who completely believes I'm brave. This is for you, then, Edith-with-a-Y-and-an-E. One foot at a time, I swing myself into the metal cylinder. Clutching my shoes and praying there's no concrete floor or hidden triple-story basement below, I slide into the unknown.

* * *

I open my eyes slowly. Mentally checking for breaks, pains, twists or any part of me that isn't where it should be or hurts more than it ought to. Nothing. I'm sprawled on my back, clutching my shoes. Safe in a puffy nest of discarded blue jackets sprinkled with white gloves. I look around the dingy walls of the basement, my eyes tingling in the musty surroundings, my nose beginning to twitch with the dust and accumulated pungency of a pile of dirty laundry. Potentially lifesaving laundry.

Glowing on the wall across from me, a red sign, showing perhaps the most reassuring word I've ever seen: EXIT. Holding on to one side, I clamber out of my jacket-filled laundry bin, swinging one leg over the side, then the other, then I hop to the ground. I scoot my feet back into my black sling-backed weapons and head for the exit door.

For the second time today, I march across the parking lot toward the sliding glass doors of the archives entrance. I'm steaming with anger and I'm more determined than ever now to see those damn photos. My theory? There ain't no photo array in that box. Which is no doubt why someone was trying to stop me from seeing it. And whoever that is certainly doesn't expect me to pursue it. Wrong.

The glass doors to the archive lobby slide open. I see Tek, arms crossed, leaning back on the guard's desk, facing the door. Waiting for me?

Tek stands with a start. I can see he looks worried as he comes toward me, arms outstretched. "My God, Charlie," he begins. "I couldn't figure out where—are you all right?"

I stop, assessing, ready to take a step backward. Ready to run. I see Tek's hair is perfect, his clothes unrumpled.

He's dumped his blue jacket. And there's no ski mask in sight. Or gun. He has on jeans and so did the person in the hall. But so do I. So does half the planet.

Tek comes closer and touches me on one shoulder. "Where the hell—"

"Where the hell were *you?*" I interrupt, twisting myself away. "I was in the bathroom for about two seconds. When I came out, you had vanished." I clench my fists, looking at the floor, my stomach churning with indecision and fear. "And then—"

Tek grabs my elbow, exactly the wrong thing to do. Again, I yank my arm away. "You vanished," I hiss. "And then someone—"

Tek holds up both hands, surrendering to my attack. "Wait a minute, wait a minute," he says, backing away. "I went to room G156, just like I told you. I waited for you there." He shakes his head, as if thinking back. "I figured there was some female thing in the bathroom, but after a while, when you didn't show up, I went in to check. And you weren't there. I came back to the security desk to wait for you, figuring that's what you did, too."

"So didn't you see me? Calling for help on those snazzy high-priced security cams?" I try to keep my voice even, but my words are spitting out, taut and tense. "Someone was chasing me. Someone who I think had a gun." I could swear Tek didn't tell me a room number. I think. He trails after me as I stalk to the security desk, questioning him over my shoulder. "You were here? And you didn't see me? On any of those stupid cameras?" I turn to the guard. "What the hell are you guarding, anyway? First base? Did *you* see me? Did you see anyone leave?"

The guard looks up from his screen as if I'm intruding.

I see the game is still underway. I guess I am intruding.
"Nope," he says, and then turns back to watch baseball.

"Hey," I slap both palms on the desk and lean across
it, trying to drag Mr. Security away from Fenway Park.
"Hel-lo. Mr. Guard," I snap. "I called for help on your not-
so-security cameras." Then I slowly stand up, realizing
soon all this mystery will be solved. Through the miracle
of videotape. Whoever's chasing me was also on camera.
And therefore, on the security tapes.

I turn to Tek. "Let's get that video. The security video.
Then we'll know the whole story." I cross my arms in
front of me, my jaw tight and my eyes narrowing. "Get
it." If it's Tek on that tape, he's trapped.

Behind me, I hear a rattle and clink of metal on
linoleum. I turn to see the guard sliding his chair away
from the televisions.

"Sorry, ma'am," the guard says. He picks up a scatter-
ing of black markers that are strewn across his desk, then
deposits them, one by one, into a bright blue coffee can.
"There's no tape in those cameras. It's just surveillance."

Your tax dollars at work.

"It was probably nothing, your imagination," Tek says.
"Did you actually see a gun? Did anyone actually threaten
you? Or even say anything?"

"Well, no," I say, thinking back. "But he—grabbed
my wrists."

"And let you go, apparently."

"But I hit him. With my shoes. It must have hurt him."
I watch Tek's face, checking for a wince of memory. I
should try to check the front of his pants, too, to see if
my shoes left any marks. Except whoever it was had on
that jacket. And I still can't figure out why—*wait*. It's got
to be about the photos.

Someone doesn't want me to see them. What else could be the motive for trying to scare me away? If Tek's the hallway bad guy, he'll come up with some reason we can't get the photos today, or we should come back, or he couldn't find them. Some bogus reason to hide the evidence that will set Dorinda free. This morning's bizarre confrontation, now that the fear is dissipating in the normalcy of the lobby, might even be worth it. To find out who's side Tek is on— the side of justice? Or his own future? Here comes the test.

I look at Tek with as sweet a smile as I can muster. "You're probably right. My overactive imagination. So let's get back to the reason we came." I flash another smile and adjust my hideous blue jacket. "Those photos from the Sweeney case. Shall we go get them now?"

I tuck my hair behind my ears and wait for the brush-off. I can hardly wait to hear it.

"Well, we don't have to do that," he says.

I knew it.

"Oh, no?" I begin, trying to keep the sarcasm out of my voice. "Why?"

"Because they're already here," Tek says, flashing a smile of his own. He pulls out a brown corrugated card-board box from behind the security desk. It says "Evidence," in red capital letters. Underneath, in black marker, someone's block-printed "Sweeney."

As I watch, dumbfounded, Tek lifts the lid, placing it on the counter, and then pulls a manila envelope from the box. He carefully unwinds a thin red string from around one paper disc, then another, then back to the first.

Holding the envelope open over the counter, he tips out the contents. A batch of glossy eight-by-ten photographs slides across the marble. Tek spreads them apart, one by one, putting them in a row, each one perfectly visible.

There are six photographs in front of us. All women. Five of them are mystery faces. The last one has dark hair pulled back in a ponytail. A peaceful smile, a touch of makeup on a middle-aged and still-pretty face. It's Dorinda.

"Your tax dollars at work," Tek says. "You need copies?"

Chapter Fourteen

Botox jumps onto my lap, pretending it just happens to be where she was going to sit anyway, and turns several times, swiping her tail across my face, making sure her calico body is situated in exactly the right place. I lean over her, dealing eight-by-ten photographs like a hand of poker onto the glass top of my living room coffee table. No matter how I look at the black-and-white lineup of middle-aged women, it's a losing hand. For me. And for Dorinda.

My phone is tucked under my chin, and I hear the answering machine kick in. "Hi, it's Franklin and Stephen. We're away from the phone, so—" There's a click and a silence, and then a real voice interrupts.

"Hello?"

I waste no time on pleasantries with Franklin. "Me," I say. I lean back on the couch, propping my bare feet on the edge of the table. Botox, with a glare, rearranges herself on my gray sweatpants, almost spilling the glass of white wine I'm holding. "Fun day at the archives. Got the photos and almost got killed."

I spew out the entire story from blue jackets to labyrinthine halls to identical doors to laundry chutes. To guns. To the vanishing Tek. And non-guarding guards.

"Just another day at the office," I finish. "And to top it

off, the photo array looks totally by the book. We've got to show them to Will and Rankin at some point, but if this is what they displayed to the witnesses that night, and they picked out Dorinda, so much for the botched ID theory."

Botox sweeps her tail across my face again, and I bat it out of the way. "You get anything? In Swampscott? Please tell me you did. Save the day."

"I did, actually," Franklin answers. "But you're okay, right? Not hurt? Hang on, I have to put down the groceries and get my notes."

I take a sip of wine as I wait, glancing at my front door, checking that the security chain's in place. Tek said he'd put in a report about what happened—*might* have happened, as he put it—in the archives. And I'm certainly going to file a report of my own, just to make sure it's on the record. But I'm happy to be home with my door chained. Even if there's not really any danger.

"Okay, listen," Franklin says. "I went to the bar, The Reefs? Where Ray Sweeney was last seen. The owner was here, a guy named…" He pauses, and I can hear notebook pages flipping. "Del DeCenzo. *D-e-C-e-n-z-o.* He says he wasn't there the night of the murder, but he was the next day when the cops came with a picture of Dorie. The bartender ID'd her, right away. Some patrons, too. Pointed right at her, he said. But here's the scoop."

"Did you find out about the bartender? Who he is? Or is it a woman?" I ask.

"It's a man, Charlotte, and I did, but hang on. Like I said, here's the scoop on Ray Sweeney. DeCenzo had one word for him. And I'm quoting now. 'Asshole.'"

"Lovely," I say, taking another sip of wine. "Evocative."

"I thought so, too. He's a real poet. But anyway, Del describes Sweeney as a loudmouth, a town politico with, as he described, 'illusions of grander.' And he was trying to, as Del so delicately put it, 'screw them' on the price of liquor licenses. Sweeney'd apparently visit all the bars in town, cadging liquor. Expect to drink free. 'Like we owed him,' Del said. 'If we didn't pour up, we figured he could yank our licenses, somehow.' Seems like Ray was not number one on the Swampscott popularity charts."

"Fun town," I say. "Corruption, extortion, and a murder. So the bartender picked out Dorinda? Where's he now?"

"Yeah, that's probably not a good use of our time," Franklin says. "He's 'in the wind,' according to Del. Only worked there a week or two, then split. And the witnesses who saw the photos, all strangers. He has no idea who they are or where they are. Police might know, I guess. Speaking of which. Tek's ex-partner?" I hear the notebook pages again. "Name's Claiborne Gettings. Moved to Detroit. Retired. I suppose we could call him."

I stare at the photos and they stare glossily back at me. Telling me nothing. "So if Dorinda was at the bar drinking with her husband, like everyone in the bar re-members, she couldn't have been at work. But if the time sheets and tapes are correct, she was at work. Only one can be true."

I hear a click on my phone "Rats," I say. "Call waiting. I'll—"

"Could be Will," Franklin says. "Call me back."

Franklin hangs up and I push the button. I mentally cross my fingers that Franklin's right. It's Will. Dorinda's saying yes, and this day will end on a high note.

"Hello?" I say. I can almost sense Will's voice ready to speak on the other end.

"Hi, um." I hear.

It's Penny. I glance at the clock on the mantel. It's just

after nine. Outside, in the real world of vacations and oceanfront cottages, the last of the sun is disappearing, so maybe Penny and Josh just got back from dinner. Or an early movie. But why would Penny be calling me? Maybe something's wrong.

"Hi, Penny," I say, steeling myself for bad news. "How's everything in Truro?"

"Fine."

So I guess there's nothing wrong. There's a pause on her end and I'm not sure how to fill it. Or if I should. She's eight, she certainly knows how to talk on the phone. Intimidated by an eight-year-old. Doing fine here.

"So what's up, Penny?" I continue. I take my last sip of wine. "Did you go to the beach today?"

"Yes." Pause, pause. "Dad wants to talk to you." I hear a fluster of motion on the other end. I think I can make out Penny's voice saying "*You* talk."

"Hey, sweets." Josh's voice wraps me in warmth, almost as if he's in the same room. I stroke Botox, head to tail, and she leans into my touch, purring.

"Hey, *you* sweets," I say. "Nice to hear from Penny," I add, laughing. "Not much of a talker, huh?"

"She's been loading my new cell phone," he says. "At age eight. She's choosing ring tones, putting numbers in speed dial, all that. I'm instantly ancient. I thought it would be fun if we called you together."

"Yeah, apparently not exactly her idea of fun. Anyway, it's wonderful to hear your voice. Tell me everything." No need to fill Josh in on my archive adventures with Tek. Or whoever.

As Josh talks, I leave the perplexing police photos behind and walk down the long hall to my bedroom, hearing about the battle for beach parking permits, the covey of bright umbrellas on the sand every day, the trips to Jam's Deli for coleslaw-soaked turkey sandwiches, the swarms of kids boogie-boarding and digging for shells. "Everyone's reading the same two books," he reports. "All that's missing is you."

Holding the phone between my shoulder and cheek, I peel off my sweatpants and hang them over two or three others on an overflowing hook on the back of my closet door. Sand and sunshine, huh. So far, there's been no summer for me. I stick my tongue out at the glum-faced blonde in the mirror, which makes her smile in spite of herself. Stop complaining.

"Lobsters tomorrow, right?" I say. "And perhaps, that shower?"

"It's tonight I'm thinking about," Josh purrs. "Penny's off, up in her room with her new goldfish. Flo and Eddy. And that leaves you and me, alone. Wish you were here," he whispers.

"Tomorrow," I say. Botox has already curled up in my open suitcase, announcing her decision that it's actually a new cat bed. She's pretending she doesn't know Jen the pet sitter will be visiting twice a day this weekend. "I can't wait. I'll be there soon as I can after work. I promise." And I mean it.

I see the shoes first. Even all the way from the double glass entrance doors leading to the Special Projects Unit, I can see the black patent platforms, precariously high, attached to slender ankles. I deduce, as I slowly approach my very own office, that someone other than me is sitting at my very own desk. Wearing those shoes.

That's pretty nervy. And since I don't see Franklin's shoes, she's clearly there uninvited.

I'm almost at the door, staring at patent leather the whole way, when one shiny toe begins to tap, telegraphing an entitled impatience. That's even nervier. I'll tell you who's entitled. I'm entitled to my own desk.

I arrive at the door. Of course. *Poison.*

And not only is Susannah sitting at my desk, she's clicking into my computer. She turns, apparently unaware of the expanding list of office protocol don'ts she's amassing, and claps her bling-spangled hands.

"Oh, fabulous, you're here, Charlie," she says. "Happy Friday." She actually waves me toward Franklin's chair. "Have a seat. Let's dish."

My brain is sparking with short circuits and liable to burst into flames, so I compromise by leaning against Franklin's desk.

"Hey, Susannah," I say. "Any good e-mails this morning?"

She waves at my computer, sarcasm flying right above her hyper-coiffed head. "I'm not checking my e-mail, Charlie, but thanks, though. Now. I had the boys in MIS install what we're calling a 'Susannah schedule' on your computer. See this star on the desktop?" She clicks a few keys and shows me a new icon. "Click here, every morning when you come in, and you can log in the outfit you're wearing. It'll keep track of all your clothes. So you don't, you know, repeat?" She tilts her head, as if she's my Malibu Barbie TV sorority sister. "You know? Do you love it? I mean, do you *love* it?"

"It's fabulous," I say. "I can hardly imagine how I lived without it."

"Now," she continues. "Also on this Susannah schedule is the timing for the Charlie's Crusade promos.

Shooting, editing. Then air dates. As you can see, the graphics are done."

She clicks a few more times, and the double *C*'s appear again. "Do you love it? And then we're editing in eight days. On the air in ten, or whenever we get the big green light."

"You know, Susannah, the Charlie's Crusade story, from our end, is not really on the same schedule as the promotion department. You know?" I pause, checking for a glimmer of comprehension. None. "We're on the trail, of course, and the story could certainly be compelling and successful. But I'm still somewhat concerned, as I've tried to say, that we're—"

"Kevin says you always come through, and warned me you investigative types always worry too much," Susannah says, with a dismissive wave. "And the news director is never wrong." She stands up, gathers her portfolio from my desk, then looks me up and down, her face registering something like bewilderment. "Black linen slacks and sandals? White T-shirt? Jean jacket? Are you…" She searches for a word. "Undercover?"

"Just headed to the Cape, after work," I explain. Who is she, my mother? I risk another stab at sarcasm. "I'm not on the air today, obviously. So I won't be entering this in the computer, is that how it works?"

Susannah looks relieved. "Well, then, I'm sure that's fine. Have a—oh." She turns back to the desk and picks up a pink slip of paper. I can see it's from Franklin's "while you were out" pad. I've never needed one of those, because I don't answer anyone else's phone. And no one else answers mine. Until apparently, now.

"Your phone rang," she says.

I can't even think of a polite response. Happily, she

doesn't wait for an answer and hands me the paper. "Your mother called. She said to tell you she needs to see you."

I slowly stand up, staring at the pink paper. I forget about office protocol. "Did she say why?"

"No, she didn't."

"Like, needs to see me, come over when you have a chance?" I persist. "Or needs to see me, get over here right now?"

"Ah, she didn't say," Susannah replies with a tiny shrug.

Susannah may have had more to add before she teetered out of the room, but I'm already grabbing Franklin's phone and punching in Mom's number. I think I can hear the clicks as the second hand ticks forward on our big wall clock. "Come on, come on," I mutter. "Answer."

There's a click, and a whir. A mechanical voice begins its canned reply.

"The patient you have dialed…" I look at the receiver, then slam it down.

"Chocolate?"

I'm baffled. I thought I'd be facing a swarm of doctors, or worse, one grim-faced surgeon shepherding me into a private corner. Instead, Mom is holding out a gold-foiled box of square dark chocolates, untouched, each nested in its own shiny ruffle.

"Take one, dear," she urges. She's not offering the selection to me, of course, since her vision of my weight coalesced during my preteen years. When my dress size was "chubbette."

The white-coated soap opera wannabe adjusting Mom's quilt offers a camera-worthy pout. "Aren't you a devil," he says. He clicks Mom's heart-rate-and-respiration monitor back onto her finger, then inspects the assortment. "These things are e-vil."

"Mom?" I step closer to the hospital bed, dangling the pink message slip between two fingers. "You said you needed to see me?" Did I miss something here?

Mom, still wearing a perky hostess smile, lifts a quick "wait a minute" finger. The nurse, temptation resisted, bustles out with a promise to return. As soon as the door closes, Mom slides her candy into her nightstand drawer and pats the bed beside her.

"Sit down, Charlotte." She looks around the room, although obviously we're alone. "Listen dear," she says. "I'm going to need to recuperate at your apartment. I don't think I can stay here any longer."

"Of course," I say, hoping my face hasn't turned green. Over the years, I've learned just to agree with Mother, then wait for her to change her mind. Then I get the brownie points without having to actually do whatever it was. I sit in the cozy club chair, though I'm nowhere near comfortable. "But Mother, why?" I continue. "You were supposed to be here for at least two weeks. To make sure all your sutures heal properly. And I thought you loved it here. And your doctors are here, all your nurses. People can watch out for you. Monitor you."

"Well, they're not doing a very good job of watching someone, at least," she says, and her voice grows softer, even conspiratorial. She fiddles with the silky fringe on the throw pillow she's now clutching across her chest. "It's all very hush-hush, but when my door is open, I can see things. Going on. People are walking too fast. Stretchers, going by. People I don't recognize." She pauses. "You know what I think? I think someone has…well. I tried to find out on my own, of course, but no one will give me the time of day."

"Mother, I—"

"So. You need to find out the truth for me. You do the investigative reporting, sweetheart. So investigate. And Lord knows if people are dying after cosmetic surgery, well, I'll simply have to leave. Immediately. And that's not all."

"But Mother, might that not be jumping to conclusions? Seeing the worst? There are a lot more reasons people might be hurrying. It's a hospital."

"And what's more," Mom continues, "I know you spoke with Dr. Garth, of course. But now I believe we'll have to find you another surgeon. I'm not going to be responsible for putting my own daughter in danger. I could never forgive myself if anything happened to you."

I blink, staring at my mother, who continues to talk as if I'm listening to her. I'm not. My mind is about twelve miles away, in a now-empty home in Swampscott. Where another mother, and another daughter, faced potential life-and-death decisions of their own.

A knock on the door, and Mother's mouth clamps shut. She narrows her eyes at me, then in a quick motion, pretends to be asleep. She quickly opens her eyes again, checking to make sure I'm in on the ruse. Then she goes back to "sleep."

I go to the door and open it quietly. The nurse is back, but I block his entrance to the room, sliding out into the hall and closing the door behind me.

"Mother is napping," I say pleasantly. "And she seems to be on the mend. Might I ask you a somewhat strange question? And forgive me, I'm sure everything is fine. But Mother seems to think, well, was there a problem? Was there some sort of bad outcome in someone's procedure?" I'm expecting the nurse to hedge, or more likely, just deny there's anything unusual.

Surprising me, though, the nurse glances down the corridor. I follow his gaze. There are only closed doors.

"I can't tell you what's happening," the nurse whispers. Another furtive hallway recon. "It's all private. You're a TV reporter, you certainly know the federal privacy laws regarding hospital patients. But you know the center has an impeccable record, you can look that up. And I can have a doctor reassure your mother." He purses his lips. "I can promise you no one died," he finally says. "Or got into—trouble. If that's what she's worrying about."

He steps away from the conversation. "I'm on duty," he says, turning away. "I'll go check on your mother later."

He takes one step, then turns back with an expression I struggle to read. Like a teenager with a juicy secret. Dying to tell.

"I'd tell you if I could," he says. "Honestly, nothing's wrong. I mean, would I be here if something was wrong?" And he pads away down the hall.

My hand on the doorknob, I'm torn about which way to go.

In? What if Mother's in danger? What if there's a big story here at the hospital?

Or out? Because I think I have the answer to the murder of Ray Sweeney. I think I know who did it. And if I'm right, it'll be the story of the year.

Chapter Fifteen

I can't leave my mother. I don't think there's anything actually threatening her, but I can't just run out when she seems to be so upset and fearful. I go back into her room, where she's now sitting up, hands clasped, eyes wide open, staring grimly at the muted television. She's changed the channel away from home improvement. Now she's watching *Forensic Files*.

"Mom," I say, trying to sound reassuring. "I did a little research with that nurse. You know, your chocolate guy?"

Mom looks at me, waiting. Her stretchy white bandages, still wrapped around her face, make her look like an owl. An owl with two black eyes.

"And you know, I really think you might have misinterpreted something."

Even in owl mode, Mom's face sets, like it used to do when I was pleading to stay up later or explaining why I was reading *Mad* magazine instead of doing homework. Not what she wants to hear.

I touch her arm, insisting. "Really, Mom. Don't worry. And I'm sure I can find out what's going on. If there's something going on. But I'm convinced it's nothing dangerous. Really. But I have to call Franklin, okay? I'll stay with you as much as I can, I will, but I'm supposed to be at work So I'll have to explain where I am. And I can't use my cell phone in here, so—"

Mother waves at the vintage princess phone on her nightstand. "Perfectly good phone right here," she says. "Is it not?"

It is, but I'm going to be discussing murder. And dead husbands. And I don't want to do that around her.

I back out of the room, talking all the way. "I'll be back in a flash," I say. "Nothing is going to happen. Watch TV. Just stop watching those forensics shows. They're making you paranoid. Watch something upbeat instead. Positive. You love Martha Stewart, right?"

And before she can answer, I'm out of the room and down the hall. I pull my cell phone out of my bag as I almost run to the front entrance. By the time I power through the revolving doors, the phone is ringing.

"Franko," I say. I begin to pace the sidewalk in front of the surgery center. "It's me. It's the daughter. I mean, the daughter did it." I gulp, knowing I'm talking too fast for Franklin to make sense of it. Still, I have to spill this. "Dorinda knows her daughter—Gaylen something? The one who was asleep at the time of the murder? You know. Did it. She's guilty. Her mother is protecting her. We've got to track her down."

Silence on Franklin's end of the line. I can almost hear his brain churning through the evidence we've uncovered so far. "Oh, man," he says. "And that could explain why the tapes and the time sheets seem correct—they are. Dorinda was actually there. At work." He pauses. "Okay, Charlotte. I think I'm with you. But devil's advocate, okay? Why did the bartender and those witnesses pick her out of the photo lineup? Dorinda, I mean?"

"Well, here's the easiest answer," I say. "They're just

wrong. A bunch of drunks, late night, dark bar. And you know people don't really look at strangers, especially if someone's arguing. They try to stay out of it. Pretend it's not happening. And the photos weren't even shown until the next day, remember? So they were probably hungover, too."

Still pacing, I flutter a little "no problem" wave to a curious security guard. "Still," I continue, "someone didn't want me to get those lineup pictures from the evidence box, that seems clear. Maybe it's Tek. Maybe it's Oz. There's something wrong with those photos—and there's something wrong with the witness ID. We just have to find out what it is."

"We should take the photos to Will and Rankin," Franklin suggests.

"But here's the thing, the main thing," I say. "Dorie is innocent. She's protecting her daughter. She confessed to protect Gaylen. And that means our story would be revealing Gaylen's guilt. No wonder Dorie doesn't want to talk about it. Talking to us is the last thing she'd do. She doesn't want us, or anyone else, to prove she's innocent. Because it means sending her daughter to prison."

I can hear Franklin tapping on his computer. "I'll see if I can find Gaylen," he says. "And I'll check our archive video again, see if there's a recognizable shot of her on tape."

"And hey, I'll call Will Easterly. Maybe he knows where she is." I stop pacing, and plop down on a green wooden bench in front of the hospital. The security guy is eyeing me again, like no one talks on cell phones in front of hospitals. I grit out a smile, signaling there's still no problem. Which, I realize, is completely not true. I'm supposed to leave for the Cape in—I look at my watch—four hours. I've got to explain to Mom that even though

I'd love to, I can't stay with her every minute. And I really, really want to check with Will Easterly about Gaylen's whereabouts. My conscience is killing me and all I'm trying to do is the right thing. Whatever that is.

"The little bitch," I whisper to Franklin. "She knows her mother is protecting her and she's letting her do it. Can you imagine? It's because her mother gave her every-thing she wanted, probably. Her father, too. Until he, I don't know, did something. To alienate her. She's so beyond spoiled and self-centered. She's killed her father and is letting her mother take the fall. She leaves her own mother to rot in prison. And the mother accepts it."

"Daughter dearest," Franklin answers.

The first thing I see is the fish. About a dozen of them, give or take, fluttering and diving in a massive turquoise aquarium. A cascade of bubbles fizzes to the top, past a stand of coral and a lace-like fan of whatever that stuff they put in fish tanks is. The hum of some ventilation motor and the flickering lights in the tank make Will Easterly's office seem anything but lawyerlike. A psychi-atrist's office, maybe. Or guidance counselor.

Or music teacher. Up against another wall, a modest upright piano, stacks of sheet music piled beside it. Will comes around from behind his desk, hand extended.

"Welcome to my office," he says "And my home. Figured I might as well use one of the rooms for work. Not much call for me to join one of those big Boston firms." A smile appears, then vanishes, on his face.

He still has a haunted look, I think so every time I see him. But I guess I don't know how he looked before. He goes to the fish tank and taps in a trickle of fish food flakes. Two orange-striped Nemo-looking fish ascend, silently, to the surface. I remember Penny and her new pets. Flo? And Eddy? Maybe I can get some secret fish info from Will, win her over with my fish knowledge. I check my watch. Darling Franklin promised to come babysit with Mom while I see what I can discover about Gaylen. I owe him big.

"So as I said on the phone," I begin. "I've started to wonder about Gaylen. Wonder if, you know, that's why Dorinda won't talk with us. Did you ever consider it? That she was trying to protect her daughter?"

Will nods, still staring at the fish. "It did, at some point, cross my mind. That Gaylen might have done it. But then Dorinda confessed, and you know the rest. And it is kind of out there. I mean, Dorinda…" He turns to look at me. "She's not crazy. She knows what prison means. She knows right and wrong. But she adored Gaylen."

"Adored?" I say. "Past tense? She doesn't anymore?"

"Won't talk about her, not at all," Will says. "She utterly refuses. It's as if Gaylen doesn't exist. And it's sad. I gather, at one point—at least I've heard—they were very close."

"Well, where is she, anyway? And what's she like? I mean, this is strange to ask, but do you think she could have killed someone? Her father?"

Will shakes his head. "Wish I had an answer for you."

"And where—"

"Wish I had an answer to that, too. I have no idea where she is."

We both stare at the fish for a moment. I'm watching their tropical yellows and blues flash though the waving seaweed and rising bubbles. Maybe fish will be good for Penny. Maybe I'll go buy a goldfish toy, whatever that would be. Maybe we can bond over fish.

"I have to talk to Dorie." The words come out, though I hadn't planned to say them so brusquely. "Especially now that Gaylen may play such a key role."

"Ah. About that. Dorie called this morning." Will's face sags and turns even more mournful. "She says no. And she told me to tell you, stop asking."

I consider my options. That takes about one second, since I don't have any options.

"Then let me tell you something to tell her," I say, as pleasantly as I can. Sometimes you've got to make a bold move to get a big story. "Tell her I know what happened. I know Gaylen was not asleep the night of the murder. I know who really killed Ray Sweeney, and it wasn't Dorinda. It was Gaylen. And if Dorinda doesn't want to talk to me about it, fine. I'll just have to do the story without her. But she's not gonna like it."

Everyone on the planet is driving to Cape Cod. The speed limit is fifty-five miles an hour. Which, of course, a real Massachusetts driver is going to ignore. Right now, however, all of us are going about zero miles an hour. Route 3 South is a parking lot. From here to the top of the next rise, I see an endless line of bikes, boats and surf-boards bungee-corded to the cars beneath.

It does make it safer to dial a cell phone, I think, searching for the positive. Mine of course is in the back seat, but with this traffic snafu, I put my Jeep in Park, twist across the seat back and sling my entire tote bag onto the front seat beside me. I always promise myself I'll take out my phone before I start a journey and I always forget.

I punch On. Just as I hear the *dootle-oot* warble sig-naling it's powered up, a barrage of angry honking swells into highway crescendo. Startled, I turn to face the car behind me. In the front seat, a driver wearing wraparound sunglasses, face contorted, is apparently yelling. At me, from the way he's pointing. And from the look on his face, it's probably good I can't hear the particular words he's saying. I turn to look out my windshield and see why he's so incensed. The jam is over. No one's in front of me.

Slamming the Jeep into Drive, I give a little so-sorry wave behind me, and head south. But I can still use the phone. I punch a few buttons, keeping an eye on the road of course. Mom answers on the first ring.

"Mamacita," I say. I smile. I haven't called her that since middle school, my first Spanish class. "How are you? Just checking in. I'm on my way to see Josh. Did Franklin come over?"

"Yes, yes, he's such a darling," Mom says. "He brought me *Bride's Magazine,* the sweetheart. We're talking about my invitations. And your dress. Which, I might add—"

The highway signs announce I'm almost at the Sagamore Bridge. The graceful steel-arch structure spans the Cape Cod Canal, the dividing line between the real world of the mainland and the vacationland beyond. It's also a notorious cell phone dead zone.

"Mom," I interrupt. "I can't wait to see. But I'm worried you're still upset, and before I lose you, I want to make sure—"

"Lose me?" Mother asks. "You're not going to lose me, Charlotte. Don't be silly. Franklin brought in Dr. Garth. Everything is fine. I was apparently wrong, can you imagine? Now. Franklin also told me about that daughter. Gaylen, is her name? What kind of a name is that?"

"You know, Mom," I say. I'm wondering if this conversation is going to be worth it, or whether it will end in some sort of battle. "Let me ask you. Do you think…would a mother go to prison to protect a daughter?"

"Charlotte, dear, a mother would do anything to protect a daughter," she says. "If you had a child of your own, you'd never have to ask such a question."

I sigh, regretting the whole topic.

"It's what I was telling you this afternoon," she continues. I can tell she's warming to her subject. I won't have to say another word for miles. "If I thought you were in danger, I would do whatever was necessary. Franklin tells me you think that's what happened? That this Dorinda person let herself be sent to prison to shield her daughter?"

The traffic slows again, cars pacing themselves to enter the highway rotary, a confusing and ridiculous undertaking obviously designed by highway engineers on drugs. It looks like a grade-school experiment in centrifugal force. Drivers are supposed to wait their turn to enter a spin of circling cars, all going fifty miles an hour. Problem is, for Massachusetts drivers, taking turns is as foreign a concept as rooting for the Yankees. If you manage the rotary properly, you can get off at the exit that takes you over the bridge to Cape Cod or the one that takes you south toward the ferries to the Vineyard and Nantucket. If you blow it, you're headed back to Boston. Or circling endlessly until someone takes pity and moves over to let you through.

"Well, that's what I was wondering," I reply, trying to monitor the spiral of cars and assess my chances of getting in and out without going around five or six times. "But I mean, do you think—"

"Charlotte, there's no question—"

There's a hum and a buzz. And the connection is gone. Mom is probably still talking.

I take the last watery slurps of my no longer fizzy Diet Coke and, readying myself for the scariest part of the trip, I chant the mantra of Massachusetts drivers. "Vehicles already in the rotary have the right of way." The moment there's an opening, I blast the Jeep into the whizzing traffic.

Truro's always a little bit father away than I remember. Every time I get to Orleans, one after another roadside emporium pushing taffy and T-shirts, I think I must have already passed it. And every time as I persevere through the touristy hustle-bustle of Eastham, I remember that means there's half an hour to go. Which gives me some quiet time, finally, to think.

Twisting open the new Diet Coke I got at the Pick 'n Pay, I'm thinking about Gaylen. So here's the precious daughter, the result of a shotgun wedding. I picture the prom queen, sobbing quietly, being lectured by her world-weary mother. Being reminded her beauty would fade, and her only chance at happiness is to forget her high school Romeo and latch on to the up-and-coming Ray Sweeney.

Poor Dorie had to break the news to her despondent but desperate sweetheart. Channeling some kind of made-for-TV movie, I see the red-eyed Dorinda. In my daydream she still has on her tiara, since that's the only picture I carry around of her. So here's Dorinda, tearfully explaining grown-up reality and maternal orders to her soon-to-be discarded Romeo. What's his name. CC. Even knowing the futility of their teenage declarations, they bitterly vow never to part, and then heavyhearted but flaming with desire, they embrace, and then—

The video in my head screeches to a halt.

Maybe CC Hardesty was actually Gaylen's father.

Maybe that's why CC left town so quickly. Enlisted, then exited. Maybe that's why Dorie agreed to marry Ray with such haste. And that would mean Ray Sweeney is not Gaylen's real father. So Dorinda knew it. And possibly CC. But did Ray? Does Gaylen?

I try to count months, see how the wedding date meshes with Gaylen's birthday, but I don't have enough specific information to do the gestational math. But theoretically, it could be true. So imagine Dorinda's despair. Her daughter's real father, killed in some faraway military explosion. Perhaps never realizing their teenage lust and passion had resulted in a child. Or, worse maybe, did. Later her daughter's stepfather, notorious, with a predilection for inappropriately young girls, makes disgustingly unwelcome advances. Maybe that proves Ray knew he wasn't Gaylen's biological father.

The only people Dorinda ever loved. CC: dead. Gaylen: fighting off a sleazy creep she thinks is her father, only to give him a fatal push in a final burst of self-protection. So Dorinda, finally, gets to take control. She takes the fall for Gaylen, sacrifices herself so her daughter, at least, can have a life. Not exactly a foolproof plan, since it relies quite a bit on Gaylen's ruthless selfishness. But maybe that's the proof I'm right. Ungrateful child to the end, Gaylen disappeared the moment the prison doors slammed shut, and lifted not a finger to exonerate the mother she knows is innocent. Anyone who is unfairly incarcerated would unquestionably want to talk about it. Unless there were an ulterior motive.

I like this theory. And Will Easterly will soon have to break it to Dorinda. I now know her secret. If she doesn't talk, I'm going to tell.

I see my turnoff onto Pamet Road, and navigate the

final curves of my journey to the weekend. For Josh's sake, and Penny's, and my potential future with both of them, I won't call Franklin about my revelation until tomorrow. On Saturday. He knows as well as I do, there are no weekends in TV.

Chapter Sixteen

The white lace curtains over the open bedroom window flutter in the breeze, letting in the day. The morning sun feels different on the Cape. Maybe because there are no buildings to block it, maybe something about the pollution, or the wind across the ocean. I look at the empty space and rumpled pillow next to me, and allow myself a lazy playback of last night.

Happily, Penny had claimed what she labeled the princess room, a cozily bay-windowed whitewashed bedroom on the second floor. Tagging behind Josh and me as he gave the tour of their rented summer cottage, Penny showed how she installed Flo and Eddy on the dresser and ensconced Dickens in special stuffed animal bed made of the blue-and-white throw pillows from her bedroom love seat. The princess seat, she called it.

Josh's bedroom is downstairs. And while Penny was finishing her vanilla frozen yogurt with only-white jimmies on top, her father had stealthily moved my suitcase into the same room. We were fairly certain the solidly sleeping Penny would never hear us, especially after we'd let her stay up too late watching *Mary Poppins* until she fell asleep, sated with popcorn, on the rumpled couch.

Josh carried her upstairs, then finally we were alone.

And although we attempted to muffle each other's late-night laughter with pillows, that made the whole hide-sex-from-the-eight-year-old escapade even funnier. Finally, desire and longing won over stealth. Time and place forgotten, Josh and I lost ourselves in lust and comfort and passion. And, as he repeated many delicious times, in love.

I run my hand across the yellow flowered sheet, back and forth, over the empty space Josh left behind. Remembering his words. His touch. This is what people do, if they're lucky. A cozy home, summertime, kids with sand in their shoes and sunscreen on their noses, the smell of bacon and coffee in the morning, memories in the making.

When Mom was my age, I calculate, I was off in college. I never thought about her and Dads, someplace on vacation, cozy and happy. I've seen snapshots, wavy-edged and falling out of those glue-on triangular photo album corners, but they've always been from another time. Me age three, with curly hair and a floppy sunbonnet, standing barefoot on the beach at Lake Michigan. Mom looking like Deborah Kerr in a structured black bathing suit and dark glasses. Dads squinting, holding a towel, looking out of his urban element, surrounded by water and sand. They don't seem like real people, that family from the past.

And yet, someday Josh and Penny will be captured in photographs like that. And me with them. Maybe. And I wonder why I've never thought before, that's why people take photos. To try to capture happiness. Without the memories, though, the photos are just pieces of paper.

I roll over and scrabble though the pile of watch, beeper, reading glasses, water bottle, hand lotion, and Blistex on the nightstand beside me, looking for my cell

phone. Talk about ungrateful daughters, focused on themselves. I dial the hospital. I've been thinking about Mom
the mom, not Mom the person. Who probably, who certainly, just wants the same things I do. Love. Contentment. Family. And I'm part of her family. I need to let her
know I understand. She just wants me to be happy.

"The patient you have called…"

Should I leave a message? I hang up the phone,
deflated. But resolute. *Later.*

Penny's dropping Cheerios into a glass of milk, then
fishing them out, one at a time, with a spoon. Droplets of
milk splash on the kitchen table as she retrieves the pieces
of soggy cereal, then puts them into her mouth. Josh, at
the stove with his back to her, is prodding a frying pan of
sizzling eggs with a spatula. Both are wearing bathing
suits, flip-flops, and Bexter Academy T-shirts. Exactly
what I'm wearing. If someone didn't know better, we
look like a prep school prof's family cozily summering
at our second home on the Cape. Another proof appear-
ances can be deceiving.

No one's noticed me yet. Somehow, I'm intimidated by
this entrance. Am I part of the group? Do I sidle up beside
Josh, wrap one arm around him and take over the eggs?

Or am I company? Which means I casually announce
my arrival to both of them, as if last night never happened
and tonight won't either.

"Over easy? Or sunny-side up?" Josh says, turning to
Penny. His spatula is dripping butter onto the stove top,
then onto the linoleum floor. I notice his arms are getting
nicely tan and his hair still looks like morning. He sees
me, and smiles as if he's seen his best friend. "Oh, good
morning, sweets," he says, with a private wink that makes

me weak in the knees. Then, all business, he points to me with the buttery spatula. "Just in time for eggs."

"I only want the white parts," Penny replies, ignoring me. "The yellows are too runny and yucky. They make my toast sticky. Which is dis-gusting." Another Cheerio, released from arm's length, plops into the milk.

I finesse my entrance, giving Josh a casual-looking touch on the back which I hope Penny categorizes as "pat" and Josh categorizes as "there's more where that came from."

I pull up a chair across from Penny. She continues to play the Cheerios game, ignoring me. I pull a spoon closer to me—it's old-fashioned and stubby, diner style, stainless steel—and I spin it on the navy-blue tabletop. "Think I can keep this on my nose? Without holding it?" I ask. Ultra-casual. I hold the spoon by the handle and put its bowl on my nose, talking around it. "Bet you I can."

Penny looks at me, suspicious. She pauses, but then apparently can't resist the temptation to prove me wrong. "No way," she says. She blows her bangs out of her eyes. "Uh-uh."

Pushing the spoon toward her, I offer her the challenge. "Try it," I say. "I promise it can be done." I glance at Josh, who's now turned down the burner under the eggs, and is watching our mano a mano. "Try it, and then I'll show you how," I say. "It's cool."

Penny takes the spoon, pursing her lips. From her wary expression, I can tell she suspects this is some kind of grown-up trap. But she wants to know the trick.

She puts the spoon on her nose. It instantly falls off. Picking it up and staring at it with deep concentration, a flare of insight crosses her face. She licks the spoon. And tries it again. And again. Each time the spoon falls with a clatter onto the kitchen linoleum.

Josh scoops up the spoon and hands it to me, challenge in his eyes. "What do you think, kidlet?" he says to Penny. "Shall we make her show us? And what if she can't do it?"

Penny stands by her chair, hands on her little hips, her tanned legs poking put from under her oversize T-shirt. "We'll make her…" She shifts her weight back and forth, tapping a thoughtful finger on her check. She's apparently eager to plan my retribution. "We'll make her…do the dishes by herself!"

"Yes!" Josh agrees, pointing to her. "Do the dishes by herself. Love it. Except however, what if she can actually do it?"

This is more perplexing. Penny shifts back and forth a few more times. "If she can do it…" she says slowly, "I'll help her with the dishes." She plops back into her chair, crossing her arms in front of her. "But I know she can't do it." Then the earth moves, as Penny directs her comments to me. "Can you?"

I put the spoon against my open mouth, cover it with my other hand, and give a puff of moist breath. I quickly paste the bowl to the end of my nose, then take my hands away. The spoon hangs, suspended. For at least two seconds. I snap it up before it falls. "Ta-da" I sing out, as Josh applauds. "The magical spoon."

Penny's eyes go wide, then she grins, processing what she's just seen. She dashes around to my side of the table, snatches the spoon from my hand and hands it back to me. Demanding. "Show me," she says. "That's totally awesome."

As Penny and I discuss the spoon technique, Josh brings breakfast dishes to the table. We all practice between bites of fried egg and toast. Penny's yolk, I noticed, remains perfectly intact in the center of her plate, only a fringe of white encircling it. She comes around behind me, curious, as I show her how spoon reflections can be upside down. Putting her hand on my shoulder, she peers at her topsy-turvy self. It's the first time she's ever touched me.

Josh clears the table, and gives Penny a meaningful look. "Dish duty for you, kidlet," he reminds her.

Penny looks at me, pleading. I almost melt onto the floor. "Um," she says. "Could you help me?"

"Of course," I say. "But how about…let's leave 'em for now. Do the dishes when we get back from—"

"The beach!" Penny interrupts, flinging both hands into the air.

"Beach it is," Josh agrees.

And then the phone rings.

It's not for me. Franklin would use my cell. And if it's for Josh, it can only be—

"Hello, Victoria," I hear Josh answer. "No, we're…"

"Mom!" Penny yells, and runs to scramble for the receiver. I'm left at the kitchen table, staring at my still-white legs and my unreliable future.

Fine. If they're on their phone, I can be on my phone.

"Did he leave a message? He just said, call him? So, did Kevin call him? Did he tell you what he said? Why would Oscar Ortega be calling our news director? Why wouldn't he call me? Or you? Why wouldn't Tek do the calling?" I finally wind down my barrage of questions, but Franklin is still quiet on his end of the line. I drag my toes through the sand beneath the tree swing in the back yard, trying to process his perplexing news.

"Are you finished?" Franklin says. "As I told you, you can ask me anything you wish. But as I also told you, I

won't know the answer. I don't know any answers. All I
know is I got an e-mail from the news director. In it,
Kevin said he'd gotten a call from Oscar Ortega, and that
I was supposed to find you, and have you call him. He
probably e-mailed you, too, but I assumed you hadn't
checked or you would have called me."

"Call Oscar Ortega? I'm supposed to call Oscar Ortega?"

"Call Kevin," Franklin says. "Jeez, Charlotte. Why
don't you just call him instead of asking me lists of un-
answerable questions?"

"But it's Saturday," I say. "You think Kevin's at the
station?"

"I'm closing my eyes to see if I can get any psychic
vibes," Franklin answers. "Let's see. Is…Kevin…at
the station…."

"Hush," I say. "I'm trying to figure this out. And even
if Kevin is there, Oz certainly isn't at *his* office. Damn
it." I wrap my arms around the swing ropes, twisting im-
patiently. Josh and Penny are loading the car. I've got to
go. But I need to call Kevin. Do I? Nothing's going to
happen today. I hope. No matter what, though, I've still
got to fill Franklin in on my Gaylen theory.

"I have to go," I begin. "But two things. One, you call
Kevin, say where I am, and see what's up. I'm reachable
on my cell. Unless we're at the beach. Then leave a
message. There's just nothing I can do—I'm here, he's
there. The other thing? Listen to this." I plant my feet on
the ground to stop the swing, and lean forward, elbows
on my knees. "I was thinking about Gaylen."

The wash of the waves, hypnotic and serene, almost
takes me away from my reality. The sand is baked warm
under my toes, and seagulls screech overhead. While

Josh has gone off to get sandwiches, I'm trailing behind Penny, who's scampering in and out of the water, pretending she's alone. From time to time she scoops up a shell and tucks it into the already sagging patch pocket of her T-shirt. She's soggy and sandy, and seems blissfully lost in her day.

The beach at Race Point is crowded with color, humming with motion, dappled with sun and shadow. It's windy, as always, but that just makes the waves sparkle and dance. One of those days you get a glimpse of where Monet was coming from. I glance back at Penny. And she's suddenly too far away. Too far out in the water.

"Penny," I yell, running after her. "Come back this way." I don't want to spook her and I'm not sure if I'm being overcautious. But how can you be overcautious when there's an eight-year-old in the Atlantic Ocean? My feet splash into the cool salt water, sticking into the sandy bottom, my progress instantly slowed by the pull of the waves. I don't take my eyes off her. Or the wave that seems to be coming too close.

In an instant, Penny is engulfed.

Running as best I can, I don't take my eyes from the spot I last saw her. I know she wasn't anywhere near over her head. The water was only knee-deep. But I caught the glimmer of fear and surprise in her eyes as the water unexpectedly knocked her legs out from under her. I plunge toward her, seeing only an arm and a flailing leg.

We arrive at the surface together, sitting on the sand, the water all around us, the waves receding as if the moment never happened. Penny's clinging to me, red faced, gasping, wiping the water out of her eyes, her hair in dank strands, dripping into her face. Her pale green

T-shirt floats into puffs, billowing around her, and she looks like a waterlogged little flower. She's fine, but afraid.

"I thought… I was… I didn't know…" Penny gulps, trying to breathe and talk and hold back tears at the same time.

"You're all right now, sweetheart," I say, pushing her dark curls away from her sand-streaked cheeks. "I was watching you the whole time. That wave just took you by surprise, didn't it?"

The water is calm now, peaceful and unthreatening. To anyone watching, nothing happened. I smile at her, reassuring, not letting go. "Nothing is going to happen to you. I won't let it."

I take her by the hand and help her to her feet. The water, so clear we can see the tweedy sand underneath, is just up to her knees. "Ready to go back to the blanket? Or want to stay in a while?"

"Um," she says. "Let's walk back." She keeps my hand as we slosh to the shore. "I wasn't scared," she insists.

"Well, hey," I say, slowly. "It's okay to be a little bit scared. The ocean is big, right? And kind of unpredictable. That's why you always swim with a pal."

She's quiet for a moment as we walk. "Like you?" she asks.

"Yup." I say, not letting on that my heart is so full I can barely talk. "Like me."

I take a few steps through the water, then as we amble slowly back to our blanket, decide to go for it. "Penny, honey. You know, you could call me Charlie, if you like."

She purses her lips, kicking the water as she walks. "Yeah, that's what Dad told me, too." She stops and turns to me, the water now tickling her ankles. She looks like she's going to cry. What just happened?

"I don't want two moms," she says. Her voice quavers. Her mouth is frowning so deeply it must be wrenched from the depths of her little soul. "I don't."

I crouch down to her height, keeping her hand and taking the other. She looks at me, dejected little face, hair still dripping, soggy T-shirt drooping off one thin shoulder. "Penny Gelston," I say. "You only have one mom. You'll always only have one mom."

Penny blinks, silent. A droplet, maybe a tear, traces down her cheek.

"Everyone has just one mom," I continue. "And she'll always be special, no matter what." I swallow, holding back my own tears a bit. I guess the watery incident with Penny was more frightening than I had admitted. Or maybe it's something else. "You know, my own mom is getting married this summer. My dad died a while ago. There'll be someone new in my life, too. But I'll always love my real dad. That doesn't change."

"So," Penny begins, slowly, as if I've given her another kind of lifeline. "We could be like friends? But my mom is still my only mom?"

"Of course," I say. "Exactly right." I stand up, and we begin to walk together, back to our place on the sand. A familiar figure carrying a brown paper bag comes into view across the beach and waves to us as he comes nearer. "Here's the secret." I lean down, and whisper in her ear, "A heart always has room for more love."

Chapter Seventeen

The moment I step across the threshold of the news director's office, every shred of remaining weekend warmth and contentment gets sucked away into a black hole of apprehension. It all seemed so promising—Josh, loving, attentive, and breathtakingly male. Penny, beginning to open up. Even Mom. We spent Sunday together, and even though she's still sometimes woozy with pain-killers, we actually had a real conversation. Tonight, I'm going back for dinner. If I live. Because now, Kevin O'Bannon's chrome and glass domain might as well be a crime scene in progress. With me as the victim.

Kevin, barricaded behind yellow-stickied stacks of *Broadcasting Magazine* and black-boxed résumé tapes, motions me to come in. He flips two fingers in a gesture that I'm supposed to translate as "and close the door." Susannah's skulking on the couch, punctuating the tension by tapping an expensive-looking pen on her ever-present folder.

The back of my neck goes clammy. My hands can't find a place to go. Kevin's sitting. Susannah's sitting. I'm standing. They ain't planning to give me a raise. Or tell me I've been nominated for another Emmy.

"Charlie," Kevin says. His voice is full of foreboding.

"May I play something for you? And you see what you think of it. It's a voice mail message. I saved it for you to hear."

Like I have a choice. "Of course," I say. "Franklin and I tried to call you over the weekend, but—"

"I got your messages, too." he says. Kevin swivels to his telephone, and punches on the speaker.

"This is Oscar…" I hear. In those four syllables, my already shaky Dorinda story begins to wobble like a dying top. Ortega's terse words continue to spit through the phone.

"Your Charlie McNally," his voice booms, "has lost her objectivity. She's clearly in league with those ultraliberal misguided do-gooders, all of them, soft on crime. And you're allowing it to happen. Perhaps even encouraging this conspiracy to derail my candidacy for governor."

Ortega's basso is so profundo, the tiny speaker actually shudders, struggling to transmit Darth Vader through a plastic box on Kevin's desk. If voice mail could breathe fire, this one is doing it.

"I won't have it, O'Bannon. You pull that woman and her sidekick off this so-called story," the disembodied voice demands. "Or your next message will be from the FCC."

His slam of the receiver must have rocked the Richter scale. Kevin looks at Susannah and she points her pen at him. He looks at me.

"How on God's green earth," Kevin begins. His voice is softer than usual, and he sounds like he's straining to stay under control. He clamps his lips together, making a thin white line across his reddening face.

"F. C. Freaking C?" His voice rises with each letter, and he stands, palms on his desk, and shooting lasers. "You told us this was a sure thing," he says. "You told us there was no problem."

I frantically search for equilibrium. I never, ever, told

them it was a sure thing. Quite the contrary. How many times did I warn Susannah? I look at the queen of lies, sitting in smug silence on Kevin's couch. She heard the message from Oz, then threw me under the bus. But wailing "I did not" is not going to save me. Or the story.

Using every ounce of phony confidence I can muster, I take a seat in one of Kevin's fake leather guest chairs. "Do you love it?" I ask, deciding on my tactics. "I mean, do you *love* it?"

Susannah looks baffled, hearing her own favorite saying tossed back at her. *Take that, consultant girl.* Her forehead doesn't even twitch as she tries to frown. I decide to think about that later.

"Seems to me that Oz doth protest too much," I say. "You think if he wasn't nervous about the outcome, he'd call you like that? I mean, for someone to call a major market news director, essentially threaten him? Only one reason for that." I hold up a finger. "Big fear. And that means there's a big story. Correct?"

This started out as a gambit to take their minds off the specter of the FCC. But as I warm to my theory, I realize I'm right. Why would Oz care so much, if he didn't think we were sniffing around something he was trying to keep quiet?

Kevin leans back in this chair, crosses one ankle over a knee. He swivels, just a few degrees each way, just enough to register there's some thought process occurring, then turns to Susannah, silently questioning. Continuing the pantomime, she shrugs.

"See?" I persist. "It makes our story bigger. I'm certain of it. Just let Franklin and me keep going. And there's more." I quickly sketch out my theory about Gaylen.

"So your move, obviously, is either to ignore that

phone call—" I cock my head toward the phone "—or to call him back and say we're still in a research phase. Say we always get both sides of the story, we're eager to do an interview with him when the time comes, and we'll stand behind whatever we put on the air." I pause, gauging whether Kevin and Susannah realize the logic of this. Am I the only one in the room thinking about journalism?

Kevin nods. "First amendment. Freedom of the press. Justice." He rubs his chin, probably trying to channel Edward R. Murrow.

What would Ed do? I send Kevin messages via ESP, and cross my fingers under my suit jacket.

"Two weeks," Kevin says. He shoots his silver cuff-linked wrists, his engraved initials glistening in the pin-spotted track lights. "You're on the air in two weeks."

"Gaylen's disappeared, according to everyone I talked to." Franklin's flipping through his spiral notebook as we regroup in our office. He's just back from this morning's round of interviews up north. I've filled him in on the news director's ultimatum and both of us are feeling the pressure to produce.

"Question one," says Franklin. "Was CC her father? Here's a quote from Myra Matzenbrenner—'That's what we all thought.' And when I asked whether she had any idea where Gaylen went, she said, 'The girl changed her name and left town.' That's the Swampscott scuttlebutt, anyway. As Myra put it, 'You wouldn't want to be seen on the streets every day as the girl whose mother killed her father.'" Franklin lifts an eyebrow as he reads from the page. "Then Myra goes, 'If he *was* her father.'"

He flips his notebook closed. "She says CC died when Gayien was about ten. Apparently Dorinda got a phone call from the Navy or whatever, informing her. So that meant CC was out of their lives for good, father or not."

"But she doesn't know where Gaylen is now, bottom line," I say.

"Right," Franklin answers.

I think back. "Wonder if Poppy Morency knows," I say, slowly. "Wonder who gets the money if the house sells."

"Wonder if Tek knows, or Oz," Franklin says. "They have 'ways' of finding people, right? Gaylen was there the night of the murder, obviously. You'd think they might keep track of her."

"Yeah, I'll do that now, call Oz and ask." I put on an ingenue face, and perform my fantasy question to the attorney general. "We're thinking you all put the wrong person in prison? And, oh by the way, do you guys know where Gaylen is hanging out these days?" I give Franklin a thumbs-up. "That'll do it. The A.G. will be delighted to help us on this story. Maybe even send Tek over to consult."

"You know, it's Tek I've been thinking about," Franklin says. "Did you ever get that witness list he was supposed to send? And that day in the archives—"

My phone rings. I should let it go to voice mail so we can plan the rest of our day, but I can't resist a ringing phone.

"McNally, News," I say, yanking a stubborn snarl out of my irritatingly twisted phone cord. Then, suddenly the tangle doesn't matter.

"Hi, Will," I say. The sound of his voice makes me sit up straight. My future may depend on this phone call. I look at Franklin, and silently mouth the name, *Will.*

Franklin holds up both hands, showing me crossed fingers.

Then, as Will begins to list details of what's necessary

to visit MCI-Framingham women's prison, I grab a pencil and scrawl out the news.

It only takes one word.

YES.

"So Dorinda Keeler Sweeney said yes," I say, closing the door to Mom's room behind me. "Suddenly the world is a happier place." Holding a mammoth bunch of starkly white tulips in one arm, I lean over and give Mom a quick kiss on her still-bandaged forehead. "How are you, Moms? Didn't they say you should be feeling better by now?" I peel away the slick brown paper from around the flowers and scout for a vase.

"Our family heals slowly," Mom says. "And Dr. Garth is annoyed with me for walking too much. Apparently that's aggravated my tummy incision, or some such. It's not closing up quite properly." She pushes a button on the console beside her bed and a humming motor sits her up little higher. She winces at the motion, a flash of pain crossing her face.

I see her eyelids flutter and I take a step to help, but she waves me away.

"I'm fine, dear. I just keep taking my pills. And I just keep thinking it'll be worth it, when Ethan and I are sunning our newlywed selves in the Islands, and I'm happy in a bathing suit for the first time in thirty years." She pauses, considering. "Twenty years. And there's a vase in the bathroom."

I arrange the waxy white tulips, their graceful stems and pointed green leaves, in a tall crystal vase as Mom prattles through the latest on her wedding plans. Peonies, Pachelbel, shrimp, choosing someone to officiate. I'm still focused on my Dorinda news. For a day that began inauspiciously in Kevin's office, things are looking up in Charlie world.

"…and of course, your dress," Mom is saying. She points to a pile of glossy magazines on one of the nightstands. "And don't you think I'm right about the leopard-striped leggings and the marabou feather mules?"

"Huh?" I answer. I've been faking my half of the conversation with "mmm-hmm" while I think about my Dorinda interview.

"You're not listening to me, Charlotte dear," Mom says. She points an accusing finger, trailing her heart monitor wires like some gothic jewelry, but I can see a twinkle in her eye. "Are you thinking about your story? You're just like your father. I could always tell, back then, when he was off in his own world, wishing he was pounding on that old typewriter of his. Or interviewing some ne'er do well."

"Thanks, Mom," I say. A wave of affection—and memories—suddenly and surprisingly makes my eyes a little misty. I see Dad's face, his black-framed glasses perched on his head, pencil tucked behind his ear. I thought it was "dorky" at the time. None of the other kid's fathers wore a pencil. Now I often put one in just the same place, and think of him whenever I use it. I wish he knew that.

"Do you miss him?" I ask.

"Of course, I do, dear." Mom reaches out a hand, as if I'm the one who needs to be comforted. "Your dad will always be part of me. Close to me. When he died, I was…well, I tried to be strong for you and Nora. Being someone's mother, that's a full-time job. It doesn't stop for disaster. Or when your children grow up." She smoothes the pink-and-white checked quilt that covers her, almost up to her chin. "You girls, you helped me through it. There were times when I—" She stops. "How did we get on this subject?"

Fine. I'm selfish and self-centered and should be thinking about my mother, but all I can think about is Dorinda. Plus, whenever I'm researching a story, I always turn to experts for advice and information. Maybe I've got one in this very room.

"Well, Mom," I say, "you're right. I was thinking about my story. Remember I told you Dorinda Sweeney agreed to do an interview? And you and I talked about how far a mother might go to…well, I'm just trying to decide how to ask her if she's sacrificing her freedom for her daughter. It just seems so unlikely. That someone would do that. Doesn't it?"

"Ah, Charlotte." Mom elevates her bed a little higher. Even with her bruised eyes and bandaged head, she manages to look almost regal. "You know I'm proud of you, don't you? That I realize what a success you are, in your career. All those Emmys. You know that, don't you? "

I'm not sure where she's going with this. Although her praise is reassuring to hear, I know Mom well enough to predict there's a "but" coming up.

"But…" Mom doesn't disappoint me. "With all your flashy and fast-track life, I'm still not sure if you understand human nature. Or maybe it's because you've never had a child of your own."

Don't go there, I silently plead. Do *not* go there: The joy drains from the day, as I sit, silent, wondering yet again why every conversation with her winds up about me and my failings. I look at my feet, wishing I could look at my watch.

"You think I don't still worry about you?" she asks.

"You think I don't look in the mirror and get surprised, every time, at who's looking back?"

I look up, puzzled not only by her words, but by a tone of voice I've never heard from her before.

"When I think of you," she continues, shaking her head carefully, "I can still see you as a child. I still see me as a young mother. I heard your first word, I smelled that sweet baby shampoo in your hair. The first book you ever heard, I read it to you. We listened to music. Practiced the alphabet. You're still that little girl to me, and it almost makes me cry every time I see you, all grown-up and on your own. I would have done anything for you. Still would. That's my job."

I pull a tuft of pink tissues from a pearl-inlaid lacquered box on her dresser. The white tulips seem a little hazy, I realize, as I dab my eyes. Then I see Mom needs a tissue, too. She takes the one I offer with a smile of thanks, but then waves it at me instead of using it.

"You think I'm criticizing you," she says. "I know you do, and I wish—I wish you wouldn't. Majoring in Shakespeare. Husband. Children." She smiles, tucking the tissue under a cuff of her periwinkle satin bed jacket. "Plastic surgery. Those are all your decisions. I only want you to be happy. Like your Dorinda. She wants her daughter to be free. She's doing her job."

I think about love. I think about justice. I think about loyalty. I think about sacrifice, and the choices parents make. And their children.

There's a tap on the door. "Mrs. McNally?" A white-coated attendant, the same one who reassured me there was nothing ominous about the hospital activity Mom thought she noticed, enters Mom's room, wheeling a cloth-covered dinner cart. He smiles as he sees both of us.

"And Miz McNally. I saw in the guest book you were here. Nice to have you with us." With a clang of silver-plate, he whisks the cover from a platter of assorted cheeses. "I managed to snag you some delicious apps from the kitchen." He looks around, then closes the door.

Mom waves the platter away, but I'm focused on the food, realizing my Greek salad with no onions or croutons lunch was long ago. Then I hear a little noise, a mixture of a sigh and a hiss. When I look up, the nurse, his back pressed to the closed door, is looking at us, waiting for us to pay attention.

"I'm not supposed to breathe a syllable, but I have to tell you," he says, his words tumbling out. "I'm very fond of you, Mrs. McNally, and you, too, Charlie, if I may call you Charlie." He pauses and purses his lips, apparently considering whether to go on. I'm transfixed, Gouda in hand, waiting for what's coming next.

"But Charlie, you said your mother was worried. About all the activity. And I just don't feel comfortable with that. And you'll probably find out about it anyway," he says, using the classic rationalization of someone about to spill a secret.

The nurse takes a few steps forward. Then he puts both hands on the foot of Mom's bed and whispers a name.

Mom's eyes widen. I put down my cheese.

"She's here, getting a little work done," he says, his eyes glistening with conspiracy. "But no one is supposed to know."

"Yeah, it was hilarious," I say to Josh, holding the phone on my shoulder. Botox is pretending to sleep, so I attempt to climb into bed without disrupting her. She shifts, begrudging me a spot. "So, he says, all her security guards put on white uniforms? Like nurses? So the tabloids wouldn't know she was there for all the surgery. Apparently the nurses were in a battle royal. Union types, the shop stewards, were enraged the place would let bodyguards masquerade as medical staff. But most were cozying up to the phony nurses, trying to get an audience with their fave rave from the movies."

I pull my comforter up around my neck, and tuck the phone between my face and the pillow. I wish Josh were here in person. I know he's in his bed, too. When I close my eyes I can almost feel his arm across my shoulders. Sleeping alone, these days, feels more alone than it used to.

"No, I can't get you an autograph," I say. "From her, at least. How about one from me?" I snuggle in closer to the phone. "In a place, say, where only I could see it?"

Chapter Eighteen

The razor wire around the prison glitters tauntingly in the July sunshine, daring the bad guys inside—women, actually—to escape. And keeping the law-abiding citizens out.

I feel like the poster child for good guys as I step out of the sunshine and into the institutionally yellow-tiled entry hall. This is the evil twin of the sleek state archives. The place is barely air-conditioned. Smells like stale everything.

I dig my state-police-issued reporter ID out of my purse and hold it up to the thick glass window of the guard's desk. The guard looks up, assessing, then she slides a pink piece of paper halfway though a metal slot. I see her hand, ragged cuticles and bluing veins, next to mine, tanned from the Cape, manicured and soft. Inside, outside. "Request-to-visit form," she says, terse and businesslike. She's said this a million times, and she'll say it a million more. No need to elaborate, no need to change. She points to a black cord dangling over the edge. "Pen. Fill it out."

I carefully print my name and social. U.S. citizen, yes. Convicted of a felony, no. Journalist, yes. Nervous, yes. Although that's not on the form. I hand the pink paper back to the melancholy-looking guard. Somehow feel I should try to connect with her. "Thanks," I say. "Nice day."

"Wouldn't know," she says through the metal grate. Her patent-billed cap shades her eyes as she reads my paperwork, then she feeds it into what looks like a fax machine. She cocks her head toward a bank of lockers. "Everything in there," she orders. "Everything. No cell phones, pagers, belts, receipts or keys. Wedding ring, medic alert, you can keep. And the locker key."

"I can take in my notebook, though, correct? And a pencil?" I ask. I know I can.

My stuff stowed, I hear a phone ring. The guard answers, then points to a sliding door. The rasp of a buzzer cuts through the silence. "Into the trap," she says. A massive metal door rumbles open. I step in and it closes behind me.

Metal detector. Pat down. Another buzz. Another sliding door opens, then clicks closed with a mechanically final clang. I'm inside.

I'm on the way to meet Dorinda Keeler Sweeney.

Another thing Mom was right about. It's impolite to visit someone's home without bringing a gift. What I brought to offer to Dorinda Sweeney is her freedom.

Problem is, she doesn't seem to want it.

The "no-contact room" is painted rancidly avocado. The walls are cinder block. No windows. A wall of thickly aging Plexiglas goes ceiling high between us, years of cigarette smoke and handprints filming Dorinda's face with a yellowing veneer. The phonelike receiver that connects us is up to her ear, but so far, she's all yes or no answers, not really participating. She refuses to give any details of the murder and insists she'll walk out if I keep asking. I wouldn't call this an interview. It's more like a monologue. Mine.

"But why did you confess?" I ask again. I figure I owe

her the respect to lay my cards on the table. "Look, Dorinda. I don't think you killed Ray Sweeney. But I think you know who did."

"I told Will…" she says. Her voice is steady and she looks me in the eye. "I told Will to tell you. The truth is the truth."

Her nails are bitten to the quick but her granite eyes are solemn, her posture graceful, head high. She blinks, her fingers wrapping and unwrapping on the receiver.

My visit can last fifteen minutes. Twenty at most. I need to keep talking, even if she won't.

"But I found the nursing home time sheets," I say. I lean forward, my elbows on the wooden counter, beseeching her. The surface is pockmarked, gouged with remnants of countless initials, numbers and imperfect hearts. Marks of time and fear and hope. "We have the tape, Dorinda. The eyewitness identification was obviously wrong. You were at work, not in the bar. Your lawyer—"

Then I hear a change in the silence. The receiver is clamped to my ear, and the muscles in my hand tighten as I feel her change her mind. I pause, scanning her face. It's unsettling to be talking to someone on the phone but still be able to see them.

"What?" I ask.

Her chest rises and falls, the fabric of her too-large cotton T-shirt folding gently as she moves. Even a size small would engulf her. She's wearing what look like hospital scrubs, patch-pocket top, draw-string pants. Hers are faded, drab. I see why they call them fatigues. Dorinda is the month of March, bleak and colorless.

Suddenly she smiles. Nothing could have surprised me more.

"You know I've seen you on television. I admire your

work," she says. It's as if we're having a cup of tea in a cozy luncheonette instead of a grim institution with correction officers hulking at the door. "Will told me what you think, that I'm protecting Gaylen. But on this story, you're wrong. I'll tell you what you need to know. Then you need to, please…"

Her forehead furrows, and she leans her face close to the glass. "…leave me alone."

Dorinda fidgets in her metal folding chair, crossing her legs, uncrossing them. She's wearing what look like Keds, scuffed, one edge fraying and threadbare. Velcro flaps instead of shoelaces. Tube socks. She shifts the receiver to her other ear.

"I worked the overnight shift at Beachview. For hours, it was just me and the clients. I had the run of the place. You saw the time sheet book. I just filled mine out when I finally got to work that night. Went to work, went to the bar, went—home. Then came back to Beachview."

She looks down, briefly, then back at me. "As for the video—I just took the tape from the night before, and changed the label. Changed the date stamp. Destroyed the tape that showed I wasn't there. I'm the only one allowed in the meds room that time of night. And trust me. Every night looks the same."

"So you're saying the tapes and time sheets were a cover-up? And it really was you at the bar?" My notebook is burning a hole in my pocket, and I'm longing to take it out to capture her exact words, but I'm afraid that will intimidate her. What she's saying is unforgettable, anyway.

"Ray was—" Dorinda's eyes flicker to the guards by the door, and she cups one hand over the receiver to mask her words, whispering as she looks back at me "—a bastard. He was disgusting, and worthless and…and…

and…manipulative. I've talked about it with my counselor here. I can't even imagine what he wanted to do to Gaylen."

I'm trying to process these disturbing details, assess whether I really believe them, and dig for more information at the same time. Change the date stamp? With every answer I get, it feels like the Dorinda-is-innocent story is fading into fantasy. I have about ten minutes to resuscitate it.

"And where is Gaylen?" I ask. "Do you see her? Write to her?"

A look crosses Dorinda's face, too fleeting for me to read. "She's disappeared," Dorinda says. "She was so confused and angry, she vowed she'd never see me or speak to me again. I don't know where she is." Dorinda shakes her head, as if erasing a memory. "I don't blame her. Look what she got in the deal. A creep for a father. A murderer for a mother." Her shoulders almost shudder. "Far, far away is where she is, that's what I'd say."

"So, no idea where? Really?" This is somewhat hard to believe, a mother not knowing where her only daughter is. But I guess when the mother is behind bars, it's easier. "Gaylen was what, twenty-one years old back then? And living at home? Do you have a picture of her?"

Dorinda's face softens as she reaches into the front pocket of her shirt. With two fingers, she extracts a snapshot-size photo. I can't see who's in it, but from the back I can tell it's tattered around the edges, one corner repaired with transparent tape. "Only this one," she says, staring at the photo. "Gaylen threw it at me when she left. Mine got lost somewhere when I came here, but we each had one, made copies. It was always my favorite. From when she was nineteen."

She carefully places the snapshot flat against the glass, a proud parent showing off her daughter. I see a teenager in Levi's and a Swampscott High hoodie, smiling and giving the peace sign. I don't have to memorize her face. I don't have to ask Dorinda for a copy. This photo is already stored in my phone. I was right. It looked a lot like Dorinda, but it wasn't. Gaylen. Of course.

"You know, Dorie," I begin, "if Gaylen were being abused by Ray, if he attacked her. Or threatened her. And she pushed him down the stairs to get away, she'd never be convicted of anything. You don't need to protect her. If she killed him in self-defense, she'd…"

Dorie's face tightens as she slides the photo back into her pocket. "Her father never touched her. I made sure of that. Gaylen was asleep that night. Asleep. Just like I told the police. Just like I told Will. And that's all I'm going to say." She clamps her arm across her chest and leans back. Body language for *I'm done.*

I suddenly comprehend all the time and space and conflict that separate Dorinda the prom queen from Deadly Dorie the convicted murderer. How do we get where we are? At what point do our decisions become our destiny? The door clanging shut behind us doesn't have to be made of steel. It can just be made of time. *Yeah, fifteen to life in Framingham,* my cynical reporter brain puts in. Still, I know the prison sentence is not only for Dorinda, but also for her daughter.

One thing for sure, she consistently calls Ray Gaylen's "father," not "stepfather." Do I need to reconfirm who Gaylen's father is? I do. I check my watch. Doomed.

"I saw your prom photo in the yearbook," I say. I'll try a new tack. "With your friend CC Hardesty?"

Staring at me, eyes welling, Dorinda slowly takes

the receiver away from her ear and, still holding it, drops her arm to her side. As if to make sure she doesn't hear any more. Then, even more slowly, she brings the black plastic phone back to her face. For one moment I get a glimpse of the girl who once danced and curled her hair. I can almost see the memories unreeling in her mind.

"I think of him every day. He was…" She shrugs. "He was my first love, what can I tell you? He was wild. Possessive. My mother thought he was—a bad egg, she called him. Made him all the more desirable, of course. He was Romeo in the Swampscott spring play, when I was Juliet, did you see that in the yearbook? A born actor. He would call me Juliet all the time, swear he loved me just as much. When I got the phone call from the Navy that he'd been killed…"

Suddenly, her eyes turn resistant. "What about him?"

Now here's the part in the soap opera where the organ music swells, and they cut to the tease of tomorrow's show. The announcer's voice intones the questions: Is Gaylen actually the boyfriend's daughter, conceived in one stolen night of passion before a loveless forced marriage? How will the hapless reporter, desperate for answers, find a way to ask such a delicate question? And what—big organ chord here, da-dummmm—will be the answer? Wait until tomorrow's episode of—

Except this hapless reporter doesn't have until tomorrow. I have now.

I can feel my foot jiggling under the counter. All I have to go on here is town gossip and a hunch that makes this a story for Danielle Steel instead of Diane Sawyer. Two choices here. Ask. Or don't ask.

"Dorinda," I begin. I pause. Suddenly the phone

receiver feels sticky. I switch ears and begin again. "Dorinda, forgive me. I just have to check all the facts. In researching what happened that night—"

"I told you what happened," she snaps.

I hold up a hand, apologizing. "I know," I say. "Just let me ask you two more questions. Three. Was CC Hardesty—"

Dorinda bursts into laughter, the alien sound ricocheting off the cinder-block walls. I stop, surprised into silence.

"Was he Gaylen's father?" she says. "Is that your question?" She shakes her head, as if she's hearing a familiar story. "Wish I had a nickel for every time someone tried to ask me that. I know it's what everyone thinks. I've heard the gossip, too, you know? I've lived it. But no, Ray Sweeney is Gaylen's father." Her mouth twists, regretting. "More's the pity."

"Did CC know Gaylen was born? Did he ever come back to town? Could he have seen her when he did?" A thought skitters through my brain. "Did he ever meet Ray? He had to know him, right? CC spray painted the sidewalk with your names."

"Never came back that I knew of," Dorinda says. "His family's long gone. No reason to."

"Except to see you," I say.

"But he didn't," Dorinda replies. "And then he was killed." She looks past me, and I turn to see what she's watching. A blue-uniformed guard points meaningfully to the clock on the wall beside her, then gives me the wrap-up signal.

Dorinda taps on the Plexiglas to retrieve my attention. "I'm sure your heart's in the right place. I know you're a good person. That's why I told Will I'd talk with you. But stop wasting your time with me, all right? You should try to help someone who needs you."

And then she hangs up the phone.

What have I learned? I interview myself as the guard leads me through the long dingy hallway back to the outside. Do I think Dorinda is guilty? Yes. Maybe. No. But if she faked the time sheets and the video, after killing her husband, that means it wasn't even an accident. She planned it. No wonder she confessed. First-degree murder is life without parole. With her plea deal, at least she has a chance to get out in fifteen years.

I turn to the guard, who's silently escorting me. She's an imposing package, broad-shouldered and stocky, with tiny graying dreadlocks tucked under her cap. Her wide black belt carries metal D rings for clanking pass cards, a tiny flashlight and a silver whistle. The embroidered name over her breast pocket says Off. Delia Woolhouse. Might as well give it a try. I hold out a hand. "Officer Woolhouse? I'm Charlie McNally, from—"

"Didn't even need to check your name on the sheet, Miz McNally. Know who you are from the tube," the guard says. Her tough exterior melts as she stops and bestows a wide smile, shaking my hand. "You tough, girl."

"Thanks," I say. "You, too. And call me Charlie. Could I ask you—"

"Walk," the guard instructs. She points the way. I walk.

"Does Dorie have any other visitors?" I say. "Have you seen anyone here?"

"Not many," the guard replies. "I'm in charge in this block, so I'd know." She pauses, thinking. "Her pastor from that Unitarian church in Swampscott, for sure. And the battered women's counselor from the place in Lawrence. 'Bout it."

I sigh. Great. A church and a woman's shelter. Two places where anyone who knows anything is sworn to secrecy. Still, it's better than nothing. "What place in Lawrence?" I ask.

Officer Woolhouse grabs a metal handle, then drags open an expanding metal grate, leaning her whole body into the motion. As the grate collapses, it reveals a massive sliding steel door behind it. The guard pushes a square aluminum plate on the wall and the door begins the grumbling mechanical progress that will put me again on the outside.

"Don't know," the guard says. She lifts her hand in farewell, then points the way back into the sunshine. "Shouldn't have told you what I did." She grins again. "It's off the record, Miz—Charlie. Just like they say on *Law and Order*."

Chapter Nineteen

"Not only does she insist she's guilty, but it seems like she planned it. And then she tried to cover it up." I try to prevent my voice from rising as I replay my infuriatingly unrewarding prison interview to Franklin, Oliver Rankin and Will Easterly. The CJP conference room, headquarters for what Rankin annoyingly keeps calling Team Dorinda, is beginning to feel more like the loser's locker room.

"I'm thinking our story is just about down the tubes," I say. I can't even begin to imagine the meeting where I'll have to explain this to Kevin and Susannah. I tilt back in my upholstered chair, clamping both hands to my head in defeat. "It's a house of cards. Collapsing on all of us."

I point to Rankin. "You, Oliver—if Dorinda is guilty, the CJP is going to take a real hit if Oz decides to nail you over taking her case. Will, it'll look like you're frantically trying to regain your reputation, but it may just highlight your embarrassing past." I shrug and snap my chair back to the table, propping my chin in my hands. "As for me and Franklin, we're just—ah. I don't even have words for this disaster."

"Did she tell you how she killed him? How she managed it all? You saw how delicate she is." Will's pacing, staring at the floor, not waiting for any of us to answer. He yanks open his tie with a frustrated intensity and wheels to face us. "You know she's innocent. This whole thing stinks. Something, or someone, is driving her to this. To have confessed."

"Gaylen, you mean," Franklin says. "I agree. I think our next step is to find her. I'm still not convinced Ray was her father, by the way. Remember, that guard told Charlotte about the church and the women's center, and I'm wondering if they might know where she is."

Something stirs in my brain as Franklin explains our ideas for locating Gaylen, but it skitters away before I can retrieve it.

Oliver Rankin's confident voice interrupts my thoughts. "Fruit of the poisonous tree," he says. "We don't have to prove who actually killed Ray Sweeney. We just have to show the investigation was botched. Or that Dorinda was coerced into a confession. By the police, or person or persons unknown. This is about getting her a new trial, folks."

"Fruit?" Franklin says.

"Of the poisonous tree," Will answers. "Oliver is theorizing if we can prove her confession was a consequence of some improper act, something illegal, a judge might—"

"Give Will another chance to prove what he thinks is the truth," Rankin finishes the sentence. He focuses on me. "Give you a chance to show the public some good old-fashioned journalism. Justice for Dorinda. And it'll be back to the political drawing board for Oscar Ortega."

It's not what I was trying to remember a minute ago, but Ortega reminds me of Tek. And the photos. Which I have in my bag. They're one of the reasons we're here.

"But here's the problem," I begin. "Dorinda's got an explanation for everything we think might exonerate her.

And the eyewitnesses—the bartender and those custom-ers—all picked out her picture in the Swampscott police lineup." I try to dig out the photo file as I'm talking, which causes my voice to be directed under the table. I curve myself back upright, still mid-explanation. "Tek's supposed to be e-mailing me all their names, but I haven't heard from him yet."

I place the manila folder on the table and deal out the photographs, one at a time. Six faces. Five strangers, and one familiar.

Rankin and Will come around behind me, looking over my shoulder at the photo spread that three years ago convinced police and prosecutors Dorinda was a killer.

Six middle-aged brunettes, no scars, no moles, no unusual characteristics. All could be somebody's suburban mom. All dressed like they're ready to pick up the kids at soccer or head to the Stop & Shop. One in Red Sox T-shirt, one in a turtleneck with the Ralph Lauren polo pony, one in a designer sweatshirt. And of course, Dorinda.

"Who are the other people?" Franklin asks. "Where do they get those photos?"

"They must have gotten Dorinda's from her home, an album, something. The others? Sometimes they're cops wives. Or even cops," Rankin replies. "They find people who match the description of a suspect in some way. That's supposed to keep it fair, so the suspect isn't the only one wearing glasses, for instance. They don't want someone to say 'she kind of looked like that.' They only want positive IDs."

"But, damn it. In the best of circumstances, remem-bering what someone looked like is not easy," Will says. He leans across the table and picks up the photo of Dorinda. I twist around to watch him. He's staring at the photo as he continues. "Especially if it's in a dark place. And the suspect is a stranger."

"I mean, this was a bar, near closing time, people had been drinking," Franklin says. "It just all seems so—"

I look back at the photos, trying to imagine whether I could pick out Dorinda after seeing her once, as a random stranger. The Ralph Lauren preppie, bobbed hair and bangs, doesn't look like her at all. The Red Sox woman has freckles. The one in the sweatshirt—I pull my reading glasses from their perch on top of my head and look closer.

"Hang on a second," I say. It's still too dark in here to see close-up details. Frowning, I search for better light. Finally I take the photo to the coffee station at the end of the room. I flip on the light over the sink, and hold the photo underneath.

I must have made some sort of sound, because Franklin comes to stand beside me, pulling the photo closer to him. "What do you see? There's nothing but a woman who's not Dorinda wearing a black sweatshirt."

I'm trying to contain my excitement. I'm almost afraid to say anything. I could be wrong, of course. But with growing certainty, I know I'm not. A breath of life creeps back into our story. It may not be the story we started with, but if I'm right…

I ease the photo out of Franklin's hand and carry it back to the conference table. I offer the picture to Rankin and Will. Will takes it first.

"The logo on her sweatshirt," I say, pointing. "How would you describe it?"

Will looks at me, then Rankin, baffled. "Uh, okay…" He brings the picture closer to his face, then away again. "It's a shield," he begins. "Some kind of a crest? It has letters—*S* then *J*. Then it says 1969." He shrugs and hands the photo to Rankin. "Some clothing company founded in 1969. Right?"

"Wrong," I say. I take the photo back, and this time, give it to Franklin.

"Puff Daddy," I say. "I mean, P. Diddy."

Franklin grins and starts to nod. "You rock, Charlotte," he says. "You're right. It's the logo of Sean John, Diddy's clothing line. You know, the music mogul. The rapper."

Rankin and Will exchange a bewildered glance. Will gestures the floor to Rankin. "So?" the attorney says.

"Well," Franklin says, his smile beginning to match my own, "Charlotte and I are researching counterfeit clothing. It could be our next story. Anyway, as a result, we're familiar with all the logos. All the designer logos, the ones that get copied and resold.

"So?" Rankin repeats. "You two have lost me here."

"So," I reply, "We know the 'founded in 1969' thing is a gimmick. A marketing ploy to make the company seem more established, I guess. But Sean John's clothing company—the women's part—was founded in 2005. Nobody was wearing a sweatshirt like this in 2004. They didn't exist." I know I'm talking too fast, but this is what we'd been hoping for. Some glitch in the police procedure. Some flaw in the technique they used to put Dorinda away.

I take the picture back, then point to the logo. "You see? This had to be taken after 2005. At least a year after the murder. No one was shown this photo in the summer of 2004. Couldn't happen. Someone who didn't know fashion fell for the 1969 date, but no question—this array is fake."

"Designed to make all of us go away, you think?" Franklin takes the photo back and looks at it again. "It's as if they're trying to…" He looks at me, searching for words.

"Change history." I finish his sentence.

"And there's no one who could have designed this cor-ruption of justice but Mr. Oscar Ortega," Rankin says. His chair creaks in protest as he swivels, back and forth. I can almost watch his mind calculating.

"Or Tek Mattheissen," I put in. "And what if it's not the only time? What if they're cleaning up a series of frau-dulent witness identifications?"

"This is a cover-up of the worst kind," Rankin contin-ues, accelerating into performance mode. "Planting false evidence." He smacks his fist on the table. "Three years after the fact." Smack. "Police and prosecutorial miscon-duct." Smack. "Obstruction. Yes." He shoots the fist in triumph. "Ortega is going down."

"And Dorinda could be freed," Will says. He's picked up her photo again, holding it with both hands, looking at it, not at us. "When a judge hears about this."

The guys' voices tumble over each other, the volume rising as they share ideas and strategies. But an unpleas-ant reality insists on ruining my discovery. I sit down at the far end of the table, by myself, trying to think.

We can prove this photo array was not the one shown to the witnesses after the murder. And that certainly proves there's some outrageous police misconduct. But as for Dorinda? That's what's annoying the hell out of me. It could be a knockout blow to Oscar Ortega and the D.A.'s office. But it doesn't for a moment prove Dorinda is innocent.

I cross my arms over my chest, bummed that my Perry Mason moment of detection triumph doesn't insure Dorinda's freedom. I calculate the impending losses. Dorinda's freedom. Rankin's reputation. Our story. My job.

But on the other hand, I realize, slowly unwinding from my defensive posture, it doesn't prove she's guilty, either. Even if Dorinda actually was in the bar, it doesn't mean she killed anyone. It doesn't.

It must all go back to my adventure in the archives. That must have been Tek, trying to scare me off the trail. And when he couldn't, I'm guessing his slimeball Plan B was to bring out the phony photos. But I'm not going to let some half-assed attempt to frighten me send me cowering back to covering cat shows, no offense to Botox. There are people who know the real story. What really happened that night. We just have to find them.

"Tommy who? Bennigan? " I keep my eyes on the road and one hand on the wheel while I scrabble in my purse for a pencil. "Hang on, Franko. Got to get a…" I find a pencil, but of course it's broken, so I toss it into my Jeep's backseat and scrounge for another. "I'm amazed you got the police report this fast. Imagine, they're actually following the public disclosure law. Probably a first in the annals of the Swampscott PD. Okay, got the pencil."

"It's Bresnahan," Franklin says, then spells it.

I write the name on the little notebook I keep clipped to the sun visor.

"Tommy Bresnahan, according to this police report, was the bartender the night of the murder," Franklin continues. "Latest whereabouts, according to the report, U-N-K. Apparently he was the fourth bartender in four months. Easy come, easy go. Cops told me the bar owner's apparently working the place himself now. DeCenzo, remember? He's given up on hiring outsiders."

"Well, you can find this Bresnahan if anyone can," I say. "Do bartenders need licenses or anything? Moron!"

"What?" Franklin responds. "Moron? How should I

know if they need licenses? I can find out, though, but gee…"

"Not you," I reassure him. "Some idiot's decided up here in the city of Lawrence, a red light means go. Which makes my green light mean stop. Anyway, how about this for our afternoon plan. You want to try to track down this Bresnahan? And what about Tek's partner on the case? The guy in Detroit."

I steer around a corner, trying to read the street signs, but of course this is Massachusetts, so there aren't any. "You get them, and after I find Gaylen—cross fingers— I'll head to Swampscott and see if I can sweet-talk the bar owner into giving me more info on this Bresnahan. I bet DeCenzo has job applications, paperwork, something. But it'll have to be later when his place opens."

The house numbers on what I think I remember is Eckman Street are getting higher, so I'm pretty sure I'm headed in the right direction. And then I see the house.

"Listen," I say. "I'm just pulling up in front of the Lawrence Collective. If we're lucky, and we often are, that little ingrate is going to be in my clutches any moment now. And Dorinda is one step closer to getting her life back."

As Franklin clicks off, I realize Dorinda's life may not be the most rewarding to "get back," if her daughter is guilty of killing the hardly lamented but nevertheless dead Ray Sweeney. Her own father, if Dorinda is to be believed. I know Franklin still thinks CC Hardesty is the father. If CC knew about Gaylen's birth, maybe he thought so, too. And I wonder what Gaylen believes.

Before I can give myself a good answer, I realize I'm at the inconspicuously ordinary front door of the Lawrence Collective, a dingy clapboard three-decker. I know from a story we did a few years ago on battered women that it's a front for a hideaway. A shelter for women who don't want to be found. It offers a roof, good food, anonymity— and counseling. The guard said Dorinda's counselor was based in Lawrence. Only two places here do prison counseling. One told me they didn't go to Framingham, so this is the only place left she could be. And if she's here, maybe she'll know what really happened.

I push a small square button on a dingy intercom screen. There's a blast of static, then a wary voice buzzes back. "Yes?"

I look up, remembering they'd rigged the tiny lens of a surveillance camera above the door. I smile into it and wave, then answer. "It's Charlie McNally, Channel 3." The directors here turned out to be good sources for the shelter story. If I'm lucky, they'll still be around.

A grating metallic click snaps the lock open. Crossing my fingers, I go inside. When I locate the director, Rosemary Pannatieri, and tell her waht I'm after, she looks at me as if I've lost my mind. She throws a plaid-shirted arm across my shoulder as we walk through the empty living room toward her nook of an office. I remember it's basically a closet. An actual closet with the clothes bar still in place above her desk. There's room for her chair and a visitor's. And that's all.

"If I didn't love you so much, I'd throw you right out of here," the shelter director says, pointing me to the needlepoint cushion padding the visitor's seat. "You're asking me for information about a client? Mind you, I'm not confirming anyone is a client. But you know the rules, Charlie. Confidentiality is our middle name—no, it's our first name."

She takes a covered rubber band from her top drawer

and tames her tangle of curly salt-and-pepper hair into an unruly twist. There's a smile in her dark eyes as she looks at me again. "You never give up, I know. And that's why we love you. But you ain't getting one word from me."

"Can I just ask," I begin, "if you've ever—"

Ro holds up a weary hand. "Nope," she says. She points to one ear. "I can't hear you. In fact, I can't hear questions at all."

"But I—"

"I seem to remember you're a coffee girl," she says. "Don't want you to drive all the way back to Boston caffeine-free. Come grab a cup in the kitchen and we'll talk about old times. But that's all. Your stories made a lot of difference to the women here, and I'm grateful."

I follow Ro back down the hall, past closed doors and an array of children's drawings and finger paintings on sheets of newsprint tacked to the walls. Multicolored rainbows. Big yellow suns. Crayon green trees with circles for leaves. Stick-figure children with outsize feet. No houses. No faces. I count my blessings for a moment, marveling at the cosmic roll of the dice that landed me and my mom in safety and security.

A slender figure, back to us, is chopping carrots on a wooden cutting board. She turns, skittish, as we step through the doorway. Knife in hand, her face flares into fear. "It's okay," Ro reassures her. We're not introduced and she turns back to her chores.

Ro pours coffee into two mismatched mugs, hands me one and points me back out the door with hers. "Dinnertime soon," she says quietly, "and I don't want to scare any of our clients, you being here." She smiles. "No offense."

As we stroll back toward the front of the house, chatting about nothing, Ro points out the new couch, chairs and throw rugs she's purchased with a state grant she managed to wrangle. A chaotically colorful room is filled with toys and easels and towers of blocks, train tracks laid out in a sprawling figure eight.

"We're getting there," Ro says. She knocks on the wooden door frame for luck. "And no trouble to speak of."

We arrive at the triple-locked front entrance, and both deposit our empty mugs on a doily-covered side table. She clicks open one dead bolt with a snap, then another. Then turns back to me.

"Look, Charlie," Ro says, "you know I can't tell you about any clients. But it's not a breach to tell you we do have a volunteer counselor at Framingham. Getting her degree in psychology, focusing on domestic violence. Her name is Laura Maldonado."

"Is she—" I begin. Maybe she's Dorinda's counselor.

"Who she talks to, what they talk about? That's one hundred percent off-limits," Ro answers. She pats me on the shoulder, opens the door and waves me out. "Dinner-time soon. Our staff and clients need privacy. But as always, it's nice to see you."

"So much for that brilliant idea," I mutter out loud as I head down the flagstone path. "Good coffee, zero information." It's still early evening, the sun's still up, neighborhood kids flash by on bikes, a menagerie of dogs happily chasing after them. I dig for my keys as a navy-blue car with an unfortunate dent in its passenger-side door attempts to parallel park in front of my Jeep.

She's never going to make it. I trot around behind my car, afraid to get in her way, and wait while she makes another attempt. I hear the grind of her gearshift as she backs into place, see her rear tire bounce against the curb. No wonder there's a dent in her door. Girl cannot drive.

Smiling, I position my key to open the Jeep's door and glance up as the driver climbs out into the street. My key never makes it into the lock.

I can't be sure, but the journalism gods may have answered my prayers. I just wish they would have told me what to say.

"Excuse me?" I figure that's as good an opener as any.

The girl turns toward me with a polite smile, questioning. She's twenty-something. Wearing a plain white shirt and a dark cotton skirt tied with a colorful scarf. Bare legs, little navy flats. A bulky brown leather bag, almost bigger than she is, hangs over one shoulder, with a rolled-up newspaper sticking out its unzipped top. Could be a college student? Coming home from her summer job as a salesclerk? I don't know. But I do know her brown eyes. I know her cheekbones. I recognize the oval shape of her face and the wave of her almost-russet hair. I have her picture in my cell phone.

"Yes?" she replies. Then she frowns. "Oh, I didn't hit your car, did I?" She walks closer, eyes fixed on my front bumper.

This is Gaylen. My mind is racing. Of course. This is where she lives. The shelter. This is where she's hiding. The possibilities in my brain shift, rearrange, and then click nicely into reality. This is how Gaylen gets to see her mother but disappear from the rest of the world.

"Laura?" I ask. I'm low-key. Casual. Unthreatening. She'd never know my heart is beating so fast I can barely breathe. If she bolts, I'm screwed. "Laura Maldonado?"

She stops short, her face registering confusion, then suspicion, as she takes a cautious step backward. Her car keys are still in one hand, a tube of pepper spray and a silver whistle dangling from a metal key ring. I see her glance at them, shift them, as if she's worried she'll have to physically defend herself or call for help.

"Do I know you from somewhere?" she asks, her forehead furrowing. She's still taking tiny steps backward, away from me and toward her car.

I'm taking tiny steps forward. Toward her. And toward some answers. "You're Laura, right?" I confirm. She nods, only just, but says nothing. "I'm Charlie McNally, Channel 3 News." I'm almost close enough to reach out and touch her. "And this morning I had a long talk with your mother."

Laura—Gaylen—whirls around, scrambling for the proper key, one hand reaching for the car door handle. With a step, I plant myself between her and the car, leaning against the still-warm metal, preventing her from opening the door. I'm the tiniest bit anxious about the pepper spray thing, but I'm betting she won't use it.

I smile at her, attempting to telegraph how much a threat I'm not. "I know who you are," I say softly. "And I'm so sorry."

Laura/Gaylen is breathing in little puffs, her chest rising and falling, her eyes darting. She looks like a frightened child—she *is* a child—caught in a lie, trying to calculate if she can get away with it. Then with one quick motion, leading with a thin shoulder, she darts for the car door. But I'm taller and stronger. And I'm not going to budge.

"Gaylen?" I continue, keeping my voice low and steady, "I understand you don't want people to know who you are. I respect that. And I can keep a secret." I pause. "If I need to."

I scout up and down the quiet street, cars in driveways,

the last of the kids inside. The dinnertime lull in a summer night. "Look," I say. "Walk with me. Once around the block. Just hear me out."

"You can't—" she begins. Her eyes narrow warily and suddenly she looks much older. Sadder. Suspicious as a mistreated animal. Then her nose goes in the air, and she looks at me from under her lashes. "I don't know what you're talking about," she says. "And if you don't leave me alone, I'll call the cops."

"Want to use my phone?" I ask pleasantly. "I'll wait with you while they come." I elaborately adjust the sleeves of the thin sweater tied over my shoulders and tuck a strand of hair behind one ear. I call her bluff. "But of course, when the officers ask your name, if you don't tell them the truth I will."

Her shoulders sag. The sneer disappears from her face.

"Once around the block," I coax, taking advantage of the chink in her armor. I take her elbow gently, and guide her away from the car. "I think your mother may be innocent, Gaylen. Do you?" I feel her stumble and take her arm more protectively as we walk.

"I don't know," she whispers. She looks at me with a flash of dread. "If she didn't kill Ray…"

Ray. Not Dad.

"…who did?" Her head goes down, eyes on her feet, as we continue along the cracking sidewalk, patches of random grass and yellow-headed dandelions poking their way into existence. "And why did she confess?"

"Well, that's what I'm wondering, too," I say. "Wondering if you had any ideas about that."

We walk in silence for a moment, a cawing flock of starlings settling into the scrawny municipal trees lining the sidewalk. I can't figure this girl out. If she's guilty, she would be defensive, somehow. And she's not. It's as if she's really asking me, *why?* What's more, this is not the self-centered kill-your-father-and-leave-your-mother-to-rot-in-prison psycho brat I'd imagined. There's something about her expression, her weary demeanor, the way she stretches her tension-strained neck. She looks so much like her mother that—

"Gaylen," I say. "It was you in the bar that night. Wasn't it?"

Chapter Twenty

The story of the whole night spills out. Gaylen describes it almost faster than I can even envision it happening. Yes, she admitted, *she* had been in the bar, not her mother. Arguing with her bully of a father, bitterly, loudly, because she wanted to move out, into an apartment of her own. And as always, he'd refused, laughing, and told her he'd never allow her to leave. Her father pounded down tequila. She'd had two margaritas. She'd been dizzy, they'd hit her hard. They'd walked home, still arguing. He was aggressively, intimidatingly drunk. She'd stalked off to her bedroom and collapsed, still dressed, on top of her bed.

The next morning, her mother shook her awake and told her Ray was dead.

It had taken her more than once around the block to tell her story, as the evening waned into the breezes of a New England summer night.

Now curled against the back of the worn and anemically once-red booth in the Bizzy Bee coffee shop, Gaylen has her head down, her eyes covered with sunglasses. I've yanked my hair back with a clip and put on my reading glasses, hoping my do-it-yourself disguise will fool any Channel 3 viewers. It doesn't matter. Weary-looking customers in work shirts, nurses' uniforms, oil-stained jeans silently stir coffee and pick at tired sandwiches, stolidly ignoring the intense conversation of the two unfamiliar women in the corner booth. So far, actually, I'm mostly listening. Bursting with questions and dying to take out a notebook, but I know it's better to wait. She seems ready to talk. Let her give me all she wants. And then, maybe, I can even get more. Could I be sitting with a murderer?

We both have iced teas, our second refills. The condensation drips down the nubby sides of the tall plastic glasses. Gaylen jabs at a wedge of lemon with her straw.

"Gaylen? Should we talk about what happened that morning?" I put my chin in my hands, leaning toward her, trying to convey my willingness to listen. "You've been hiding for a long time now. You've given up your life. And your mother—if she's innocent—has had her life unfairly taken away. I can't believe that's how you'd want to spend your life. Or your mother to spend hers. Is it?"

Gaylen's still staring at her tea. Now, with one hand she twists the glass, around and around, smearing a puddle of water on the speckle-topped plastic table. All I hear is the buzz of background café conversation and the slosh of the ice in her glass. Finally, she looks up from under her lashes.

"What do they say in TV?" she says. "Off the record?"

I'm definitely not having that conversation. "Listen, Gaylen, like I told you," I say, ignoring her question. "The Constitutional Justice Project, Will Easterly, Oliver Rankin—they think your mother is innocent. My producer and I are researching the story. This train has left the station."

No answer from Gaylen.

"So let me ask you this," I begin. "And we're on the

record. Back then, did you mother tell you she killed—
" I pause, just briefly, my mind registering my uncertainty
that Ray Sweeney was actually Gaylen's father, another
complicated subject "—she killed your father?"

"She confessed," Gaylen says. She takes a deep
breath, a gesture so consuming I see her shoulders rise,
then fall, then sag. She looks me in the eye, challenging.
And says no more.

"Gaylen? That's not what I asked you." I meet her
eyes. "Listen. I'm going to lay this out for you. I don't
think your mother is guilty of murder. I think she's protecting someone. And I think it might be you."

This is a risky tactic. She might leap out of this booth
and try to head for the hills. I reach across the table and
put one hand, gently, on her arm. "If your mother is protecting you—it means she loves you very much. But it
means she's going to spend most of her life locked away.
Behind bars. Because of you. Is that what you want?"

Gaylen leans against the back of the booth, her eyes
assessing, her expression uncertain.

My hand is still on her arm, but I slowly take it away.
"You want to visit your mother in prison, just see her once
a week, not even be able to touch her? Or hug her?"

Gaylen's face begins to crumble. I can almost see her
will disintegrating. She's what—twenty-four years old?
Twenty-five? She's gone through hell. And she's probably
still there.

"Have you ever talked to anyone about this?" I persist.
"I bet you haven't. You could have just run away. But you
didn't. I know it's because you don't want to lose your
mother, Gaylen. That means you truly love her. Do you
think this is the best way to show it?"

"I…I…I don't know," Gaylen says. "Mother…I…

she—confessed." The word *confessed* comes out twisted, as if she doesn't like the taste or sound of it. "She says she remembers what happened that night. I *don't*. And she refuses to discuss it. She told me to disappear, Charlie, but I couldn't do that." She sighs, a bone-rattling full-body sigh, and briefly puts her face in her hands. "I changed my name and I left Swampscott. But I couldn't leave her. And if she didn't kill my father, why would she say she did?"

"Well," I begin, taking a tentative step onto shaky ground, "because—"

"I know why she would," Gaylen interrupts. "Because she thinks I killed him."

And there we have it. I'm still, silent, waiting.

"And what if I did? And I don't remember? Am I supposed to go to the police and say, 'Excuse me, Officer, I might be guilty of murder but I don't know'?" She puts her hands back to her cheeks and speaks through her fingers. "You're right. I've lost my mother. And I've lost myself. And I want us back."

The streetlights click on, illuminating the storefronts of the quiet street outside our window as the two of us sit across from each other, measuring our options, Gaylen's looking more and more fragile. And I don't blame her. I push forward another step. "You're studying domestic violence, right? If Ray Sweeney hurt you, even threatened you, and it was all an accident, you know that—"

The whir of my cell phone, set on vibrate, buzzes insistently and audibly inside the purse tucked beside me. Damn. Who could be—? *Mother.* What if something's wrong? I hold up a finger, shake my head in frustration. "I'm so sorry, Gaylen. It might be my…" I pause. "I need to take this."

I flip open my phone. Franklin's voice crackles through the receiver. "I'm at Swampscott PD," he says. "Chief's office." His voice is terse, and I can feel the tension even through the annoying hiss of our static-filled connection. "Found Clay Gettings." Something something. "Detroit." Something something. "You at the bar?"

I can barely make out his words as the connection weakens. He's still talking, but it's becoming more impossible to comprehend. At least this is good news. We knew Claiborne Gettings, the other cop who investigated the Ray Sweeney murder, had moved to Detroit. If Franklin's found him, he could confirm the lineup photos we saw were not what cops showed the witnesses back then. At least, he could if he's not in on the cover-up.

I see Gaylen shift in her seat. She's eyeing the back of the restaurant. If she's looking for the bathroom, I guess that's fine. If she's looking for a back door, that could be disaster. I hold up a hand, stopping her, as I try to get a word through the buzz.

"Franklin?" I say. "Can't really hear you. You found Claiborne Gettings? That's great." I glance at Gaylen, who seems to have settled back into the booth and is digging for something in her tote bag. "Where? Will he talk to us?"

"Dead." That, I can hear. "Drowned. Behind the Lynn docks."

A flare of static is not all that makes me wince. This is no coincidence.

"Apparently he came to town last week for some family thing," Franklin continues. "They found him this morning."

"An accident?" I ask, although I fear I know the answer.

"No," Franklin says. "Signs of a struggle, police say. Seems like someone wanted him out of the picture."

I hear a voice in the background, apparently talking to Franklin. Finally Franklin comes back to the phone. "Gotta go," he says. "Seems like they might have a suspect. Later." And he's gone.

I stare at the dead phone in my hand, trying to process Franklin's news. Then Gaylen passes a business card across the table. Its edges are splitting and frayed. It's creased and worn. I can see it once was white. And I see whose name is on it.

"Did you say Clay Gettings? The cop who investigated the murder?" she asks. "I've been carrying around his card, all these years. He said if I ever remembered anything, to call him. I just couldn't let go of it, somehow." She tucks it back into her wallet, a physical reminder of another time. "Did you say *accident?*"

"Ah, Gaylen, I don't know, really. That was my producer, Franklin Parrish, who's at the Swampscott Police Department. Apparently there's been an incident." Things are moving too fast, and I feel as if the china plates on sticks I'm attempting to juggle are about to come crashing down. I was just connecting with her, I could sense her opening up and I don't want to lose her. "Go back, Gaylen, to what we were talking about. That's the most important thing. Are you willing to face your past? And your future? Can you help us find out what really happened?"

Gaylen bites her lower lip. I can see tears welling in her frightened eyes. She's forlorn and forgotten, a non-person trying to carry an impossible secret. Trying to make an impossible decision.

"Do you think I killed my father?" she asks. "Or do you think my mother did?"

And now she's asked an impossible question.

"Do you?" I reply. I do know the answers, I decide. But I want to hear what she says.

"It's the reason I didn't leave," she says. "I've been hoping, praying, that by staying near Mom, seeing her, being with her, I could convince her to tell me what happened to our family. And I try to help other women in trouble—it's the only way I can keep myself from feeling horribly guilty. I know she never loved my father, and he did have his problems. They barely spoke. And we…we fought, you know? But like any father and daughter. I think he loved me. I do."

Gaylen's petite face turns wistful, and the furrows in her forehead soften. "Mom and I had a secret symbol, when I was growing up." She holds up two fingers in a V.

I think back to the photo of her I still have stored in my phone. I thought she was giving the peace sign. But apparently it was more than that.

"It meant 'to us'—the two of us, you know?" she continues. "In it together? Now we're still that way. In it together. But our lives didn't turn out the way we'd planned."

Lights in the restaurant snap off, the farthest in the back, then another, then another. I squint through the approaching darkness. One white-aproned waitress, leaning wearily against the counter, points meaningfully to her watch. I smile when she holds up two fingers, but of course she means they close in two minutes. When I turn back to Gaylen, she's touching her eyes with a blue-flowered paper napkin.

"Maybe you can help us." Her voice has dropped to a whisper. "You're right. And I know it. She's sacrificing her life for me. I can't let that happen. I'd rather know the truth than let her suffer one more day."

* * *

"Absolutely and completely not guilty," I say to Franklin. The phone is tucked between my shoulder and my cheek as I attempt to sweep up the pellets of cat food Botox has scattered across the kitchen floor. She's figured out how to shred open the pre-packaged pouches of Tender Vittles, so if I dare to arrive home too late for her tastes, she simply serves herself. She has to maintain her "if you don't come home I could die" act, so after she opens the pouch, she only eats one or two of the puffy brown morsels and disdains the rest. I'm ravenous, too, having survived today on about six cups of coffee and a gallon of iced tea. Happily, the digital timer on the nuke is ticking down toward "reheated" for my usual low-fat soon-to-be-unfrozen lasagna.

"Gaylen could have taken off, you know? Disappeared?" I continue. "Instead she hides out in a shelter and sneaks in to see her mother. And now she says she wants to find the truth, too."

I nudge Botox out of my path with the edge of my flip-flop and adjust the phone. I'm still in my work uniform of pearls, slacks and sweater set, but I'm finally out of my heels. And the tick of the microwave is making me feel as if I'm right out of Pavlov's lab.

"I told her we'd protect her identity, as long as we can at least, so she won't run. I think she won't. She's clearly devoted to her mother. You'll be shocked, how much they look alike, so no surprise the witnesses got it wrong. Especially if they were only shown one photo. But Franko, here's—"

"Charlotte," Franklin interrupts. "Think about that night. The two witnesses—impossible to find. The bartender—missing. Claiborne Gettings—dead. Right now, the only person available who knows what photographs, or photograph, they used that night is Tek Mattheissen. And he's going to say they all chose Dorinda from a legal, appropriate array. And he's going to remind everyone she confessed. Gaylen could confess from now until kingdom come that she's guilty. No one is going to care. Oz and Tek Mattheissen want Dorinda Sweeney in prison. They *need* her in prison to pave their way to power."

My microwave beeps, and I almost cry with happiness. "Got to call you back," I say. "Lasagna time." My phone makes the call-waiting click. *Food,* my brain wails. *Now.* "Other line, Franko," I say, "I—"

"Charlotte," Franklin persists. "One more thing."

"Let me see who's calling. I'll be right back." Without waiting for a response, I click to the other line. "McNally, News—I mean, hello?"

"Charlie, it's me," Josh says. "We're home. I'm sorry to call you this late, but—"

"Hey, sweets, never too late for you. Hang on," I say. "Got to get rid of Franklin." Without waiting for a response, I click back. "What?" I say. "I'm so sorry, it's—"

"Charlotte, just be careful," Franklin says. "If Gaylen didn't kill her father, and Dorinda didn't kill him…"

In the midst of juggling two phone calls, imminent starvation, a beeping microwave, a delicious boyfriend and a neurotically prowling cat, I see where Franklin is going. If Dorie and Gaylen are innocent, that means someone else is guilty. It means Dorinda is sacrificing her life to protect an innocent person. And one more thing.

"It means—"

"Yeah," Franklin says. "It means there's someone else. Dorie's unwittingly protecting the actual murderer. A killer who's still out there."

We're silent for a second, then I realize…Josh. "We need to talk about this," I say. "But I have to call you back. Josh on the other line."

I'm impatient to hear Josh's voice. We've only grabbed the briefest of phone connections over the past few days and I'm having serious affection withdrawal. They're probably going to find me sprawled on the kitchen linoleum in a low-blood-sugar coma, but I can't ignore him. Passion trumps hunger. I click the button to get him back.

It's a dial tone.

A droning, taunting, unmistakable indication that Josh has hung up. Either he's annoyed with me for putting him on hold. Or something is wrong. And if something is wrong, my—boyfriend—called me for help. And I put him on hold. My stomach suddenly hurts so much that any future thought of hunger is impossible. My only concern is Josh. And why he's not still on the other end of the line.

"Damn," I mutter, as I punch in the wrong numbers. I'm calling his home, I realize. But he's in Truro. With Penny. I'm an idiot. Why didn't I hit star six-nine and just redial?

Another ring. No, wait, he said he was home. Why are they home? They're supposed to be in Truro. Another ring. No, they're back this week. Josh has some Bexter Academy faculty seminar. Of course, everything could be fine, and I'm just so tired and hungry that the most normal phone call in the world escalates to soap-opera drama.

"Hello?" It's Josh.

"It's me," I begin. "I'm sorry—"

"Charlie," he says, interrupting. "Can you…can you

come over? It's Penny, she's…" He pauses, and in the background, I hear a little girl crying.

Josh filled me in on the car phone, as I, mourning my abandoned lasagna, crunched a meal on wheels of about a million salted almonds and one protein bar. As a result, I'm no longer starving and also semi-prepared when I enter Penny's pale green-and-white-striped bedroom and see the empty fishbowl on her glossy white chest of drawers. Penny is sitting on the floor, leaning back against the side of her bed, but all I can see are her bare feet and a tiny bit of her tanned ankles. She's pulled the daisy-covered bedspread over her head.

"Pen?" I say, taking a step onto the fluffy green rug. "It's me. Um—Charlie." I sit down beside her and pull the daisies over my head, too. The two of us are in a tented world of our own. In the hazy fabric-baffled light, I can see her red nose and tear-matted eyelashes.

"Flo," she says. "And Eddy." Her wisp of a voice, morose and melancholy, pronounces their names as if from a roll call of fallen heroes. "Got white."

I tuck my arm through her elbow and stare with her at the gauzy underside of the bedspread. "Poor fish," I say. "You loved them, didn't you? They were good fish. And we will miss them."

We sit in silence for a moment. Penny makes no move to pull away. I hear a little snuffle. She uses one sleeve of her ruffly pink T-shirt to wipe her nose.

"Should we talk about them?" I ask softly. "What's your favorite story about Flo and Eddy?"

"They were cute fish," Penny replies after a moment. "They would swim after each other. And they liked when I gave them food. And they were pretty in the sun. Like gold."

"Like little treasures, right? And they loved you, too, don't you think?"

I hear Penny breathing, sniffing a few times, as if she's considering. "Yes," she says. "They did."

"Creatures like goldfish, they aren't like us humans," I say. "They live a long time for fish, you know, sweetheart? But it doesn't always seem like a long time to us." I pause. "So, we will miss them. But we were glad to know them."

Penny pulls her feet back under the spread, wraps her arms around her legs, then plunks her chin onto her knees. "I knew it would happen," she says, still staring into the flowered cotton. "Everybody I love…goes."

I don't know how to be a mother. I don't know how to deal with a little girl who feels as if the rug has been yanked out from under her still-uncertain little legs. Who thought she knew what she could rely on and how her world works until suddenly, through no fault of her own, it doesn't anymore. Penny's bereavement isn't only about fish. And this isn't the first time today I've been faced with this.

"You know, Pen," I begin. "I was talking to someone else today, who's missing someone. Someone she loves very much. And you'll never, ever guess what she does. Want to hear?"

A sniff from beside me, then the back of her hand unabashedly wipes her runny nose. "I guess," she says. "Was she missing her fish?"

"Nope," I reply. I edit the story a bit. "She was missing her best friend."

"Uh-huh."

"But they had a secret signal, you know? And she showed it to me." I look down at Penny, who's turned her face up to mine, inquiring. I nod, as if I have some profoundly valuable information. "It's very powerful. And it means—it means no matter what, you're a team. And it means no one is going to leave. Even if you're far apart, you're together."

"What is it?" Penny whispers. Her brown eyes are wide, leftover tears still clinging to her lashes, but she's turned toward me and she's put one little hand on my knee. "Can you tell me it?"

I nod, closing my eyes briefly to emphasize the gravity of the moment. "I think we should take off the quilt, okay? The secret signal is better in the light."

With a careful hand, Penny deliberately peels back the quilt. Her thin brown hair clings to the fabric as she curls out from underneath. I lift up my end, too, and turn to the little girl who's looking so expectantly at me.

I slowly hold up two fingers. "Do like this," I instruct.

Staring intently at my example, she carefully arranges her right hand in the peace sign. She holds it up and a watery smile begins to form.

"Like this?" she asks.

"Perfect," I say. "Now. Any time you give me that sign? I know you're on my team. It means the two of us. And you know what? Do you think we should go show it to your Dad? Let him in on the secret sign?"

A glimmer of anticipation begins to erase her sorrow. She carefully reties the drawstring of her baggy purple cotton pants and pushes her pearlized white plastic headband back from where it's fallen down her forehead. "Think Dad will get it?" she asks. "That it's like, the two of us? Me and Dad? And we'll only know it?"

"Just you two." I nod solemnly.

"Yay," Penny says. She practices the sign again, then scampers toward the bedroom door. As she enters the hall, she turns around, a smile—almost a smile—on her face. "And, um, you'll know it, too."

And she's gone.

The patterns on the ceiling are different in Josh's bedroom. My apartment is third floor, too high for the lights of traffic. When I snap off my night-table lamp, it's dark. Here in Josh's bed, I can watch the shadows flicker on the white walls, the headlights from passing cars rising and falling, crosshatches of shadow floating by through the window blinds, appearing then disappearing.

"You're good with Penny, " Josh murmurs. He spoons closer and nestles one arm over me. He tucks his hand around me.

"Ah, well, she's adorable," I say, snuggling in. "And, you know, it's kind of a journey for us both." I breathe in the scent of Josh's arm, wondering, as always, how he can unfailingly make me feel so female. "Life is unexplored territory, you know? For a little kid?"

I think about my mom. How she taught me about putting the peanut butter on first, how to ride on the El, how to make a new friend. She comforted me when I failed the driver's test and when I didn't get invited to the prom. Even though she keeps telling me not to come visit, maybe, now, it's my turn to comfort her. She just won't say it. I smile into my pillow. Seems like thinking about being a stepmother is forcing me to think about being a daughter. Maybe I need some exploration there, too.

"And I kind of feel, well, Penny and I are exploring together," I continue out loud. "Each other's worlds. And what we mean to each other. Must be hard for her.

"Josh?" I say softly. I can feel his breath on my skin, even the touch of his eyelashes. For a while tonight, there was no thought of anyone or anything except the two of us. No sounds that could be translated into actual words. Our private passion was all that mattered. If he's still in that world, I don't want to interrupt. I love it there, too.

But my eyes are wide open and my mind is racing ahead.

Chapter Twenty-One

Bars are creepy in the morning. At night—with the lights and the crowds, and the haze of perfume and hairspray, and the reflections of glasses and earrings and whitened teeth in the requisite room-long mirror—you don't notice that there are no windows. So as I step through the thick wooden doorway into The Reefs, the blazing July sunlight is snuffed out, and I'm dumped into dank timelessness. I know it's morning, but it could be any time. What's making The Reefs even creepier, this is the last place Ray Sweeney was seen alive by anyone except Gaylen. And maybe whoever killed him.

I plop my folder and my second latte of the morning on one of the chest-high round tables—high tops, they call them. Draping my black linen suit jacket over the back of a long-legged wooden chair, I wait for Del DeCenzo to finish his phone conversation.

Waiting seems to be the developing theme of my day. This morning I waited outside Kevin's office, drinking latte number one and watching CNN with no sound. Kevin eventually came out, and told me he'd gotten some nuclear-level threatening letter from Oscar Ortega, reiterating his continued opposition to our "political motivation" and "ratings lust." Which I thought was a bit overdramatic. Kevin then reminded me the station was counting on our story to win the July book. Which I thought was a bit over-confident.

Then I waited while the tech support guys unhooked every single wire from my computer and installed a new hard drive. Which prevented me from checking my email and printing out my story notes for an indescribably long time.

But good things did come, as they are proverbially supposed to, after I waited. There in my mail box was the long-awaited info from Tek Mattheissen listing the witnesses who identified Dorinda in the bar. I'm here trying to understand why those witnesses got it wrong.

Del's still talking. Back to me, for privacy I suppose. The bar owner is leaning one elbow against the wall, while his other arm gestures animatedly. His voice is too low for me to hear what he's saying, but his body language telegraphs a battle in progress. I open my overstuffed folder, my bible for the investigation. Might as well look at the list again.

Tommy Bresnahan. The number-one name on Tek's witness roster. Tek neglected to indicate Bresnahan was the bartender—thanks for nothing—but now I can see if DeCenzo confirms it. And then, maybe he'll help me find his former employee. I shake my head, picturing the bar on the night of the murder three years ago. If Bresnahan identified the person in the bar as Dorinda, that's just bull. It was Gaylen, I know that now. She remembers Bresnahan served her margaritas and her father tequila shots. And a twenty-one-year-old is not a forty-year-old. To the liquored-up strangers minding their own business in a dingy bar, maybe. But Bresnahan? That's hard to believe. Either he's got serious vision problems or an ulterior motive. Or the police were so convinced it was Dorinda he figured he should just agree.

And then, after all, she confessed. So it didn't matter if the cops strong-armed anyone.

I hear DeCenzo click his cordless back into the wall-mounted holder. As I look up, he's coming toward me, taking a long slug from a tall thin can of some energy drink. I'm wondering if he also owns tanning salons, since every inch of visible skin is baked an unlikely copper. He towers intimidatingly over the bar, brush-cut graying hair and military bearing, his Reefs T-shirt straining across a hypermuscled chest, a white canvas apron tied around his waist. Maybe owns a couple of gyms, too. Probably serves as his own bouncer.

"Assholes," he says. He crushes the can and tosses it into a wastebasket, then gestures to the phone. "They're raising the price of ice, now. Ice. It's just some damn cold water, for cripes' sake. How much can ice cost? This place is a frickin' Alcatraz around my neck." Del grabs a thin white towel and wipes it across the bar, back and forth, apparently contemplating the escalating price of ice. Franklin described this guy perfectly. A real poet.

"So, young lady," he says, tucking the damp towel into the waistband of his apron. He hands me an envelope. "This what you want? I thought I was done with you TV types. Talked to your—" he shrugs "—conductor?"

"Producer," I say, keeping a straight face. I shift position on my too-high chair and fight a losing battle with my suddenly too-short black skirt. "Thanks so much for digging this out. It's his job application, right? The one for the bartender who worked here the night of the murder…." I pause, hoping he'll fill in the name.

"Jerk," he says. DeCenzo leans back against the stainless steel sink, crossing his arms over his T-shirt. He's wearing more jewelry than I ever would, a couple of shiny necklaces, one dangling a massively curlicued *D*. A rock of a diamond ring flashes on one hand and a chunky gold ID bracelet glints on the other wrist.

"Jerk Bresnahan." He shakes his head. "I move to town from Detroit, what, three years ago? I must have hired, what, a million guys to tend bar? How hard can it be? But no, this guy's spooked because someone who was in the bar dies, for cripes' sake. Ray Frickin' Sweeney. Who had it coming, if you're asking me." He pauses, narrowing his eyes. "Don't mean anything by that," he says. "Don't write that down. Anyway, like I told your…"

"Producer," I say.

"…I gotta keep records," he finishes. "That's how I know this guy didn't even pick up his last paycheck."

I open the white envelope, which has a coffee stain on one end. I pull out a copy of a prefab employment application. Place of birth: Salt Lake City. And then, there's the brass ring. Tommy Bresnahan's social security number. Which someone has circled. Bingo. Now I can find him.

DeCenzo is still talking. "Came all the way from someplace like Wyoming, he's telling me. Utah. He's all about how he's born out there, skis, bartends all the resorts. I say, fine, one margarita's pretty much like another. Police arrive. He bolts."

"And you haven't heard from him since then?"

"Rains it pours," DeCenzo says. "You call, and he calls. Couple days ago. Said he might 'stop by.' Get his paycheck. You kidding me? Not in this lifetime, I told him. Nobody does that to—"

"Did he leave a number?" I interrupt. Things are looking up. "Say when he would stop by? Where he was?"

"Negatory," DeCenzo says.

Things are looking down. I open my folder on the bar and pull out the list of witness names. "How about the other witnesses that night? Do you know a—" I glance at the list. "Joe Perry?"

"The guy in Aerosmith?"

"Was the guy in Aerosmith here that night?"

"No."

"Then, no," I say, forcing a smile. "How about a George Kindell?"

"It was summer," DeCenzo says. "Tourists out the wazoo. Coulda been anyone."

"One more question, maybe two," I say. I measure his bulked-up arms and daunting chest. I remember how Ray "Frickin'" Sweeney was launched down the basement stairs. And I wonder how I can casually ask a muscle-bound monolith where he was the night of a murder without getting launched someplace unpleasant myself. Maybe I'll just find that out later.

I flip through my folder for the copies of the photo lineup pictures. "How many photographs did the cops show witnesses that morning?"

"How many?" he says. He pushes his lips to one side, then the other, his face straining with the effort to remember. Or maybe with the effort to count. "They didn't show them to me. Like I said, I wasn't here the night it happened. Anyway, what's this about? She confessed."

I select the photo of Dorinda and turn my folder around so DeCenzo can see it. "This person look familiar to you? Is this a photo they showed?"

"Like I said, I didn't—" The bar owner pauses, puts

his hands on his hips. "What are you trying to pull here?" His voice is suddenly stony, suspicious. "You trying to pull the wood over my eyes or something?"

"Pull?" I'm baffled and look down at my open folder. Paper-clipped pages of my notes are tucked into one clear plastic pocket. The other research we've collected is spread out underneath. The eight-by-ten of Dorinda is facing him, but that's not what DeCenzo is looking at. He plops one tanned finger on the prom photo, the one of Queen Dorinda and her court, the image Dr. Garth morphed into middle age. "That's who was here that night," he says.

I get it now. "Oh right, I know," I say. "But that's just a computer-altered photo of her." I tuck the computer illustration away and tap the picture from the police files. "But this is a real photo. Do you remember if this was the one they showed witnesses?"

"What I remember? Is nothing. But, hey. She confessed." He nods, as if he's making a momentous decision. "You find Jerk Bresnahan? You say I'm not giving him his paycheck, even if he does show back up. We done?"

"We done," I say. I put the photos away and close my folder, trying to keep my face pleasant and pokerfaced. It's a little tough, because a new theory is now quickly coalescing. This one features Del DeCenzo as murderer. He's a thuggish pitbull who hated Ray. He wasn't in the bar that night. That's motive and opportunity. And as a result, Del would be delighted for Dorinda to stay right where she is. I hand him my business card, standard reporter practice, and smile politely as I back out of the bar. "We done."

The view from the window in Tek Mattheissen's thirtieth-floor outer office is spectacular. A flotilla of sailboats navigates the Charles River, all sun and white sails against the redbrick facades of MIT across the water in Cambridge. I've been waiting, theme of the day, for the chief of staff about twenty minutes now, and I'll bet it's time down the drain. A fool's errand, Mom would say. And she may be right. Either Tek Mattheissen is a conniving, manipulative and violent criminal who's trying to corrupt the justice system to make his boss a big shot or he's a hapless dupe who's been tricked or convinced or bribed into doctoring evidence to make his boss a big shot. Either way, it's unlikely the attorney general's chief of staff is going to divulge the truth.

But, reporters' credo, I must attempt to get both sides of the story. Tek agreed to do the interview, thanks to Franklin's persuasive skills. As well as the fact that Tek has never met a camera he didn't like. Tek insisted he would only give a statement reaffirming the government's position on Dorinda's guilt, but that won't stop me from asking other questions. Plus, he doesn't know that I know that the photo lineup is a fake. If he figured I'd just take the evidence file and go away, that was his first mistake. His second was agreeing to the interview.

Still, I'm facing some unfortunate complications. One: Walt Petrucelli, photographer from hell, was supposed to meet me here. If his camera's not set up and ready to roll when Tek arrives, in the unwritten but nevertheless inviolable rules of the time-honored game of reporter versus interview subject, Tek gets the upper hand. Because we weren't ready, he can walk out. No interview, he wins. And I have nothing.

Two: my thin arsenal of ammunition. Tek could just deny the photos are fake. He could say the sweatshirt photo is a mistake, somehow got in there by accident. I'll know he's wrong, but I can't prove it. The only people who know what photos were actually shown are the witnesses, missing, and the bartender. Missing.

As for what I think happened in the archives, he's already taken the position that I'm a wack job. I've got no leverage—or proof—that he's wrong.

Actually, come to think of it, I've got another problem. Even if the photos are fake, it doesn't prove Dorinda's innocent. And I have no way of floating my suspicion about Del DeCenzo as murderer to Tek. He'd just repeat the two-word mantra that I'd be thrilled never to hear again: She confessed. It almost makes me wish Walt wouldn't show up.

And with that, of course, he does. I hear the clanking of Walt's goofy aluminum pushcart, a ridiculous contraption. He wheels the whole shebang across the carpet. It's teetering with battered black light kits, a tripod, and a ratty green bag of electrical cords, zipper hanging open and plugs dangling. Balanced atop the whole precarious tower, Walt's big Sony camera.

"Effing parking," Walt mutters. Some people say hello. Walt doesn't bother. He waves an orange piece of paper in the air, then stuffs it into his back pocket. "Got an effing ticket. They can pay it, they want this interview so bad." He surveys the waiting room, one arm resting on his pile of equipment, his Hawaiian shirt garishly neon against the institutionally drab walls.

"Can't do the interview in here," he says, channeling Eeyore. "Air-conditioner noise. Makes a bad hum." He scans the room, morose, as if it's been designed to make him unhappy.

"Hi, Walt," I say. "Can't help the hum, you know? But we're doing the interview in the inner—"

"Charlie, I'm so sorry." Consuela Savio strides through the door, hands fluttering to her watch, her pearls, the glasses atop her swirls of lacquered hair. She stops them on her ample hips and looks at me, shaking her head. "We'll have to reschedule. Tek—had to go. Again, I'm sorry. But things happen. Call me to resched?"

Well, there's a score for the good guys. I get to leave, regroup and come back with a few more ducks in my row. I get the upper hand. What's more, Connie's hiding something. And not doing a good job of it.

"What happened?" I ask. "Is he all right?"

Connie shakes her head again. "Police matter," she says. She pauses, seeming to choose her words. "A situation on the North Shore."

Walt's already wheeling his cart toward the door, at his happiest now that he's been granted a reprieve from actually having to do his job. But my reporter alarms are pinging into alert.

"North shore? Situation?" I persist. She owes me one for the canceled interview. "Anything our assignment desk needs to know?"

The PR flack sighs, her cleavage deepening to risky levels. She's apparently balancing the pros and cons of letting me in on the scoop. She looks at me sideways, calculating. "I suppose it's a story," she says. "And you'll find out eventually. A bar owner? In Swampscott. Found dead. About an hour ago. I don't have the name. Local police say, all preliminary, signs of foul play, assault." She smiles, weary with her knowledge and cynicism, adjusting a heavy silver earring that's fighting a losing battle with gravity.

"I was supposed to wait for Swampscott PD to put out the release. But since you're here…" She shrugs, then gestures to Walt as she walks toward the door. "But that's it. And absolutely nothing on camera from this office. You know your way out?"

"Charlie?" Walt's looking longingly at the doorway. I can't decide if he's lusting for Connie or just wants to leave.

"Yeah," I say. "You can head back. I'll walk."

Alone in the waiting room, I reach a hand into my bag, feeling for the white envelope Del DeCenzo had given me just a few hours ago. I rub one finger across it, thinking about the hulk of a bar owner who had unearthed three-year-old paperwork for an inquiring reporter. It might not be him who's dead, of course. I frown. Why is Tek involved in a Swampscott murder? It's not his jurisdiction anymore.

"Miss McNally?"

It's Oscar Ortega. Himself. His elegant bulk fills the office doorway, and he stands, waiting, one hand on the door frame. His white shirt fairly glows with starch, and there's a glint of coppery thread in his tie. Even his shoes glisten.

"Ms. Savio informed me you were still here," he says, "which makes this somewhat easier." Two blue-uniformed ramrods, Kojaked heads, big guns and shoes shinier than Ortega's materialize behind him.

My brain spins through a catalogue of possibilities but finds no answers. I know he's determined to stop our Dorinda story. He thinks I'm in league with Oliver Rankin and Will Easterly, his mortal enemies, so he's threatened my job, attacked my motives and harassed my news director. But what does "makes this somewhat easier" mean?

"Hello, Mr. Ortega," I begin politely. I dig out my reporter's notebook and flip it open. "How nice to see you. You certainly know I had an interview set up with

Tek Mattheissen this afternoon? He's not here, though, so perhaps we could sit down with you instead?"

No way he's going to talk, I know, but best defense is a good offense. Unsettlingly, I'm still curious about why I need a defense.

"I don't think so, Ms. McNally," Ortega says. Oz steps out of the doorway and into the room, his lieutenants moving around from behind him. Toward me.

Or maybe they're just going into the next room.

They're not. One of them takes me by the arm, then looks inquiringly at Ortega.

These androids have got to be kidding. I yank my arm out of the cop's grasp and take a step away, glaring at him, then at Oz.

"Mr. Ortega? What's this all about?" I say. I'm sputtering in indignation. "If this has something to do with the Dorinda Sweeney story, your tactics are beyond unacceptable." I calculate the distance to the doorway, wondering what would happen if I simply bolted. But this is too ridiculous. This is the attorney general. We're in a state office building. "So beyond unacceptable that if you don't let me leave this instant…"

Oz is still smiling, an oily iceberg, as he waves his cops to back off. But he doesn't budge from the door. He runs a pudgy hand over his head, flashing a ring, just a bit too gaudy, and a pearly cuff link catches the fluorescent light. "You're wanted for questioning in the death of Delbert DeCenzo," Oz pronounces. "He was found dead in his bar in Swampscott. Your business card was in his pocket."

Janelle Antoinette DuShane barricades herself in front of me, prowling like a protective mother lion. One panicked phone call to Kevin O'Bannon resulted in my very own lawyer, name partner in the scrappy but feared DuShane, Cornell and Suisman. She appeared like a one-woman hostage-rescue team to extricate me from the absurd but nonetheless terrifying captivity in the A.G.'s office. I'm silent, on her orders, but fuming.

Cream silk shirt fairly dripping from Toni's svelte shoulders, she clicks open her pricey patent-leather briefcase, each snap of a lock resounding thorough the tension-filled office. Then my lawyer stares disdainfully at Oscar Ortega. She's elegant, Harvard-educated and adversarial. He's silent and studiedly casual, swiveling in a massive ebony leather chair behind his perfectly paperless desk. The cop goons are dismissed.

"Let me see here," Toni says, flipping through a legal pad. "We have assault and battery by a police officer, false imprisonment, and countless violations of the United States Constitution. First amendment, fourth amendment. I can't even list them all.

"So, let's examine your options." Toni tilts her head, and taps one coffee-colored finger against a flawlessly tawny cheek. "You have none. And now if you'll be so kind, Ms. McNally and I are leaving. If you have any further questions for my *client*," she says deliberately, "you'll have to call my office. And you'll be hearing from us about your clearly illegal actions. Taking Ms. McNally into custody? Preposterous."

If I'm going to have a lawyer, I figure, just as well she's six feet tall and a knockout. But I'll be much happier when I'm out of here.

"Not so fast," Ortega says. He swivels slowly, ignoring Toni's rebuke. "Your client was the last person seen with a law-abiding citizen. A person of interest in a murder case. A person who is now also deceased. Her business card was right out on the bar. What's more, she was seen entering and leaving the premises. She—" Oz pauses, then holds out his hands as if in apology "—ain't going nowhere."

"That's absurd," Toni says. "There's absolutely no way of knowing when or how Ms. McNally's card was put in Mr. DeCenzo's wallet. A jury would laugh at you. As for my client being in some bar this morning? How on earth would anyone be able to prove that?"

Oz leans back in his chair, steepling his fingers so we know he's serious and powerful. "Your client," he says, his voice tinged with sarcasm as he savors the word, "is Charlie McNally. Her face is about as familiar as…well, let's just say, it would be supremely difficult for her to remain anonymous. Charlie McNally? No doubt about who she is. She was there. Shall we start the discussion with that stipulation?"

"Mr. Ortega," I begin. I can't stand this. I've done nothing wrong, certainly not kill someone. "We don't need to be adversaries here. I—"

Toni silences me with a glare, but it's Ortega who speaks.

"You reporters," he says, as if that word is barely acceptable in polite company. "You think you can go anywhere. Ask questions. Interfere. And then just—skate? Without any repercussions? You poke a pit bull, he's going to bite you back."

Ortega stands, leaning toward us, his hands flat on his desk. "I am the attorney general of the Commonwealth of Massachusetts. Chief of the pit bulls. My job is to solve this murder. And if your client can help me do it, reporter or not, she's going to have to do it."

Two lawyers, immovable object and irresistible force. They glare over the expanse of Oz's desk, the antagonistic silence between them almost sizzling.

As much as I hate to admit it, Oz is right. Not about the reporter thing, but about solving the murder. But I'm thinking he may get more than he bargained for. I'd been dying to confront Tek about the photographs, hoping they'd be the key to exonerating Dorinda. Now, it seems, she could get her freedom another way. Because someone is trying to take out everyone who knows about the case. Me in the archives. Clay Gettings. Del DeCenzo.

Whoever killed those people is not Dorinda. I reach into my purse and pull out the white envelope.

"Toni. Mr. Ortega," I say. Toni attempts to stop me again, but I shake my head, waving her off. I open the envelope and unfold Tommy Bresnahan's job application. "This is why I was with DeCenzo."

Smoothing out the paper on Ortega's desk, I explain who Bresnahan is, how he disappeared after the murder, and how he recently called DeCenzo, alleging he wanted to pick up an uncashed paycheck. I point to his place of birth and his social security number.

"I was going to try to find him, out West or wherever. But maybe he's not that far away," I say. "Because now I'm wondering if he did show up. Today. After I left. And it wasn't some old paycheck he was after."

Toni and Ortega examine the application, then Ortega holds it up to the light. All at once, with a quick gesture, he folds it back into thirds, and tucks it into his desk drawer. "Evidence," he says, as the drawer clicks closed. "Thank you so much."

Toni gasps. "How dare you?" she says. Her voice is seething and brittle. "My client is cooperating, much against my better judgment, and you—"

I raise a hand, interrupting her. "Toni," I say. "It's fine. And Mr. Ortega? Feel free to take that copy. Happy to help. The original, of course, is elsewhere. I certainly wouldn't carry that around. And if you'd like another copy? I have several in my bag."

"So did you bring up the photo array? What'd he say?" Franklin asks, as we walk into the Channel 3 newsroom. It's almost seven-thirty, and somehow at day's end, his pale and pristine sweater is untouched by coffee, ball-point-pen ink or copier toner grunge. Both sides of the ribbed collar of his white polo shirt are still pointed up in perfect fashion symmetry. I don't know how he does it. If I wore a buttercup-yellow sweater, it would be a Jackson Pollock by midmorning.

"Do you think Oz is complicit in that?" Franklin continues. "I mean, it is plausible that the fake photo idea was concocted by Tek alone. His colleagues at the cop shop—they didn't like him much. Once he signed up with Oz, they told me, it was worse. Bought a lot of fancy clothes, had his eye on the big time. Oh, sorry."

Franklin steps back to make way as a gaggle of studio technicians, pushing a black canvas cart overflowing with poles and light stands and dragging electrical cords moves across the newsroom floor. We promised Maysie we'd be here for the first rehearsal of her show. The production, which was supposed to start at just after the six-o'clock news hour, is running late. My dinner, yet again, is in serious jeopardy. You'd think I'd be much thinner, but somehow it doesn't work that way.

Maysie's in the makeup room. That's an event I wish I could share. Miss "I'm so natural and I'm on the radio anyway" has teased me about my extensive and constantly changing collection of lipstick and eye shadow for years. Now, I think with satisfaction, she'll want to borrow it.

"Yeah, no," I reply. I puff out a breath of air and lean against someone's desk, crossing one leg over the other. "I was going to ask Oz about the photos, you know? But then there was the whole unfortunate custody situation. Frankly, as soon as it became clear he was going to let me go, I just wanted out of there."

I shrug, trying to smooth the obstinate creases in my irreparably wrinkled linen skirt. Sitting on the bar stool was not the best. I wince, remembering what happened in that bar. Just this morning. Next life, maybe I'll choose a job where I'm a little more in control. At least where people I meet don't get murdered soon afterward.

"Kevin and Susannah, though. Loved it," I say. "Susannah actually said she wished they would have kept me longer, you know? *Investigative reporter in custody. Film at eleven.*" I talk like myself again. "She said it would be a huge ratings getter."

"She's unstoppable," Franklin replies. "Why didn't you call me?"

"Well, of course, I wanted to," I say. "You should have been there, for so many reasons. But Oz 'allowed' me to call Kevin, then I had to sit in his stupid conference room until Toni showed up."

"No, before that," he says. "I asked Walt to tell you to call me."

I roll my eyes, disparaging. "You kidding me? He forgot, the moment the words came out of your mouth. The man's a living sieve. Anyway. What's up?"

Franklin unzips his leather folder, and pulls out his copy of the Bresnahan application. He points to the "most recent previous address" line, where Bresnahan had written "732 Nelson Road, Conifer, Utah." He shakes his head. "Our Mr. DeCenzo, may he rest in peace, was apparently not much of a reference checker. I didn't even have to make one phone call. Just checked this out on GeoTracker. And Tommy Bresnahan? Could not have lived there. There's no such place."

"Let's see," I say, taking the paper. I've barely had a chance to think about what was on the form. I read it again, analyzing each entry.

"It's all about the social," I say. "We need to run it, see what we come up with for a current address." I pause and unhook my reading glasses from the neckline of my camisole. Flapping them open, I look again at the application. "The social," I say again. "Is wrong."

"Wrong from what?" Franklin says.

A new Maysie, glammed and gleaming, parades across the newsroom floor, stylist Marie-Rosina pouffing her new shaggy do with a last spritz of hairspray as she walks. Rick the makeup guy trails behind. Maysie stops in front of us, then twirls, showing off the sleek cherry-red pencil-skirted suit we chose from the selection Saks sent over. I think I glimpse the beginnings of a tummy, and it's all I can do to keep from hugging her.

"Don't touch me," she warns as she comes to a stop, catching her balance as the still-slick bottoms of her new high-heeled pumps slide on the newsroom carpeting. "My face will shatter into a million tiny pieces of foundation and my hair will collapse." She smiles. "But what do you think?"

"Not bad for a sports radio chick," I say, nodding in admiration. "You clean up like a pro."

"You've got too much blush on your left cheek," Franklin assesses. "Rick?" he calls out. "Blush emergency."

Rick dashes up with a fluffy brush, then waves it at Franklin instead. "You're a funny, funny guy. Ignore him, Maysie," he says. "You're gorgeous."

A producer calls "Places!" Maysie and her entourage hurry to the anchor desk. Franklin and I wave good luck.

"Wrong from what?" Franklin repeats.

I pull out someone's newsroom chair, revealing a stash of shoes, boots and umbrellas piled chaotically under the desk. A reporter must sit here. "Wrong from the…well, look. You know they usually assign social security numbers based on where you apply for the number. And usually, people born in the U.S. get them pretty young. So, like, mine begins with the numbers three-one. So do most people's who were born in Chicago."

"Oh yeah, I guess I knew that," Franklin says.

"You did not," I say. "But, nevertheless. Bresnahan's social begins with zero one."

"Give me a break," Franklin says. "No way you know the social security, prefix, or whatever they call it, for Utah."

I nod, smiling. "And that, my dear colleague, is the point. I do not know the prefix for Utah. However, I do know the prefixes assigned to people who were born in Massachusetts." I pause, letting my meaning sink in.

"Zero one," Franklin says. "So Bresnahan's whole history is fake."

"Yup," I reply. "Sure does sound like it. Wonder where poor Del DeCenzo would be today if he had just bothered to check some references. Looks like we've got a Massachusetts boy on our hands."

A barrage of lights flash on overhead. A blast of techno-theme music surges through the newsroom, cuts into silence, then starts up again. A blaring loudspeaker blasts the director's voice from the control room. "Mic check, please, Maysie?" he bellows. "And can we please get a move on with this?"

I turn to Franklin, torn between wanting to see

Maysie's rehearsal and needing to find Tommy Bresnahan. "You know," I whisper, not wanting to disrupt the taping, "I saw DeCenzo put my card in his wallet as I walked out of The Reefs. But Oz said police found it on the bar. If it was Tommy who killed him, I bet he knows I was there."

"Five, four, three…" I hear the floor director start to count Maysie down, then see him point to her. *You're on*, he mouths silently.

"And you're not hard to find," Franklin whispers back.

Which means I have to find him first. I sneak a look at Maysie. She's smiling and gesturing, reading from the prompter like a pro.

"Listen, Franko," I say softly. "I'm going up to the office. It's almost seven o'clock here, but that means it's still before five in Mountain Time. Maybe we can make this time-zone thing work for us. DeCenzo didn't check all of Tommy's references. Didn't check his social. But I'm going to. I've got to see if I can dig up this Bresnahan."

Franklin nods, pushing up the sleeves of his sweater. "Maysie will understand. I'm leaving soon, too. Stephen's picking me up. Want to join us for dinner?" he asks.

I shake my head, knowing once again, dinner is just a fond memory. "See you tomorrow, say hi to your adorable Stephen." I wave and turn to head back to my desk.

"Charlotte," Franklin hisses after me.

I turn, impatient to get back to work.

"Be careful tracking Bresnahan," he says. His already solemn face is filled with concern. "We don't want him to find you first."

Chapter Twenty-Two

I'm not really thrilled with the idea of going home. I sit at my desk, flipping a pencil over and over. Stalling. It's late. It's probably dark. I don't have my car. Living alone with a coward of a cat is not terribly reassuring when, as Franklin and I both know, there's apparently a bad guy out there. Still, I know Oz and his crew are certainly looking for Bresnahan. And the A.G.'s office has access to the database resources of every law enforcement agency in the country. And I faxed the job application to Rankin at CJP. So his people have it, too. We're all on the trail.

Of course, Bresnahan may not be guilty. What's his motive? But who else could it be? I tilt back in my chair, lacing my fingers behind my head. Now I'm considering Tek. As lead cop on the investigation, he could have railroaded the witnesses to identify Dorinda. He could have manipulated the case every step of the way. But why?

But Bresnahan has been hiding, successfully, for the past three years. If he's reappearing, it seems like the only reason would be to make sure Dorinda stays guilty. And stays in prison.

But how would he know that's in question? Propping my feet up on my desk, I close my eyes and I think back, retracing our steps. Franklin went to the cop shop, the local newspaper. I went to the high school library, the state archives, the prison, the women's shelter, the nursing home. We both went to the Sweeney's house. Myra Matzenbrenner's. So fine. Bresnahan could know.

My heart rate flares and I startle to reality as my cell phone rings. "You Can't Always Get What You Want," it warbles at me. Like I don't know that. I swing my legs down and check caller ID. Private call. Not Josh. Not Franklin. Mom?

"McNally," I say.

"Oh, marvelous, you're still there," a woman's voice says. "This is Poppy Morency, Charlie. "

It only takes a second to remember the preppy and efficient real estate agent who showed us the Sweeney home.

"Hey, Ms. Morency," I reply. "What can I do for you?"

I hear the clatter of traffic, a horn honking, a siren in the background. She's calling from her car. "Well, I don't know," she says. "But you asked me to call you if anyone ever showed interest in the Sweeney home? Well, of course you know that."

"Yes?" I say. I had figured it couldn't hurt to leave her my card. I always do it, a habit, even if don't think anything will come of it. Planting the seeds. You never know.

"Anyway," she continues. "After all these years, there was a man who looked at the house last, oh, week or so ago. And he was not a real prospect, I could tell. Or I thought I could tell, but today, he came back. This morning. And asked to look at it again. So we walked through it all. Again. And then—"

"Did you get a name? A phone number?" I interrupt. This is probably nothing, I tell myself. Nothing.

"Well, no, he only said his name was Mr. Montague. And he didn't leave a number. But then I realized he'd called me on my cell. And his number would be stored there. And as I told you, I admire your work and I thought—"

"That's wonderful," I interrupt again. I'm trying to stay calm, but this might be a very nice break. And it's about time we had one. "Do you have it available? I'm ready to write it down."

As soon as she hangs up, I'm punching in the number she gave me. It's not a familiar area code. I wonder if it's a cell phone.

Time slows as the phone rings once, then again, then again. This could be Tommy Bresnahan. Or it could be some poor schmoe who's perversely interested in a murder house. Or it could be, imagine that, someone who's actually looking to buy a perfectly nice home in perfectly desirable Swampscott. I hear a sound that clicks the phone into answering mode. *Damn.* I hope there's a name in the message. But no. "The cellular customer you have reached," a synthetic voice begins, "is unavailable. Please leave a number," the voice orders. I hesitate. Then I hang up.

But as I flip my phone closed, I remember I was calling a cell phone. You don't have to leave a number on a cell. My number is already stored inside someone's phone. I just don't know whose.

I stare out of my office window, watching the narrow alleyway. Watching for my cab. Watching for whatever else, or whoever else, might be out there.

I'm somewhat embarrassed by my own fears, but, I decide, better safe than—not.

Botox will be annoyed, and there'll be Tender Vittles all over the kitchen, but she'll be fine without me. I've made my decision. I'm headed for the one place I know is safe. With Mom.

* * *

The night-duty nurse hardly raises his head as I scrawl my name in the visitor's book. I'm halfway to Mom's room when I realize I, yet again, have missed dinner. Luckily, this place has better food than many of the best-known restaurants in Boston. I turn back to the nurse's station, hoping to sign myself up for some after-hours room service.

The nurse, a new one, I guess, since I've never seen him before, greets me like I'm an old friend. "Well, Charlie McNally, I heard you visited someone here," he says. The name embroidered on his white jacket says Kurt.

"Hey, Kurt," I say. "Yes, my mother is down the hall. But I'm wondering—any chance of getting food? I know it's late."

"No problem at all," he answers. He slides open a metal file drawer and extracts a leather-like notebook, puffed up and embossed like a menu from a pretentious restaurant. "Here's the menu," he says. "Look on the last page for Late Night Fare. And then just tell me what you'd like. I'll buzz the kitch."

"Hospital food, huh?" I say, "Didn't use to be like this."

I flip to the back and scan the list. I'm famished. Everything looks like exactly what I always wanted. "Cheeseburger? Rare? And fries," I say. I wish. "Well, no, the salad with chicken, actually. Diet Coke."

"All set," Kurt says, taking the menu. "In half an hour, max, we'll deliver it to your door."

Maybe I'm just hungry, I decide as I walk down the quiet corridor toward Mom's room. Nothing like low blood sugar to raise your anxiety level. Some lettuce, some grilled protein, and I'll probably feel like myself again. And head for home.

"Mamacita." I tap lightly on the door, opening it quietly in case she's asleep. But she's aiming the remote control at the television. I hear her commenting every time the channel changes.

"Boring," she says. She clicks again. "Silly. Repeat. Saw it. Saw it. Saw—hello, dear." She notices me in the door and clicks the television off. "Thank goodness. I couldn't watch one more episode of—well, I couldn't watch one more episode of anything. I guess the meds must be wearing off, since my tolerance for television has just about vanished. No offense, dear, of course."

She points to my usual chair beside her bed. "So sit right down, Charlotte. Please tell me about something more interesting than television."

"Well, actually my life is television," I say, smiling. I close her door behind me and sit down beside her. "But tonight, yes, it is pretty interesting." That's an understatement. Should I tell her I'm somewhat nervous about going home? It seems a little paranoid, here in the safety of the hospital. I should wait.

"Let's see," I say, searching for a subject. "Maysie's new show is in rehearsal. And she finally looks pregnant. I think it just happened overnight." My brain screeches to a halt—why did I bring up a pregnant person? I cross my fingers I haven't opened the floodgates of criticism. Mom, happily, doesn't take the unintended bait.

"That's nice, dear," she says. "I do hope she and her family will come to the wedding. And your Josh, of course. And Penny." She cocks her head, considering. "Do you think it would be appropriate for Penny to be my flower girl? I don't want to push, of course…"

"Of course," I say with a skeptical smile.

"…but it would be adorable to have a little girl in the

ceremony. Now that my little girls are all grown-up. How are you two getting along, by the way?"

There's a knock at the door, a quiet tap. "I ordered food," I say, surprised. "That was fast." In a flurry of embarrassment I realize I forgot to see if Mother needed anything. *I am such a selfish…* "Want to share a chicken salad?" I ask, going to the door.

"Heavens no," I hear behind me.

But when I open the door, it's not chicken and salad, it's another nurse. I catch a glimpse of an older-leading-man kind of look, face lined and worn, but the nurse walks by me so quickly I can't even read the embroidered name on his whites.

"Ten p.m. meds, Mrs. McNally," he says.

It's only nine-thirty, I think, glancing at my watch. But of course TV's made me obsessive about time.

Mom obediently holds out her hand, same as every night. "Thank you, and just what I needed," she says. She pops down several pills with a swallow of water. "Are you new?"

"Yes, ma'am," he says. "If there's nothing else?" And he's gone.

"So Charlotte, as I was saying," Mom picks up as if we hadn't been interrupted. "The wedding. Penny. You two are getting to know each other?" Mom reaches over and takes my hand. "You know, Charlotte, I'm so glad you're here. It means a lot to me that you're…" She yawns, broadly, and uses her other hand to cover her mouth. "My goodness. Anyway. That you're taking an interest in the wedding, and that you like Ethan, and that you don't mind my getting married again. I must say, dear, I thought it would be your wedding I'd be planning, not mine. But you've made your own decisions and I—"

"Of course I'm happy for you, and Ethan is a treasure,"

I interrupt, patting her hand with mine. "And it'll be lovely. Penny, I'm sure, would be beyond thrilled to be in a wedding. She's all about frills, you should see her bedroom. She's never met a ruffle or a pink thing she doesn't love." I feel Mom's hand relax, so I lean back in my chair, musing out loud about Penny.

"You know, Mom," I say. "When I'm with Penny, I kind of understand her. She'll ask a question, seemingly very, oh, ordinary. But I'll know what she's really asking. She wants to be reassured, you know, that her world won't be upset. That she'll be safe. And somehow, it makes me feel so—it's silly, but grown-up, to be able to take care of her. I keep thinking about what you said the other day about peanut butter. And first books. Now, Penny's mother and stepfather are having problems. So I'm even more determined to be there for her."

Mom yawns again. I wonder if I'm even more boring than the television. But she smiles. "Good girl," she murmurs.

"The other night she was so upset, her two beloved goldfish died," I continue. "I wasn't sure I could connect with her, help her at all. Seemed like it was a job for a mom, I thought. But you know…"

I pour out the story of our private discussion under the bedspread and my realization that Penny was searching for security. And how my heart seemed to open to her, and then to myself.

"And remember I told you Dorinda and Gaylen?" I say. I put my bare feet on Mom's quilt, scooting down in my chair, and stare at the ceiling, immersed in memories. The room is peaceful and cozy, fragrant with flowers and scented powder, silent except for the beeping vital-signs monitor. And for some reason, maybe it's Penny, maybe the wedding, Mom really seems to be listening to me. Maybe this is the beginning of a beautiful friendship.

"Well, they have this secret sign, you know? That they devised when Gaylen was a little girl." I glance down at Mom. Her eyes are drooping a little, but she smiles and nods, *Go on.*

I explain the sign, holding up my two fingers, and describe the deeply lasting connection it symbolizes. "And when I showed it to Penny, it was such a moment. Almost like I was passing along a timeless bond between mothers and daughters." I shrug, a little embarrassed by my own sentimentality. "Okay, sappy, I know. But, Mom?"

I can't look at her, because I may lose my nerve. I keep talking, my words spilling out. "You know, what you were saying the other day. You just want me to be happy. I guess I do know that. But can't you see, I've just been trying to please you? Make you proud of me? I guess we both want the same thing. Each other to be happy. You think?" I look up, worrying there's some way she's going to be offended. Or misunderstand.

But there's no answer. I wait, but there's just silence. She's sound asleep. I guess the pills have kicked in. I sigh, feeling, for the first time in so many days, even a little relaxed. I laugh to myself. That's not a word I use too much. Except when I'm telling someone else to do it.

Another tap on the door. This time it must be my food. I swing my feet to the floor, but before I can get up, the older nurse who brought Mom's pills comes back in. He closes the door behind him. *Damn.* No food.

"Yes?" I say softly. "Mom seems to be asleep now, thanks so much. We're fine. I was hoping you were my chicken and salad."

He doesn't smile back. He steps closer, holding out a

little ruffled pill cup. He dumps a pile of yellow and white capsules into his hand. "I need you to take these," he says.

For some reason, ingrained reporter training or insistence on logic, my reaction to his incomprehensible request is to check the name embroidered on his nurse's whites. There isn't one. And why does he look familiar? Graying wavy hair, taut tanned skin over cheekbones just too sharp, his mouth just too full. Attitude verging on swagger. Not a nurse.

Before I can remember I shouldn't, I glance at the nurse call button. It's on the other side of the bed. And the "nurse"? Sees me do it.

"Yeah, that's disconnected," he says. "From the nurse's station. So don't bother." He pats the place above his breast pocket, the place where a name should be. "And I see you're wondering who I am. You know, though, correct?"

I do. "Bresnahan," I say. "Tommy Bresnahan." Hiding behind nurse's whites. And lax late night security—lulled by the diva's entourage of strangers—must have ignored yet another newcomer.

"And that's why you get the big reporter bucks," he says. "But I fear you've been sticking that reporter nose into too many places it shouldn't go. That Ray…stole my life from me. Stole my Dorie from me. Now he's dead. And that's what he deserves."

His face twists, then he looks at me. He holds out his arms, as if performing.

"'My love is deep; the more I give to thee, the more I have, for both are infinite,'" he says. "That's what she said to me. Now Dorie's behind bars. And that's where she deserves to be. If she hadn't gone down for her *husband's*—" he spits out the word "—for her husband's murder, I'd have taken her out, too. But that all worked out just as I planned."

Now I'm confused. He's quoting Juliet? From Romeo and…

And that's why I think I've seen him. I have. He's the Swampscott High School Romeo. The king of the prom. He looks exactly like the computer-aged prom court photo, where he and Dorie shared the throne. But that can't be.

"CC Hardesty?" I say. "Dorie's high school sweetheart? You're dead."

"You think?" A smile knifes across his face. "Just got a Navy buddy to make a phone call, how hard is that? Doctor a couple of veterans office records at city hall? Who's gonna know? Who's gonna care? Now take your medicine."

He grabs one of my hands, twisting my wrist to open my palm, and pours six capsules into it. "Take them. You deserve it. For screwing around in other people's business. No one can know I'm alive. And you—do. But not for long." He points at me, demanding. "Do it. And then I can wake mommy dearest here right up from her megadose of narcotics. The longer you wait, the more likely Mother here won't make it either. I'd say she's got five minutes. So, your call. It's you. Or her."

I'm watching Mom's chest rise and fall. She's oblivious. I'm fighting hysteria. What drug did he give her? How much? I look at the pills in my hand, revolting little death bombs. I've never wanted chicken and salad so much. If the food arrives, this'll be over. Saved by room service. I have to stall.

I dump the pills onto the rolling table positioned across Mom's bed, then reach out and grab her hand before Hardesty can stop me. If I stall too long, though, it won't matter. This man's obsessed. Maybe I can use that. And I bet I know his weakness.

"Gaylen," I begin, clutching Mom's hand. "Did you know…?"

"Sweeney. Dorie. They took my life from me. It was time for me to get it back." He's pacing now, muttering, covering the width of the room in four long steps, then turning back. He stops, narrows his eyes at me. I can see he's losing patience. "Pills," he says. "Right. Now."

"Gaylen," I say, ignoring his demand. "Gaylen Sweeney. I have evidence you're her real father."

I pause, gauging whether this lie sinks in. "And if that's true, what have you done? You've framed the mother of your own child, sent her to prison for life. You've sent your only daughter into hiding, misery and guilt. And you're responsible."

I fleetingly wish I'd listened more attentively in my college psych classes. I hope this isn't pushing too hard. But there's no time to ponder Maslow, or whoever it was. "Listen," I say. "You leave. I'll call the nurse, and after they wake Mother I'll tell you how to find Gaylen. You and…" I play my ace, even though it's counterfeit. "You and your daughter can be together."

He barely considers my offer. "Right," he says, sarcastic, rolling his eyes. "Then you set me right up for the cops. Not for a moment of the past twenty-five years have I forgotten. Not a moment of the past twenty-five years have I wavered. If I couldn't have her, nobody could have her. I lived for it, worked for this, planned for this. I even…died for this." He laughs, without a shred of mirth. "Dorie. She ruined my life. My only goal was to ruin hers."

I can almost see the animosity, the tension, between us. Still holding Mom's hand, I try to position myself in front of her, blocking his view. I can't let him hear the silence. All the more reason I have to keep talking.

"And now you'll never know how she really felt, will you?" I say. I'm taunting him, tormenting him, as the seconds tick away. "Do you know her mother forced her to marry Ray? Your Dorie told me that. And she was so upset when she got the word that you—died—she cried for weeks. Even little Gaylen remembers. You have it all wrong."

For the first moment, I see him falter. He blinks, take a hesitant step backward. He doesn't answer.

"I know where Gaylen is," I say. "Without me, you'll never find her. And Dorinda will never tell you. You ruined *her* life—it's not Dorie who ruined yours. You destroyed your own family with your selfishness and jealousy. Because you didn't take the time to understand the girl you said you loved."

I'm breathing hard, trying to stay in control. If I can make this deal, offer him his daughter back, maybe I'll get my mother back. It's my only play.

"Two minutes," he says, pointing to the pills. "Pick those up. And I'll find Gaylen myself, thank you very much for telling me she's around here. And as for your mother dear, I would say—" he glances dramatically at his chunky silver watch "—I would say it's possible my watch is wrong."

I whirl to look at Mother, terrifyingly peaceful, quieter than quiet. Beyond asleep.

She doesn't even blink when all hell breaks loose.

Klaxons, blaring. Alarms, screaming. A synthetic voice blasts through the room, loudspeakers repeating *"Code Blue, Code Blue, Code Blue."* CC Hardesty wheels, staggering backward, as the door flies open, and a doctor, a team of doctors and nurses, all in white, careen a heavily laden crash cart into the little room.

With a shattering of glass and instruments clattering to the floor, the cart collides, crashes, directly into CC, propelling him across the room and toward Mom's bed. I leap up, and I'm yelling, yelling, yelling as I spin the rolling bed table, hard as I can, hard as I can, hoping I smash him in the chest or neck or head or anywhere, anywhere that will bring him down.

I see him slide down the side of Mom's bed. His fingers claw down the pink quilt. The yellow and white capsules roll, spilling away, bouncing onto the floor. Hardesty's collapsed, motionless as Mom. He's a white-uniformed ghost, returned from the dead. And now—

Now, I'm explaining, fast as I can, clearly as I can, exactly what happened. I grab the nearest doctor, his stethoscope almost swinging into my face as I corral him into action. "Call security, the cops," I demand. "He's given Mom some sort of, of overdose." I know I have to be calm. I won't even calculate about how much time has gone by.

I sweep up the yellow and white capsules from the floor, scooping so hard I burn my hand on the rug, until they're once again in my palm, and display them, quivering, to the still-confused physician. "They looked like these," I say. *"Do something. Now. Please."*

Three blue-jacketed hulks of hospital security guards have joined the hubbub in the now-crowded room. They're lifting Hardesty like a rubbery rag doll, his arms and legs not responding to their commands.

"Move it," one orders. "You're done." Hardesty's dazed, still staggering. I see handcuffs click into place

Two nurses hover over Mom, taking her pulse, listening to her breathing.

"Here's the problem," one says. She's holding up the dangling wires of Mom's heart-rate monitor. "These had come off her finger somehow. No wonder we weren't getting any vitals from her. We thought she'd flatlined." The nurse puts the thick black band back into place around Mom's finger. "Wonder how that happened?"

Doctors have called in a stretcher. One, two, three, they lift Mom from her bed. The stretcher is already moving out of the room by the time she's settled. I'm stationed beside it, not leaving her side.

"Well, that was me, " I explain. We're racing down the hall, me with one hand clamped to Mom's stretcher. Her face is gray, or pale. All wrong.

"CC told me he'd disconnected the nurse call button. But I knew Mom's monitor was still hooked up. So I grabbed her hand and gradually slipped off the wires. He never noticed the beeping had stopped. And as soon as you realized there was no signal…I knew you'd come. And I hoped it would be soon enough."

We arrive at a wide silver elevator. A grim-faced doctor slams a key card though an emergency switch, and I hear the elevator on the way.

"You'll need to wait down here, Miz McNally," the doctor says.

"But—"

"Someone will be with you," she interrupts. "Just let us do our work."

I look at Mom, still, small, and deep in a drug-dazed stupor. I briefly calculate how long it actually took for them to realize there were no longer peaks and valleys in her heartbeat and respiration. Almost too long. I touch her hand. She doesn't move.

The elevator doors slide open. And she's gone.

Chapter Twenty-Three

"Got your earpiece in? Can you hear the control room? Is anything happening at the gates?" Franklin's shading his eyes with a hand as he squints across the parking lot. The imposing entrance gates of the women's prison remain closed. They're bars of wrought iron, topped with razor wire. Behind them, a concrete walkway leads to bolted wood double doors. Also closed. Two blue-uniformed guards are stationed in front of them, arms crossed over their chests, staring at the Channel 3 live shot van we've set up on a strip of grass on the public side of the gates. We've got one camera focused on the prison doors and one facing me.

"We're taking this live as soon as she walks out," Franklin says, for about the fifth time. He looks at his watch yet again. "You set? They're gonna come through that door, and head straight for Will's car."

"I'm set, Franko," I say. "And no matter how many times you look at your watch, it won't make it happen any faster. The control room's watching the front door. They'll take the shot when they see her on camera and cue me through my earpiece. I can hear them. I'm set."

I puff out a stream of air, channeling calm. Just three days ago, Mom and I were almost killed by a revenge-obsessed Romeo. Now, CC Hardesty is behind bars, no bail. Oscar Ortega himself had appeared in court, asking the judge to charge Hardesty with the murder of Ray Sweeney, vacate Dorinda's conviction, and let her go free. Gaylen had sobbed through the entire proceeding. Will Easterly, red eyed and even more gaunt than usual, had actually—one of the few times I'd ever seen him do it—smiled when Judge G. West Saltonstall made his rulings. Tek Mattheissen was nowhere to be seen.

This morning Franklin and I are running on caffeine and adrenaline. We'd stayed up almost all night writing and editing our exclusive story. Part one of "Charlie's Crusade: Justice for Dorinda" is going to hit the air tonight. Dorinda and Gaylen, who have promised to talk with us exclusively, will be in part two. But for tonight we have a touching interview with Will, admitting his alcoholism and his ineffective job as defense attorney, and dramatic "we told you so" bombast from Oliver Rankin. Thanks to Poppy Morency, we're using new video of inside the Sweeney house, including some admittedly tabloid-worthy footage of the basement stairs. We've even got a brief interview with Joe B. from the nursing home. We're showing the alibi video of Dorinda in the meds room—which turned out to be authentic, of course—and the time sheets, which were authentic, too. Plus that age-progression yearbook photo of the prom queen and her court. The simulated face that launched a real-life murder charge.

I smile to myself. Mom was right again. If she hadn't forced me to meet with Dr. Garth, the picture that allowed me to recognize CC Hardesty would never have existed. I hope she's watching this morning. And I know she wouldn't miss it. She's fine, with no ill effects from her could-have-been-lethal overdose, and apparently no memory of the pandemonium of three days ago. And that's a good thing.

Back at the station, Kevin's acting as if he's heir apparent to Edward R. Murrow. Susannah's acting as if this whole story were her idea. She blew out every other promo that was scheduled and ordered Charlie's Crusade spots to run in every available time slot. Newsroom scuttlebutt says she's been hired to handle Channel 3's promotion full-time. That, I cannot face.

Of course, the newspapers and other TV stations know Dorinda's been proved innocent. But they also know it's because of us. It's a slam dunk, out-of-the-ballpark scoop.

Now, if all goes as planned, in a few moments we'll be going live as Dorinda Keeler Sweeney becomes a free woman again. Franklin is up at the prison gate, checking with the guards. He's impatient to get the show on the road, I know. I smile to myself. Not as impatient, probably, as Dorinda. And I know Gaylen's inside with her. They're going to walk out together.

"We're ready to go." Walt, in position behind his camera, interrupts my thoughts. He twists a knob on the side of his tripod to lock the camera back into place and looks over at me. "McNally?" he says.

What now? Something else broken? It's his coffee break time? "Yeah?" I reply warily. Walt's a chronic complainer. I'm expecting the worst.

"Gotta hand it to you," he says, not looking at me, fiddling intently with something on his Sony. "You pulled this off," he says. He gestures with his head toward Franklin. "You and Parrish. The real deal."

I couldn't be more surprised. I'm sincerely touched.

"Walt," I say, nodding, "that means a lot. Coming from you."

"Yeah, right," he says. He cocks his head and puts a finger to his ear, apparently listening to instructions through his earpiece. "Control room wants to know if you see anything happening. Your earpiece in? Talk into your mike, they can hear you."

I look at the tiny microphone clipped to the jacket of my splurgy new Italian suit, purchased, with crossed fingers, hoping for such an occasion. "Nothing's happening that I can make out," I say into my lapel. "Franklin's checking." I look to see if anything's changed, but he's still up at the gate. The officers are still in their "I know nothing" postures. But Franklin is gesturing, pointing to me.

And then the door begins to open.

Franklin runs, watching to make sure he's not in the camera shot, as fast as he can back to the live truck. I've got my eye on the prison door. And it closes again.

"What?" I demand. "What did the guards say? What's the timing?"

"Stand by," Franklin orders. "Stand by," he says into my lapel, then starts waving his arms in front of Walt's camera.

"They see you in the control room," Walt says. "If I were you, I'd get out the way. You're in Charlie's shot."

Franklin leaps out of camera range. And then the prison door opens again.

Walt touches his ear again, listening. "Five seconds," he says, pointing a finger at me.

"We're live," I hear through my ear. "We've got the Dorinda cam live," the director back in the control room says. "And your mike is hot. Go!"

"This is Charlie McNally, live with breaking news

from the front gates of the Framingham women's prison,"
I begin. I've been doing live shots for more than twenty
years. I've described horrific fires, chaotic election nights,
devastating floods. I've been soaked by hurricanes and
blasted by snowstorms, harassed by drunken college kids
and confronted by enraged politicians. I handled all of it,
as it happened and mostly without a hitch, on live television. Part of the job.

But I'll admit, right now, my heart is racing. There's
no snow, no rain, no screaming crowds. One woman, ac-
companied by her daughter, is about to walk out of prison
and into the sunshine. And I've never felt more challenged
to come up with just the right words. To do them justice.

"What you're seeing now is…" I hesitate. The door
was halfway open, but now it's stopped, waiting, freeze-
framed. And then, it opens again. And there they are.

"What you're seeing now is Dorinda Keeler Sweeney,
who just yesterday was granted her freedom. As you
know, she confessed to killing her husband, North Shore
politician Ray Sweeney, three years ago. But we have
learned…" I pause, watching Dorinda, in low heels and
a sleeveless shift, shoulders back, head high, and carrying
a purse for the first time in years, walk slowly away from
the looming red brick walls. "We have learned, her confession was a complete fabrication. She sacrificed her
own freedom to protect her daughter—whom she mista-
kenly thought was guilty—from being charged with the
murder. That's who you see, holding her arm, walking out
with her. Her daughter, Gaylen Sweeney." I pause again,
deciding to allow the audience a beat to take in the
enormity of the moment without hearing my voice over
the whole thing.

"Dorinda and Gaylen Sweeney will now have to

attempt to get their lives back, to make up for three years of lost time and devastating miscommunications. A mother who thought she was protecting her daughter from a life sentence in prison. A daughter haunted by the possibility she'd killed her own father. Three years of sorrow. Three years of sacrifice. Now it all ends, here in Framingham, on a sunny July morning. A mother and a daughter, free and safe. And starting over."

A lumpy silhouette rises in the window of the news director's office. *Humpty Dumpty*, improbably, crosses my mind. But Kevin's called me in, so I'll know the reality soon enough. I can see Susannah in her usual perch on the couch talking to Mr. Dumpty. Kevin's behind his desk listening. I smile my way across the newsroom, satisfied with our live coverage, psyched with our scoop, and accepting compliments from my fellow reporters.

Tonight, part one of Charlie's Crusade hits the air. The ratings are going to be off the charts. Dorinda and Gaylen are in seclusion at some apartment Oliver Rankin's provided. According to Will, they're never more than a few feet apart.

I arrive at Kevin's door. Humpty turns around. It's Oscar Ortega.

Susannah gets to her feet and starts to say something, but Ortega takes over.

"Ms. McNally," he says. He points me to a chair, as if we're in his own office. "Thank you for coming in." As if he were the one who called me. Susannah goes to Kevin's office door, closes it and silently takes her place back on the couch. Kevin hasn't opened his mouth. And I can't read their faces.

"We have a situation," Ortega begins. "We're tracking

the actions of Tommy—strike that—CC Hardesty, over the past few weeks. Let me show you." He bends down to click open his briefcase.

A flurry of possibilities explodes in my head and I try to assess what could possibly be wrong. The judge ruled Dorinda should be released, nothing can change that. We know CC is guilty. He told the cops he'd put sleeping pills in Ray and Gaylen's drinks. He'd confessed to entering the Sweeney house and pushing Ray down the stairs while Gaylen slept. And he said it was "easy." That confession is going to stick. Not to mention his attempted murder charges for drugging Mom and threatening me. That's going to stick, too.

Ortega pulls out a thick manila file folder and spreads it open on Kevin's desk. From inside he extracts several pieces of white paper, held together with a red paper clip. "This is the police report you filed, after that day in the state archives," he says. "You said someone—" he refers the report "—followed you? Chased you? And attacked you?"

"Exactly," I say. And now he's going to tell me my assailant was Tek. I knew it. I always figured it was Tek and wondered whether he was just going to get away with it. I prepare to hear the real story of that frightening morning in the archives, wondering how Franklin and I can incorporate it into our Dorinda investigation.

And Ortega doesn't know the half of it. "Situation"? Now I'll finally get a chance to confront him about the bogus photo array. His "situation" is about to get worse.

"So are you saying you know who that was?" I ask, more than prepared for the answer. This may also explain the noticeable absence of Ortega's usually ever-present chief of staff. Tek wasn't in court for Dorinda's hearing, even though he was the lead detective on the case. And he's not here now.

Oz purses his lips and leans back against Kevin's desk. Kevin scoots his chair away, his personal space invaded by Oz's physical bulk and commanding presence.

"We do," he says, putting the police report back into the file. "But you should know you're out of danger now."

I open my mouth to ask where Tek is and whether he's being charged with anything, but Oz keeps talking.

"Mr. Hardesty had been tracking you for almost two weeks now," Ortega says. "It was him in the archives. He followed you there. When Tek headed for the file room and you weren't with him, Hardesty decided to—as he put it—get that television bitch off his back."

He glances at Susannah. "No offense. When that didn't work, apparently you used your shoes? Very resourceful. Nevertheless, when that didn't work, he just kept on your trail, and waited for his chance."

Susannah gasps and puts a hand to her mouth. Even Kevin looks concerned. But I'm skeptical. "Wait a minute," I say. "That's impossible. The case is three years old, certainly CC left town afterward. Where was he? And how on earth could he know, from wherever he was, that we were working on this story?"

"There was only one person in Swampscott Hardesty kept in touch with. She didn't know he was reincarnated as Tommy Bresnahan, of course, and he hadn't seen her for years. They just communicated, sporadically, by postcard, then e-mail. And a phone call on her birthday."

"Who?" I ask. I run through the list of possibles in my head and cannot figure out who might have been CC's confidante. "Everyone thought he was dead."

Oz continues as if I hadn't interrupted. "But when you asked her about him, she e-mailed right away. He had told her he wanted to disappear. Asked her, years ago, to keep his secret. Very dramatic. And she did. Of course it was all innocent on her part. She had no idea he'd killed Ray Sweeney, and she told him everything you said. Which wasn't much, but enough to let him know you were working to exonerate Dorinda. And that brought him right back into town. He wasn't on your tail every second, he told us, said he didn't need to be, once he found out where your mother was."

"Who?" I demand. Not Poppy. Pink-fingernailed Myra Matzenbrenner? Not Rosemary at the shelter, certainly.

"Marybeth—" he checks a file "—Gallagher. Remember her?

It takes me only an instant to remember that day at Swampscott High, the day I was searching for the yearbook.

"The librarian," I say. I rewind my brain, trying to recall what she told me. Was there anything I should have suspected? But, from what I can remember, she never even hinted she was still in touch with CC. I mean, he was supposed to be dead. I shake my head. "She's the last person…"

"She's been the librarian forever," Ortega says. "And back when CC and Dorinda went to Swampscott High, she was also the drama coach. She was the one who picked the two of them to play Romeo and Juliet, she told us. Apparently that was the beginning of a 'special relationship,' she called it."

Romeo and Juliet. Of course. And in her mind, perhaps, the librarian was playing Friar Laurence, the confidant who kept Romeo's secret. Like Romeo, CC was not dead, just pretending. Marybeth Gallagher probably thought it was romantic. But she should have remembered how that story ended. A tragedy.

Oz is still talking, outlining their investigation. "But

once Hardesty realized the case was under scrutiny…" He shrugs. "He had to come back and make sure the coast was clear. And that no one could identify him as the person who was bartender that night."

The puzzle pieces fall into place. "DeCenzo," I say, solemnly. "Claiborne Gettings."

"Hardesty came into DeCenzo's bar right after you did," Ortega says. He sighs. "And too bad Gettings picked right now to come home for a visit. Hardesty nailed him, too. We think he tracked him to some bar, got him drunk, and, well…we're still investigating that one. But—"

Kevin picks up his phone and starts punching in numbers.

I'm, suddenly, flaringly, mad as hell. "My mother," I say, glaring at Oz. "And me." My mouth is dry and my fists are clenched. I stand up, though I didn't plan to, and point to Oz. "Franklin and I told you Dorinda wasn't guilty. Will Easterly knew it. Rankin knew it. We told you there was someone else out there. But you just dismissed us. And threatened to report us to the FCC. For what? Reporting the truth?"

Kevin looks up, concerned. "Charlie?" he says. "This is the attorney general…"

I'm aware that I'm crossing the line, but I'm too enraged to be polite. I plop back into the chair just to appease Kevin, but I'm still furious.

"You and Tek decided it was more important for you to protect your reputations as crime busters, right? Make your way to the governor's office? So you law-and-order types allowed two more people to be killed. Actually, almost four. Why aren't you guilty of murder, too?"

Kevin and Susannah stand up, and start talking at the same time.

"Charlie," Kevin says, making the time-out sign. "We need to talk about this like reasonable—"

"She's upset," Susannah interrupts, her ropes of pearls clanking against her notebook. "She doesn't mean—"

Oz waves them both off and shifts his position on the desk. It's the first time I've ever seen him look defeated. "We have to make decisions, the best we can," he says. His voice has lost its luster. It's hollow and grim. "Law enforcement is not an exact science. It's evidence, and instinct. And in this case…"

I know what he's going to say next. I wish I could put my fingers in my ears so I don't hear it.

"She confessed," he says.

There's a tap at the door. It's Franklin, notebook in hand. Kevin waves him in. "Kevin, you called?" Franklin says. He looks between me and Ortega, then to Susannah, then to Kevin. Then back to me, his forehead furrowing. "What.?"

"It's big," is all I can think of to say. "CC Hardesty, boy Romeo. Jealousy, obsession, rage and murder."

"Susannah," Kevin begins.

"Right," Susannah replies. She's flipped open her cell phone, and speed dials a number. "It's me," she says into the phone. "I need promo studio C, asap. New Charlie promos, airing tonight." She snaps the phone closed, and points to Franklin and me, back and forth. "You're both working late, correct?"

You bet, I say silently. "And we'll need a camera," I tell Susannah. "For the exclusive interview with Mr. Ortega."

I look at him, challenging. "Correct?"

Epilogue

I never imagined I'd see them all sitting in the same place. In rows of white and gold chairs, festooned with puffs of white tulle and nosegays of white peonies, one after the other, my friends and family and familiar faces. Some who have been happy for a long time. One who thought she'd never be happy again. My sister Nora and her husband Bix. Franklin and Stephen, heads together, reading the sleek white wedding program. Next to Stephen, Gaylen Sweeney. Next to her, Will Easterly. And though I can't see his face, I can see his arm. It's draped protectively and lovingly across the shoulders of the person sitting next to him. Dorinda Sweeney.

I don't have a seat. I'm waiting, standing in the back of an impeccably white canvas tent set up in the hydrangea-filled garden of the Endicott Estate. The rambling colonial-style mansion is big enough for an inside wedding, but when this August morning dawned fair and sparkling, we knew the tent had been the right decision. I'm waiting, in my actually not-so-terrible maid-of-honor dress, and watching through the French doors as Mom and her hairdresser fuss with some last-minute changes.

A tuxedoed string-and-flute quartet, stationed in one

corner, quietly plays music of hope and love and possibilities.

And there's Josh.

He steps through the tent's flowered entranceway, then
steps back, pantomiming a whistle. He gives me the
spinning-finger signal to twirl. "Yet again, you dazzle me,
Charlie McNally," he says. "Is that the dress you said you
were 'destined to loathe'? The nightmare in Pepto-
Bismol chiffon, I think you called it?"

"Yes, well, it wasn't so bad, as it turned out. Watch."
I twist a little, and the tiers of pale gossamer fabric swirl
gracefully around my ankles. "Kind of Ginger Rogers,
maybe. And since you're very Fred Astaire in that black
tie, maybe we can—" I pause, concerned again. "But do
I look like cotton candy?"

Josh takes my hand and pulls me closer to him. "I
adore cotton candy," he says softly. "It's deliciously
sweet, and it melts in your mouth. And it always leaves
you wanting more." He slides an arm around my waist.
"You sure you can't leave right now?"

"Daddy!" Penny, wearing a miniature of my dress and
white pearlized Mary Janes, trots up and throws her arms
around Josh's waist. She pushes herself away from him
and holds out her arms like a model. "Do you like my
dress?" She points a toe out from under her skirt. "And
my shoes? With the tiny baby pearls on them?"

Josh kisses the top of her head. When he looks up, his
eyes are misting with a glimmer of pride, and love, and
the passing of time. "I remember when *you* were a tiny
baby," he says, touching a just-curled lock of her beribboned hair. "Now you're all grown-up."

"I know," she says. "So I'm going to wear these shoes
every day." She points to the gold and white chairs. "Now

you have to go sit down, Daddy," she instructs. "We're having a wedding."

Josh blows me a kiss, then one to his daughter, and heads for his seat.

"You look so pretty, Charlie Mac," Penny says.

"So do you, sweetheart," I say, adjusting the corona of late-summer peonies circling her dark curls. Where she came up with it, I don't know. But she called me "Charlie Mac" for the first time last night at the rehearsal dinner. "Um" seems to have left the building. Lucky I had on waterproof mascara. "You all set on walking down the aisle?"

"I go first, I walk slow," Penny recites. "Step, touch, step, touch. All the way up to Ethan. Then you come next. Just like we practiced."

I hear a flurry of activity from the front flaps of the tent. It's Maysie and Matthew, both looking at their watches, shepherding their children inside. Max is focused on some handheld electronic game, which he tucks into his pocket as soon as he sees me. I notice Molly has on little kitten heels. Apparently Maysie lost the adolescent footwear battle.

Mays shoos the three of them to their seats, and gives me and Penny careful hugs, as much to protect her burgeoning stomach as our wedding attire.

"You okay?" she asks me. She turns to Penny. "And you, honey? You look just beautiful."

Penny nods, and points her toe out for approval again.

"Very nice." Maysie nods appreciatively. "Pearls."

Maysie tucks her arm through mine and cocks her head toward the front row. "That's quite a picture," she says.

"Yeah, that's what I was looking at, too," I agree. "Who'd have thought that group would be lined up together? Dressed to the hilt and at my mom's wedding?

You've got to admit, it's a memory maker. And Dorinda."
I pause, taking a deep breath, as her reality sets in. "Well,
it looks like she'll have another chance at family."

"All because of you, Brenda Starr," she says. "And
what's more, Oz will never get elected, now that Tek
finally admitted to faking that photo lineup. Voters just
don't like evidence tampering, you know? Even the Great
and Powerful can't spin his way out of that one."

"Ah, who knows," I say. "If he can blame it all on Tek,
one rogue cop? All politics is loco, isn't that what they
say? But look. Check out Will Easterly's arm." I point to
the gossip-worthy scene. "Seems Dorinda is acclimating
nicely to freedom."

A solo flute begins the gentle melody of the Mozart
Concerto in E flat. I know that's the signal the ceremony
is about to begin. "This is it," I say to Maysie. I grab her
hand and give it a squeeze. "I'm glad you could be here."

"You're next," she whispers. "Even if you don't catch
your mom's bouquet." She trots toward her seat before I can
reply. And I don't have time to think about that right now.

"All ready?" I whisper to Penny.

She smiles confidently. "I'm set, Charlie Mac."

"Me, too," I say.

I look past the rows of guests to the white canvas runner
making a path down the aisle to the flower-laden dais.
Lush pink and white peonies and lavender hydrangea,
the essence of summer, cascade down the podium, their
fragrance filling the tent. The late-afternoon sun gives the
white canvas a pink glow, a wedding decoration from the
universe that's not offered in any catalogue.

Behind the dais, Oliver Rankin, made a justice of the
peace for the occasion, offers last-minute encouragement
to a beaming Ethan Margolis. My soon-to-be stepdad, in

charcoal pinstripes and a white-rose boutonnière, fairly radiates happiness and anticipation. He looks like it's all he can do to keep his feet on the ground. Ethan pats his pocket, where I know he's tucked Mom's ring, and gives Rankin an enthusiastic thumbs-up. The audience, watching the blissed-out groom, murmurs a soft rustle of affectionate laughter.

The quartet pauses. The sweetly familiar opening notes of Pachelbel's *Canon in D* sound softly from one violin. The audience quiets, waiting.

Penny picks up her ivy-sprigged basket of white rose petals. "My turn now, right?" she whispers. Her eyes are shining with excitement.

I touch her hair, then give her a tiny kiss on the forehead. "You're the prettiest flower girl ever," I say softly, wiping away a trace of my lipstick. "And the best." I pat her on her crinolined rear. "Now do your stuff, kiddo. I'll be right behind you."

Penny heads down the aisle, carefully touch-stepping and strewing rose petals. I take a deep breath and nod to Oliver, who motions the audience to rise for the bride.

I turn to the entrance of the tent. And there's Mom.

One hand flies to my chest. For an instant, I'm unable to breathe. It's all I can do not to burst into tears. She's elegant, confident. And, I've got to admit, beautiful. This is her day.

Ready? I ask silently.

Mom settles her dove gray chiffon skirt as it catches the slight August breeze, and rearranges her bouquet of blazing late-summer dahlias.

With a soft smile, she nods and blows me a kiss. The poignant music swells behind us. We stand, eyes locked, mother and daughter, surrounded by friends and family. Slowly, Mom raises two fingers in the peace sign.

To us? She mouths the words, but I understand her perfectly.

I raise my own two fingers, and give her our signal back. "To us," I whisper. "To us."

* * * * *

It's going to be a

RED HOT SUMMER

LAURA CALDWELL

All available now
wherever books are sold!

RIVERSIDE PARK

LAURA VAN WORMER

*In New York's premier enclave, Riverside Park,
up-and-comers rub shoulders with the prosperous.*

Once happy, Amanda and Howard Stewart now teeter
on the brink of infidelity—and financial ruin.

Media titan Cassy Cochran's storybook marriage
hides a dark secret.

Beautiful Celia Cavanaugh's life is spiraling
out of control—with a naive teenage boy in tow.

Single mother Rosanne DiSantos struggled for years
to better herself…only to despise what she's achieved.

Proud father Sam Wyatt will do anything to stop his
family being destroyed by an act of desperation.

*The branches of this urban family entwine in a story
of love denied, revealed and remembered.*

RIVERSIDE PARK

Available now wherever books are sold!

MIRA®

www.MIRABooks.com

MLVW2652

In 2009 Harlequin celebrates
60 years of pure reading pleasure!

We're marking this occasion by offering
16 **FREE** full books to download and read.

Visit

www.HarlequinCelebrates.com

to choose from a variety of
great romance stories
that are absolutely **FREE!**

(Total approximate retail value of $60)

We invite you to visit and share the Web site
with your friends, family
and anyone who enjoys reading.

REQUEST YOUR FREE BOOKS!

2 FREE NOVELS
FROM THE ROMANCE/SUSPENSE
COLLECTION PLUS 2 FREE GIFTS!

YES! Please send me 2 FREE novels from the Romance/Suspense Collection and my 2 FREE gifts (gifts are worth about $10). After receiving them, if I don't wish to receive any more books, I can return the shipping statement marked "cancel." If I don't cancel, I will receive 4 brand-new novels every month and be billed just $5.74 per book in the U.S. or $6.24 per book in Canada. That's a savings of at least 28% off the cover price. It's quite a bargain! Shipping and handling is just 50¢ per book.* I understand that accepting the 2 free books and gifts places me under no obligation to buy anything. I can always return a shipment and cancel at any time. Even if I never buy another book from the Reader Service, the two free books and gifts are mine to keep forever.

185 MDN EYNQ 385 MDN EYN2

Name	(PLEASE PRINT)	
Address		Apt. #
City	State/Prov.	Zip/Postal Code

Signature (if under 18, a parent or guardian must sign)

Mail to **The Reader Service:**
IN U.S.A.: P.O. Box 1867, Buffalo, NY 14240-1867
IN CANADA: P.O. Box 609, Fort Erie, Ontario L2A 5X3

Not valid to current subscribers of the Romance Collection,
the Suspense Collection or the Romance/Suspense Collection.

Want to try two free books from another line?
Call 1-800-873-8635 or visit www.morefreebooks.com.

* Terms and prices subject to change without notice. Prices do not include applicable taxes. Sales tax applicable in N.Y. Canadian residents will be charged applicable provincial taxes and GST. Offer not valid in Quebec. This offer is limited to one order per household. All orders subject to approval. Credit or debit balances in a customer's account(s) may be offset by any other outstanding balance owed by or to the customer. Please allow 4 to 6 weeks for delivery. Offer available while quantities last.

Your Privacy: Harlequin is committed to protecting your privacy. Our Privacy Policy is available online at www.eHarlequin.com or upon request from the Reader Service. From time to time we make our lists of customers available to reputable third parties who may have a product or service of interest to you. If you would prefer we not share your name and address, please check here. ☐